THE
GIRL

WHO
BROKE

THE
SEA

A. CO...

Published in the UK by Scholastic, 2023
1 London Bridge, London, SE1 9BG
Scholastic Ireland, 89E Lagan Road, Dublin Industrial Estate,
Glasnevin, Dublin, D11 HP5F

SCHOLASTIC and associated logos are trademarks and/or
registered trademarks of Scholastic Inc.

Text © A. Connors, 2023

The right of A. Connors to be identified as the author
of this work has been asserted by him under the
Copyright, Designs and Patents Act 1988.

ISBN 978 0702 31758 3

A CIP catalogue record for this book
is available from the British Library.

Printed by CPI Group (UK) Ltd, Croydon, CR0 4YY
Paper made from wood grown in sustainable forests
and other controlled sources.

1 3 5 7 9 10 8 6 4 2

www.scholastic.co.uk

For Meg, Gilbert and Evan…
No one I'd rather be stuck at the bottom of the ocean with.

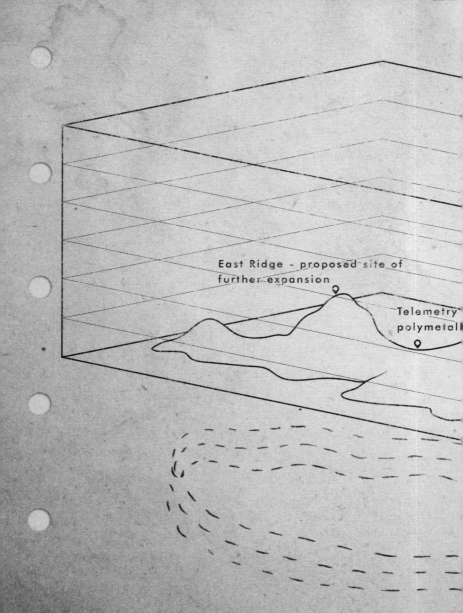

East Ridge - proposed site of
further expansion

Telemetry
polymetal

FAO Dr. Ruth Fawcett

2000M

3000M

DEEPHAVEN Mining Corp
-Primary Site

4000M

e of
harvesting

5000M

6000M

7000M

← Rift?

CHAPTER 1

**LILY FAWCETT: DEEPHAVEN PERSONAL LOG
DAY 1**

They say you'll never cross the ocean until you have the courage to lose sight of the shore. I was fine when we lost sight of the shore.

It's losing sight of the surface that bothers me.

Ch-cluunk! Claank—

"Mum?"

Ch—ch—ch—ch—ggrrrr—

"Mum, I changed my mind. I don't want to go."

Chraank—!

"I want to stay topside with Dad. I don't even *like* the sea."

Mum leaned over from where she was strapped into her seat and squeezed my hand. Outside, the articulated crane arm reached forward like a massive, yellow, steel wading bird and lowered our submersible on to the surface of the ocean. It had looked gentle in the training video, but in reality there was a jolt as sharp as a car crash, and my jaw snapped shut. I blinked in surprise, tears of shock rushing to my eyes.

Mum drew a nervous lungful of air and let it out in a shaky breath. "A fresh start, right, Lily?"

A fresh start on a mining rig five kilometres under the ocean? A fresh start four and a half thousand kilometres, two boats and a helicopter ride from the nearest landmass? That's not a fresh start, I thought. *That's desperation.*

I twisted in my seat, trying to make myself more comfortable. The straps were designed for someone taller than me, and they chafed against my neck. I watched through the porthole as our logistics ship uncoupled and moved away. Our sub rocked in its wake, the sea rising and falling around us. I felt like a flea riding on the back of an enormous animal, its great grey hide rippling as it walked.

Fifteen people floating in a tin can in the middle of the Pacific. The newest rotation of engineers and scientists on their way to Deephaven for a six-month shift. We didn't know any of them, and yet we'd signed up to live with them at the bottom of the ocean. *What were we thinking? Had things really been that bad? Was this really our best* option? I looked across at Mum, her face pale and set in concentration.

Suddenly, a beeping noise ripped through the cabin, so loud and shrill it made my teeth rattle. The rest of the crew started bracing themselves, checking and tightening their straps in a businesslike way. The thrusters roared, vibrating through the hull and my seat.

"What was that?" I breathed in the silence that followed.

Mum looked straight ahead, her jaw fixed. "I think we're getting ready to drop."

I took a deep breath and tried to settle the cage full of monkeys in my chest. Yes, I'd agreed to this. Yes, I'd promised Mum I was up for this. *But what had I been thinking?* I couldn't do it. This was a mistake. A terrible mistake. I was going to mess up, just like I always did, and it was going to be worse than ever this time.

I missed Dad. I closed my eyes and tried to imagine him. His big, soft engineer's hands, his long fingers. *Chill out, Lilypad*, he'd say.

Mum's hand closed more tightly around my own, clammy with fear.

"Mum?" I said, turning to her.

"Yes?"

There was a hopeful look in her eyes, like she thought I was going to say something brave and reassuring, something that would let her know I was going to be OK down there after all. I swallowed. I wanted to make her

3

happy. I wanted this to be the fresh start she desperately needed it to be. But a cold, dangerous feeling had risen in my throat.

"Mum, I feel sick—"

Then, several things happened at once. Outside, eight sets of vertical thrusters burst into life, pushing our submersible downwards in a great *whoosh* of grinding seawater, while inside, the sub became weightless, and in that exact same moment, I threw up.

CHAPTER 2

"Welcome to Deephaven!" Ari swept his arm proudly around the dingy sub bay like an overenthusiastic (and delusional) estate agent. "Two hundred and fifty thousand tonnes of steel, thirty-one kilometres of mechanical piping, four thousand two hundred and twenty-six light bulbs, eleven kilometres of handrails…"

And a Chief Operations Officer who's clearly been down here too long, I thought.

Ari Sigurðsson was a mammoth of a man. Six foot four at least, he looked like he was made from the same toughened steel as the rig. He'd introduced himself as we stepped off the sub, shaking my hand so vigorously I wondered if there was a piece of chewing gum stuck to my sleeve that he was trying to shake loose. His copper hair was shaved short, and his florid bronze beard looked like it had exploded from the bottom of his face. He smiled a lot: a bright, optimistic smile.

"We are the world's first truly sustainable and fully carbon-neutral mining operation," he continued, gesturing so expansively I was afraid somebody was going to get clobbered. "A unique collaboration of science and industry. A *community* dedicated to understanding the ocean depths while helping to meet the world's energy needs."

He led the way, stopping every so often to drop in another technical detail or snippet of information. "Always keep hands, fingers, feet and other appendages clear of pinch points and hinges." And we trailed after him – me, Mum, and one other family – clanging and clambering through the claustrophobic corridors.

This was our safety briefing apparently. We'd been travelling for eleven hours straight, two of them in a tiny submersible filled with the smell of my sick. I needed a shower and sleep, but regulations stated that we had to go through our safety briefing before anything else.

"Deephaven clings, limpet-like, to the side of the valley in the middle of the Clarion-Clipperton Fracture Zone," Ari intoned with obvious relish. "Nothing but three thousand and forty-seven toughened steel bolts between us and the fathomless depths of the northern trenches."

I could feel Mum's eyes on me, gauging my reaction, waiting for me to freak out. None of this was news to us. We'd spent the past six weeks at the training centre in Newfoundland preparing for exactly this, but it was different now that we were actually here.

There was a damp, salty seaweed taste in the air, mixed in with sweat and engine oil and the school-canteen odour of stale vegetables. Everything was hard steel or moulded plastic with sharp, unfinished edges. The floor was a metal grille that rattled when you walked on it. The corridors were slightly too narrow for two people to stand side-by-side, and thick pipes and electrical cables snaked around every corner, perfect for tripping over or banging shins against.

A trembling, tearful feeling quivered at the back of my throat. *This is a mistake*, my brain muttered. I wasn't good with tight spaces, or bad smells, or loud noises, and this place had all of them. *Who were we kidding?* Mum and I weren't world's-first-deep-sea-mining-rig people. Nine weeks ago I'd been a middling student at the world's most ordinary secondary school in Hertfordshire, and now this!

"Twenty-three habitation units – hab units, for short – are connected to the main rig via three and a half kilometres of nanotube polycarbonate polytunnel," Ari prattled on. "The main rig has six floors: Command Centre, Sub Bay, Recreation, Catering, Services and

7

Engineering. And the hab units house our other key functions: Operations, Reactor Room, Battery Units, Education, Science and Accommodation."

Ari paused his recital and gazed at a row of domed portholes. They looked out on to nothing but silty nothingness, illuminated by the harsh white glare of the rig's external floodlights. "You'll like this," he said, flashing me a smile and beckoning cheerily for us to gather around him. "Self-healing aluminosilicate windows," he declared. "State-of-the-art, designed by our very own in-house science team."

He took an oversized tool, an adjustable spanner of some kind, from one of his many flight suit pockets and gave the porthole a series of swift, enthusiastic whacks.

The *clangs* reverberated around the walls, and I heard Mum let out a short gasp of horror.

"See? Not even a scratch," Ari said. "I can put a crack in it if you like, show you how well it seals itself?"

"No—" Mum said quickly. She took a breath and continued more calmly. "No, that's fine, thank you."

The problem with being at the bottom of the ocean (besides the cold and perpetual dark) is the pressure, or so they told us at the training centre. Water is heavy. Sitting at the bottom of the ocean is like asking somebody to build a skyscraper on top of you. At this depth, the column of water above our heads weighed roughly five thousand tonnes, enough to turn us all into clam chowder in a

8

nanosecond if the hull was breached or, say, a porthole gave way.

"Four hundred and seventy-two Cardinal Robotic Automated Bionics — CRABs, for short — collect polymetallic nodules from the valley below us," Ari continued, jostling us down yet another corridor. "We produce four tonnes a day of nickel, two tonnes of cobalt, copper, molybdenum, and a good whack of lithium and yttrium to boot. We have ninety-six rig personnel, forty-five science and technical team and eleven children."

I glanced around at our fellow newbies: Mike and Janice Rutherford and their son, Jacob. Most of the people on the sub had been returning from shore leave, so it was just the five of us on the safety tour.

The Rutherfords look like world's-first-deep-sea-mining-rig people, I thought. Mike had aviator-style, wire-rimmed glasses and a Leatherman strapped to his waist. He didn't talk much; he was too busy taking notes, devoutly transcribing everything Ari said in a way that made me think I really ought to be paying more attention. Janice was wiry and serious looking, her face etched with a perpetual frown. She was probably a very nice person, I told myself, except that she'd caught the brunt of my zero-gravity vomit in the sub, so now she just kept sniffing her damp hair and glaring resentfully at me.

I fell into step with Jacob as we shuffled through the

pressure door. He looked about my age, sixteen, maybe a year or two younger.

"Hey. Do you think he counted the bolts himself?" I asked.

Jacob blinked at me. "Huh?"

"The bolts," I tried again. "Ari said there were three thousand and forty-seven of them. And four thousand two hundred and twenty-six light bulbs. Do you think he…" I trailed off.

Jacob regarded me with a look that was somewhere between blind panic and pity. "I'm sorry, I don't—"

"Never mind," I said.

Mum had warned me that Deephaven attracts a particular kind of person: smart, serious, ambitious types. Although she never said it directly, I was sure part of her reason for wanting me to come here was the idea that some of it might rub off on me. But I hadn't expected the profile to apply to the kids as well. Next to my scrawny, shabby and fidgety self, Jacob was all sun-scorched cheeks, broad shoulders, and a smile that you could use to sell Rice Krispies. He had a stiff, overly grown-up manner about him, and it felt like only a matter of time before he got his own Leatherman and notepad.

Ari swung through the bulkhead door like a gorilla performing a circus trick and the rest of us clambered after him. It was impressive how he manoeuvred himself through the narrow corridors. I was about the size of his left leg, but somehow, every time I tried to get through the metal pressure doors, I cracked either my forehead or my shin, and sometimes both at once. I was squeezing through a particularly tight spot when I got the pocket of my flight suit snagged on a power box clasp. I tugged, but found that I was caught, twisted at an awkward angle with one leg either side of the bulkhead and the material of my flight suit stretched tight.

"Um, Ari?" I called. "A little help, please?"

Ari bounded over and unhooked me. "Nothing to worry about," he said warmly. "Done that a few times myself if I'm honest."

I looked up to find Mum watching me anxiously and Mike glaring at me. For a second I saw myself through his eyes: a "troubled teenager" with ratty hair and an attitude problem, black eyeliner and bitten fingernails. A girl who shouldn't be here.

I couldn't agree more, I thought.

"Onwards!" cried Ari.

He paused at the narrow part of the corridor where the steel of the main rig was bolted on to a long black tube lit by two strips of light along the top. I could just see the brighter far end as it opened out into one of the other hab units.

"The hab units are connected via nanotube polycarbonate, another in-house speciality from our science team," Ari said while Mike scribbled more notes.

"Would you believe, just a four-centimetre shell made of this highly experimental and largely untested material is sufficient to hold back the immense force of the ocean?"

Four centimetres ... highly experimental ... untested...? My stomach heaved. "Um, excuse me, Ari," I said. "What happens if one of the polytunnels gets a crack? Are they self-healing, like the portholes?"

Ari nodded reassuringly. "Actually ... no," he said, seeming a little deflated. "But you're not the first to ask that, young lady." He slapped the heavy steel bulkhead. "Rest assured, these pressure doors will automatically slam shut the instant they detect flooding."

Slam shut? Like a coffin lid? I shivered.

"But what happens if you're *in* a polytunnel when that happens?" I persisted. "If the doors shut, doesn't that mean you're trapped?"

Ari didn't have an answer for that one; his mouth opened and closed thoughtfully. The group shuffled. Mum let out a faint sigh.

"You're not to worry about that sort of thing," Ari said at last, giving his beard a nervous rub. "I'm sure our technicians have thought of all that stuff. Let's head down to the canteen, shall we?" He flashed his searchlight of a smile in my direction. "If we're lucky, catering might have left a little surprise for us."

He turned and swung through the pressure door. We followed him down a long polytunnel that opened briefly

12

into one of the hab units before passing into another section. I was finding it difficult to concentrate on what he was saying; I kept thinking about all those kilometres of ocean pressing down on us, trying its best to crush us.

Mum touched my shoulder, whispering: "Everything OK?"

She adjusted a stray strand of my hair which was turning frizzy in the damp, salty air. Her face was tight, her own hair matted against her scalp with sweat. I could tell she was making an effort, trying to make everything OK because she wanted *me* to be OK. But it was hard because she was so obviously not OK herself.

"Our fusion reactor develops one point two megawatts of power and uses a plasma containment grid in the twenty megatesla range," Ari said, adding pointedly, "the Emergency Reactor Scram buttons are your friends."

He slapped the wall, nerve-wrackingly close to a large red button that was mounted there. It was behind a Perspex panel, like something you'd see in a bad sci-fi movie, and beneath it an embossed sign read:

**EMERGENCY REACTOR SCRAM — ERS
DO NOT PUSH THIS BUTTON EXCEPT
IN EXTREME EMERGENCY.**

I glanced at Mum and then looked meaningfully at the ERS, hoping to coax a smile from her. It was funny, wasn't it? A big red button with a sign underneath saying *do not push this button*. They'd told us about these so many times in Newfoundland it had become a bit of a running joke between us. But I should have known Mum wouldn't be in the mood right now. Her face stiffened, and she gave a short, sharp shake of her head to warn me off.

OK, I deserved that one. I could be an idiot sometimes. My being an idiot was part of the reason we were here, actually, so it wasn't unreasonable for Mum to worry about how it was all going to work out. I'd messed up pretty badly at home, lots of times in fact, but one time in particular. If following Mum to this new job, to her *fresh start*, as she put it, and not screwing up was the best way to make it up to her, then so be it.

"In the unlikely event of a containment field collapse, the untethered magnetic flux will try to rip us out of the ground like a daisy," Ari said, a little too enthusiastically for my taste. "The ERS buttons provide our last opportunity to eject the plasma core before that happens."

I shuddered. They'd told us about the ERS buttons in training, but they'd been careful to avoid graphic turns of phrase like *rip* and *daisy*. I reached out for balance and let my hand rest against the uncompromising metal hull. The steel was cold to the touch, wet with condensation, indifferent. It was practically *designed* for someone to pound their fists hopelessly against it as the water level rose around them. A slight vibration (the fusion reactor, I presumed), trembled inside the metal, as if the whole rig was holding itself tensely, waiting for something to happen.

"Why the signs?" I asked.

Ari scratched his beard in a way that looked like frustration. "Well, it's an expensive thing, dumping the plasma core," he said. "Not everyone could agree on how ... well ... *pressable* they wanted the buttons to be." He flashed me a wink and I forced a smile in response. "So? What do you think of your new home, young lady?"

Mum gave me a panicky look. *Be nice*, her eyes pleaded. Ari's face blazed with renewed optimism.

What was I supposed to say? The tight dampness of the rig crawled over my skin. The jangling noise of the place vibrated in my bones. When Mum had first told me she was considering a job on an experimental, first-of-its-kind rig, I'd naively assumed it would be slick and high-tech. In reality, it had a bolted-together, homemade feel, as if somebody had built it as they went along, adding hab units and new wiring as it became necessary. It had only been operational for ten years (still new by experimental deep-sea-rig standards), but the action of the sea had aged it prematurely, turning every corner and cranny a kind of cancerous brown, forming livid stains at the connection points between pipes and bulkheads.

"It's, um... It's a bit cramped," I said truthfully.

Ari's face didn't change – he still beamed at me – but it

was like someone had popped a valve inside his head and let the positivity drain out.

"Well – er… Well, yes, it is a little, I suppose…" Ari gave his beard a reassuring rub, like he was comforting a nervous pet. Then he brightened: "But it's cosy, right? And it's home! Come on. Canteen's this way."

Mum bristled as we padded through another polytunnel, the smooth polycarbonate flexing worryingly beneath us. This was more than just a *fresh start* for her, it was the *opportunity of a lifetime*. The kind of fantasy job she wouldn't even have considered if Dad hadn't moved out and I hadn't been kicked out of school. The pressure not to screw up was high.

We popped back out into the main rig on the opposite side, where the metal flooring clanged and rattled like a steel band.

Three of Ari's ops team (distinctive in their grey flight suits and blue hard hats) bustled down the corridor in the opposite direction, squeezing past us with a practised shimmy and a nod to Ari. Two men and one woman. They hammered past so quickly they made the pipes on the walls shudder.

The corridor opened out into a larger space filled with long tables and velour seating, big enough for thirty or forty people to hang out in. Another row of domed portholes studded the far wall, but I could see nothing through them except more silty greyness. The ceiling was low, the colour of old newspapers. There was a self-service food counter on the left, and a row of ancient-looking arcade machines on the right.

Looking around, I was struck by how weird it was that we should find ourselves in this place: on the one hand, we were utterly alone, surrounded on all sides by nothing but rocks and a mountain of water that wanted to kill us; on the other hand, it looked like we'd just stopped off at a motorway service station on the M40.

"Here we are!" Ari exclaimed joyfully. "Cupcakes!"

CHAPTER 3

Dad had left in the autumn. I remember that it was an extravagantly windy day. The conifers in our garden had rocked back and forth like they were trying to uproot themselves and waddle off. The previous night, the roof of our neighbour's Wendy house had ended up in our garden, pressed against our fence like a butterfly. It was like the weather was trying to make up for how little my dad seemed to care about what was happening. Like it was trying to mark the occasion for me.

I remember him standing in the doorway. A tall but slightly stooped man, his hair permanently overdue for a trim. We were waiting for Mum, who, moments before, had taken a call from the university, which was apparently more important than this. Dad seemed impatient to get going. I'd have preferred it if he'd fallen in love with someone else and was leaving us to start a new life. But really he was leaving us for a one-bedroom flat in Watford because, after seventeen years together, he and Mum had finally got bored of all the arguing.

I wanted to say something to him, but I didn't know where to start. I wanted to tell him how I felt, except I didn't *know* how I felt. I wanted him to hug me and be wise and reassuring, but I knew he wouldn't. That side of things – hugs and comfort and affection – was a mystery to him; it always had been. I loved him, of course, but I'd known from a very young age that he was somebody you had to make allowances for.

He didn't have much luggage. Just the overnight bag he always took when he was travelling and his rucksack. He was wearing his favourite T-shirt, which read:

There are only 10 kinds of people who understand binary.

Those who do and those who don't.

Look it up, it's a maths joke, he liked to say to anyone who asked. Dad worked in human–computer interaction, designing software interfaces for everything from fighter jets to fusion reactors; he liked to play online chess, although he'd never shown interest in teaching me; he liked to eat his meals at *exactly* the same time each day. The best way to have a conversation with him was to ask him about his current project, but talking to him about anything else was like shouting through a wall to somebody who was watching television in the next room.

He swung his rucksack on to his back, impatient to leave. He didn't know yet, but earlier that afternoon I'd prised every key from the keyboard of his laptop and dumped them all in the pond at the bottom of our garden.

He came back and rested his hand on my shoulder. Not a hug, not tears. But I could tell he was making an effort for me. "Chill out, Lilypad," he said. "Everything's OK. I'll video chat as soon as I'm settled in."

But I knew he wouldn't.

CHAPTER 4

Three tin-foil trays of sad-looking cupcakes were sweating under the lights on a nearby table. Each had a little marzipan disc that read: *Welcome to Deephaven!* Five of them had been eaten already, and I could guess from Ari's sheepish expression that his ops team had taken first dibs. Not that it stopped him from scooping one up for himself and slipping the entire thing into his mouth.

"So, Dr Fawcett, I hear you're part of the science team," he mumbled through a mouthful of cupcake.

Mum beamed and offered her hand; she loved it when people asked about her job. "I'm the new botanist."

Ari's eyes widened with surprise. "Botanist?" he coughed, spraying a fine mist of cupcake crumbs at her.

"That's right," Mum said. "My speciality is algae and fungi, although of course neither of those are *true* plants. I'm kind of a mycologist, phycologist, botanist hybrid… More of a botan-*ish* than a botan-*ist*, I tell my students…" She trailed off awkwardly. She added, "Dr Maximus Clarke, the Chief Science Officer, sent for me."

Her hand hovered in the air, but Ari was too busy thumping his chest to shake it.

His face had turned ashen. "Maximus?"

"Is there a problem?" Mum said, frosting over.

"They didn't tell you?"

"Tell me what?"

Ari glanced around like he was hoping there might be a handy polytunnel to dart into. He gave his beard another rub, except this time it was so vigorous I wondered if he might actually start a fire.

Mum shot me an anxious look.

Nine weeks ago, she was a lecturer at a middle-ranked university, and I was a girl whose teachers sometimes described as having "mild to moderate behavioural difficulties". Mum's job offer had come from nowhere. It had been the *opportunity of a lifetime*. An offer Mum *couldn't possibly pass up*. And it was exactly the *fresh start* she felt we needed in order to escape the royal mess I'd made for myself at school.

But, already, it was clear from Ari's face that something had gone wrong.

Ari made a loud throat-clearing sound and banged his chest one last time. "Grab a cupcake, you two. I'd better take you to see the boss." He turned apologetically to Mike and Janice. "Dr Fawcett and I need to nip down to the command centre. Shall I send someone from the team to show you to your hab unit?"

Mike looked irritated to have been cheated out of his safety lecture. "We can find our own way," he said stiffly, glancing coldly at me.

We followed Ari and passed through a dreary open-plan office stacked with ancient-looking computer terminals and chipped coffee mugs. "This is where the magic happens!" he exclaimed, gesturing around the shabby space like he was about to launch into another part of his tour.

Then we bundled into a service lift which shuddered as the door closed, and it took us, grudgingly, down to the lowest level of the rig.

"Is everything OK?" Mum asked Ari as we descended.

"Oh, sure, sure," Ari responded.

"What's going on?"

"Ah — I'd best leave that to Carter, I think."

Carter Engelbrecht was the Installation Manager, the most senior person on the rig, and Ari (Chief Operations Officer) and Maximus (Chief Science Officer) both reported to him. I hadn't expected to meet him so soon. I glanced at Mum, and she looked nervously back at me; something was definitely wrong.

"Perhaps I should speak to Maximus first?" Mum suggested.

The lift doors opened, and Ari burst out like a drowning man who'd just made it to the surface. We trekked down another twisting corridor.

Mum leaned in close and whispered urgently in my ear, "With Carter, be *nice to him*. OK? It matters what he thinks of us."

"Know Maximus well then?" Ari asked, his voice wavering a little anxiously.

"We were friends at university," Mum replied.

Ari nodded, and his look became distant for a moment. "A good man. One of the finest. Bit of a maverick, mind." We'd stopped outside a pressure door that was wider and less rusty than the rest. "Well, after you."

My breath caught as we stepped inside the command centre. *This* was how an experimental deep-sea mining rig was supposed to look. It was as dark and quiet as a library. A large screen curved around two thirds of the room, showing a digital schematic of the rig that bathed everything in soft blue light. Beneath it was a row of workstations, each with its own set of wafer-thin touchscreens, each with a technician in a gleaming white flight suit tending to it. There was no other light except a grey-blue aura from the cluster of domed portholes that looked out into the darkness of the ocean.

I was vaguely aware of Ari walking Mum over to meet

Carter, who was sitting at a desk over near the portholes, but I lingered near one of the workstations instead, drawn to what was on the monitor.

Computers are my thing. Specifically, computer interfaces. I get it from Dad, and I know it sounds limp to be into the same thing as your dad, but I can't help it, it's in the genes.

An interface is just the technical word for how humans communicate and interact with technology. Everything's an interface really. A light switch is the simplest interface you can imagine – down for on, up for off. The volume bar on your speaker. The timer on your oven.

Then you go up a level of complexity, and you get washing machines, cars and the pinnacle of consumer interfaces: laptops. But you've still barely scratched the surface. After that you get into the really interesting stuff, like nuclear power stations, fighter jets and plasma breeder systems. Dad says computers are like aliens. Not the absurd aliens you see on television who can conveniently speak English. *Alien* aliens, creatures with a completely different way of thinking and understanding the world. Dad says his job is to be a translator; he helps the computers make themselves understood.

On the monitor, there was a rig schematic, and it was *gorgeous*. It showed the rig as a sort of three-dimensional cut-out, its insides glowing with blue light. They'd shown us demo versions at the training centre, but fully operational like this, it felt different. A giant, pulsing, breathing thing, crackling with energy. I felt a shiver run down my spine. The six floors of the main rig were represented just as Ari had described them: the command floor where we were now; the Sub Bay; Recreation; Catering; Services and Engineering. And the hab units were similarly displayed as intricately instrumented modules scattered around the ocean floor. All were linked by the Central Control Network, a web of sensors and control circuits that bound the rig together like a giant nervous system. I watched as one of the technicians (*Holden*, according to his badge) navigated through the user interface on his screen, peeling back layers of control surfaces like he was dissecting a frog in biology.

It was ferociously complex. I followed the flickering dots of light that represented the shifting patterns of its systems: every door, valve, CO_2 scrubber and battery array was reporting back data from its sensors. The schematic represented this tornado of information as bands of ever-shifting colour.

Holden had the manner of an airline pilot – a very young airline pilot, whose skin still sported the reddish pockmarks of teenage acne. He was monitoring the core systems, adjusting the alignment of the CO_2 scrubbers, as if guiding us, not through the sky, but keeping us alive here against the unrelenting weight of the ocean.

But—

Something was wrong.

If I was reading it correctly, the batteries in one of the accommodation units were low, and the fusion reactor needed extra cooling water to compensate. I glanced at Holden. Surely he could see it. I'm not exactly an A student, but we'd been shown the basics at the training centre, and it was pretty clearly laid out.

"*Psst—*" I whispered. "Hey—"

Holden cast me an indignant look. He really wasn't much older than me.

"Hey, *Holden—*" I whispered again.

I knew I should leave it alone. Mum was anxious enough already without me causing trouble on my first day. But growing up with Dad had given me a knack for these things, and the information was blindingly obvious. I traced the system diagram back through to make sure I hadn't made a mistake. No, no mistake. An orange light blinked on, confirming my suspicion. Holden stared at it for a moment, befuddled.

"Holden, you need to—" Holden flashed me a mean stare. I pressed on: "You need to adjust valve 172B."

Holden had already turned away. Valve 172B blinked rapidly, practically *begging* to be pushed. *What if I did nothing?* I thought. A blackout, probably. I knew enough from our sessions at the training centre to figure that a fail-safe would probably trip out somewhere once the load got too high. But I didn't like the sound of twenty minutes standing in pitch black waiting for them to reboot the affected systems. And if I could stop it happening, that would be good, right? It would definitely reassure Mum that I was doing my best to make things work out down here; it might even help her relax a little bit.

"Mum?" I whispered. "Mum."

Mum was deep in conversation with the tall snub-nosed man whom I presumed to be Carter Engelbrecht. I turned back to the schematic.

"*Hooold—eenn…*" I hissed.

He was deliberately ignoring me. He had to be. My patience snapped. A hot gust of emotion caught me and swept me forward. Maybe it was because of the long journey. Maybe it was the anxiety of being down here, of everything being different and terrifying. I knew I was right about the valve. Holden was clearly being an ass. And all I had to do was tap the damn switch—

"*LILY!*"

Mum's shriek sounded like a whale that had fallen into a blender. I froze, my hand awkwardly close to the control interface so that there was no way I could deny what I'd been planning to do. I drew my hand back and slipped it into my pocket.

"That's probably not a good idea." Carter's voice was rough-but-smooth and unnaturally gravelly. He walked over to me stiffly, a mean-spirited Action Man in an expensive-looking suit. "Not unless you're planning to adjust the coolant flow to our fusion reactor?" He smiled widely, slowly, and placed his hand on my shoulder. It was all I could do to resist biting his finger. "I'm Carter," he said, his tone superficially friendly but shot through with steel. A tyrant with a smile. "And you must be Lily? I'd say 'make yourself at home', but you appear to be doing that already."

Holden had turned and was watching us now, his eyes smiling, the little git.

"I'm so sorry," Mum said, sounding mortified. "Lily can be a little…"

She let the words hang in the air. *I could be a little … what?* It certainly wasn't going to be anything good.

Ari joined us. He leaned over at the screen beside Holden to adjust valve 172B. I knew, vaguely, from our time in Newfoundland, that although Carter was the overall manager, Ari held authority when it came to the technical operation of the rig. He gave me a quizzical look, and I thought for a moment that he was going to tell me I'd been right about the valve all along. But then another flashing indicator caught his eye and the moment passed.

"Things might be more relaxed in academia, but we have to follow rigorous procedure here," Carter said, his icy blue eyes watching me. "A rig is a very dangerous place, suitable only for appropriately trained personnel."

I stared back at him. His suit jacket was pulled taut

over gym-tightened muscles like he was some kind of nightclub bouncer. *A suit jacket?* Everybody else on the rig was forced to wear a flight suit for safety reasons, but clearly Carter considered himself special. *If he were a user interface*, I thought, *what would he be?* Some kind of high-tech weapons system, a laser-guided missile, perhaps.

I could feel him judging me, packing me into a neat little box in his head and labelling me: *troublemaker*.

If I lost the eyeliner, managed to stop biting my nails, and stood a little straighter, would people look at me differently? I wondered. No. It would still show through. Carter had me pegged as a troublemaker, and the fact that he was probably right only made me more annoyed.

"Now ... where were we?" he said, turning back to Mum. "As I was saying, I'm sorry you've had a wasted journey, but the position for which you were hired is no longer available. You should have been notified topside." He gave Mum a condescending look. "An innocent error, I imagine, but we will of course offer you compensation for your time."

"I'm afraid I don't understand," Mum said. "I have a contract—"

"The contract that brought you here has been nullified, Mrs Fawcett."

"*Doctor* Fawcett," Mum corrected him automatically.

"I'm sorry, *Doctor* Fawcett," Carter said, making it sound like no kind of apology at all.

"Dr Maximus Clarke, the rig's Chief Science Officer, explicitly requested my assistance," Mum continued.

"Maximus Clarke is dead, Dr Fawcett."

Somehow, the library-quiet of the command centre grew even more intense. Holden and the other technicians turned and watched us keenly, the way you'd watch a seal that had been cornered by a killer whale.

Mum made a small choking sound and her hand rose to her mouth. She sat heavily in a nearby swivel chair, tears welling in her eyes. *Don't cry*, I thought desperately. *Not in front of him.* I didn't want Carter to see her upset, and I knew she wouldn't want it either. Mum didn't like crying; she always said crying just didn't do any good.

She drew a short breath and composed herself. "Wh… How did it happen?" she asked in a voice that was almost steady.

Good, I thought. *Good for you.*

"Please." Carter gestured for her to follow him over to the big cluster of domed windows. I followed too.

The command centre was slung beneath the main rig like the egg sac on a spider, extending over the edge of the valley. On the other side of the glass (sorry, *aluminosilicate*), external floodlights reflected off the murky water. Through the haziness, I could just make out the jagged line of rock dropping away, falling, and then rising again, and then dropping abruptly into blackness. I felt myself wobble, made dizzy by the drop. Deeper still, I could see the dim red glow of the telemetry grid – the fifty-kilometre-square lattice of homing beacons that the CRABs used to navigate when they harvested the polymetallic nodules the rig had been built to collect.

"Two weeks ago, Dr Maximus Clarke took an unauthorized EVA in a company-owned submersible—" Carter broke off and smiled, revealing teeth that looked like a row of gleaming bullets. "That means *extra-vehicular-activity*," he explained. "A fancy way of saying that he left the rig."

"I know what EVA stands for," Mum replied tersely.

"He descended seventy-five metres in depth and five kilometres laterally in that direction towards the east ridge," Carter continued. He pointed out into the greyness, his voice flat and devoid of all emotion. "At that point his telemetry went dead. Our rescue team has been unable to find any sign of him."

Mum shook her head disbelievingly. "Surely there's something you can do?"

"We've searched, Dr Fawcett. Believe me, our teams have spent hours combing every foot of that part of the ocean. There's nothing."

"But have you notified the police? There will need to be an investigation. Surely there is some kind of procedure—"

Carter looked gravely at her, a slight, patronizing curl in his lips. "It's natural that you don't appreciate how different things are down here, Dr Fawcett. It's not like being topside; we manage our own investigation, and the police get notified of the results. Everyone down here understands the risks that come with the job." He held out his arms in a gesture of defeat. "The ocean is a big place, and the currents are hungry. I'm sure I sound callous to you, but Maximus would be the first to agree. Wherever he is, he's long dead by now, and I have quotas to meet."

CHAPTER 5

"This is Dr Maximus Clarke with a message for Dr Ruth Fawcett," the grainy, juddering image intoned. "Ruth? I wish I could speak to you directly, but the connection down here is too slow for real-time communication."

It was July, that weird, dead month between utterly messing up my GCSEs and the end of term. I'd come home to find Mum in the kitchen, sipping a glass of wine and playing this video on her laptop.

"What I have found is … incredible. I believe it to be a new species of euglenoid. It is eukaryotic, and I suspect, a previously undiscovered form of protist. It possesses a structured bioluminescence and a remarkable ability for macro-organization; it exhibits a higher-order microbial intelligence at a level that has not been observed before…"

I snorted. "Would you like a side of croutons with your word soup, Mum?"

Mum didn't answer, and I could see from the intensity of her expression that this wasn't just another one of her regular academic clips. I watched over her shoulder. Maximus Clarke was a vigorous-looking man, a little older than Mum, with an angular face and a jerky, excitable way of moving.

"I know it's a big decision," Maximus implored, leaning closer to the camera. "Trust me, I never imagined myself in a place like this either. But … do you remember when we spoke after Maya died? I was nothing; I was grief. And this place … down here … it saved us, Evan and me. It helped us make a fresh start."

What does this guy mean by down here? I wondered, worry blossoming inside me.

"I know your situation with Lily is different. I understand why you might feel that this is not the right time. But I need you, Ruth. I need your expertize."

I bit my thumbnail. I didn't like that he'd mentioned my name. That meant that Mum had already been talking to him, and, more importantly, that she'd been talking to him about *me*.

And what did he mean by *your situation*? What had Mum told him?

We *were* in a situation, I supposed. I'd always been kind of difficult — *troubled*, as my teachers liked to say. I break things sometimes, on purpose; I don't know why. But after Dad moved out it got worse. Then something else happened, something big, something I'll never be able to make unhappen. It made Hanna, my best and only friend, hate me, it made *everyone* hate me, and it led the school to decide that I was no longer welcome back for sixth form in the autumn.

So now Mum was worrying about the effect it was all having on my "confidence", and the slow car crash my education had become.

She hit a key and the image juddered and jumped to a later part of the clip.

"Ruth, you know this isn't really my field. I need an expert. Remember your work on mycorrhizal fungi? Nobody cuts across the disciplines as you do, and I am certain your insights will make a difference. But we need to act quickly. There are … *politics* involved, and if we don't find proof soon, the discovery might slip through our fingers. I can make all the arrangements, just tell me what you need." Maximus leaned forward, his eyes shining. "Just come, for heaven's sake, Ruth. This could be the opportunity of a *lifetime*."

I didn't like him; I didn't like what he was saying; I didn't like the evangelical zeal in the way he said it. Mum scraped the video forward again to the end, like she was looking for something. She still hadn't acknowledged me; I was starting to wonder if she'd even heard me.

"I hope you'll give my offer serious consideration," the video concluded.

"What offer?" I asked.

Mum sipped her wine without turning. "He's offering me a job."

"A job?" I asked. "Where?"

"On Deephaven. It's a mining rig."

My stomach squirmed and twisted like it was trying to get out. A *mining rig*? Like … a coal mine? Soot-blackened miners from Yorkshire? Surely not that.

There were situations and there were *situations*, I thought. Mine was the kind of situation where I might have to make do with a less good sixth form, or I might have to study independently or something. It wasn't a situation where Mum went to work on a *mining rig*.

"Are you serious?" I asked. "What about me?"

Mum looked distant, almost bewildered, like she didn't quite believe it herself. "I told him no at first. But there is something to what he's saying. Deephaven is different from other rigs. They have a whole science team working alongside the rig operations. They have families there."

"Families?"

"You could come. That's the whole point. They have a school. A really very good school, in fact. Perfect for you. They can cater to your A-levels."

"What about my friends?"

Mum turned and gave me a weary look. She didn't have to say it: *What friends?*

"I'm sixteen, I don't want to live on a mining rig."

Mum said nothing for a while, then she said, "It would be an amazing opportunity."

"For who?"

"It would be a fresh start. We *need* a fresh start after … everything."

I could see in her face that she was serious. She was really considering this.

"Is it close?" I tried.

"It's quite near the International Date Line."

I took a moment to process this. I had meant *is it close to here*, which I knew was a long shot, but I had to ask. I wasn't sure where the International Date Line was, but from my vague recollection of my Geography GCSE it was somewhere in the middle of the Pacific, and that meant it wasn't close to *anywhere*.

"Like … it floats?" I said, incredulously.

"No," Mum replied. "It's at the bottom."

"Underwater?"

"Yes," Mum answered patiently.

"What about Dad?"

Mum frowned. When Dad had moved out it had been on the understanding that he wouldn't be too far away – he only lived a few minutes' drive from us right now, and he visited most weekends. But if we did this, he'd be all on his own; I wouldn't see him for months at a time.

"You're actually considering this, aren't you?" I said, anger creeping into my voice.

"I think so."

Mum's calmness was unnerving.

"Why does he want *you*?" I asked. "Are there even any plants down there?"

"Not as such," Mum said carefully.

"But you're a botanist."

Mum closed her laptop and took a long swallow of wine. "Technically," she said, her voice oddly detached, "euglenoids are classified as both plants and animals."

CHAPTER 6

**LILY FAWCETT: DEEPHAVEN PERSONAL LOG
DAY 2**

They told us at the training centre that we should keep a log of our time here. They said it was important for our mental well-being, which tells you a lot about this place, if you think about it. They also taught us basic submersible operation, emergency waterlock and evac procedures, and what to do if your helicopter ditches in the ocean. But I didn't really listen to that part. I mean, it's not like I'm actually going to use any of that stuff, is it?

When things go wrong down here, you die.

Just like Maximus did.

The day after Carter's bombshell, Mum left our cabin early. She had plans, she told me, people to see, emails to send. She had a hunted look about her, the kind of look you get when you've packed up your whole life for something only to be told that your old friend and new boss is dead, and your exciting new job no longer exists.

I stayed in our cabin, alone, trying to unpick how I felt about the whole thing. Mum talked about this as being our *fresh start*, like this was *our thing*, but now that we were here it was clearly *her thing*, and I was just in the way. She was the scientist. She was the one whose old university friend had just offered her the job of a lifetime. I was just … inconveniently large luggage.

She'd given me a choice about coming here. Go with her to Deephaven or stay with Dad in Watford. Technically, I was old enough to get a place of my own, but nobody had thought that was a good idea.

I'd chosen *here*, although I was starting to regret it already. The worst thing was that Mum probably thought giving me the choice was one of those grown-up, empowering things you do with troubled teenagers, but it meant that I never got to know what *she* wanted. Did she *actually* want me here? Or was it just that she felt like she didn't have a choice?

She came back late in the evening looking more exhausted than ever.

"Well?" I asked. "Are we really getting sent home?"

Mum forced a smile. "Don't worry, I'll figure something out."

It didn't sound promising.

She flopped into the armchair next to me. Our cabin was ridiculously tiny, a shoebox for a very small pair of shoes. There were two beige armchairs; a desk that folded up and latched on to the wall because it blocked the bathroom door when it was down; and a tiny kitchenette with a kettle, a small sink and two mugs.

"How was your day?" she asked.

"Fine," I said.

"What did you get up to?"

"Oh, er … reading, mostly."

She looked troubled. "Did you get out of the cabin?"

"Yes," I lied. "I went for a walk."

The truth was, I'd hidden in our cabin all day, trying to sleep off jet lag, eating the last of my travel snacks and watching old movies from the Deephaven downloads catalogue. I didn't feel up to facing the rig on my own yet. I'd known it was going to be weird down here – they'd warned us about that enough times at the training centre – but I was starting to worry that I really might not be able to cope. Too many things were too different. It felt too easy to end up in a restricted area or accidentally step out of a waterlock and flood the entire rig. I'd seen the rig layout a thousand times and practised operating a bulkhead door a dozen times in training, but it all felt different now.

Besides, the thought of meeting the other kids, the possibility that my social life between now and university might consist of nine more Jacob Rutherfords, was starting to freak me out.

I made Mum a cup of tea to avoid her penetrating look, taking the opportunity to quietly clear up some of the empty sweet wrappers I'd left lying around. The kettle was just big enough to boil two mugs of tea, but the stainless-steel sink was too small to actually wash either of them comfortably. I dumped milk powder into the foamy brown liquid and watched it dissolve.

"Even if we stay, it won't be the same down here without Maximus," Mum said, almost to herself. "And there's his son." The thought seemed to come to her suddenly. "As far as I know it was just the two of them; he'll be on his own now. They'll want to send him topside as well."

Poor guy. I wondered what had actually happened to Maximus. We'd spent the last nine weeks learning about all the ways the ocean would try to kill us down here, but I hadn't expected to be confronted by it right away. *Was it quick?* I wondered. Had something structural failed in the submersible and the full weight of the ocean rushed in and crushed him in a millisecond? Or had it been a slow leak? I shuddered at the thought of Maximus all alone in the dark as the water levels rose, wondering if he'd drown or freeze first.

"What will we do?" I asked.

It wasn't as if our old life was waiting for us back home. School had made it quite clear that I wasn't welcome back, and Mum's job at the university had been filled almost immediately.

"Well, we'll take it one day at a time," Mum said. "I have some time booked with two of Maximus's senior team tomorrow. We'll see if they have any ideas."

"Like what? Carter said your contract had been nullified."

"Carter doesn't have final say on everything, you know that," Mum replied. "Deephaven is a collaboration between the mining companies and the universities. The Consortium only gets mining licences in return for hosting the science team. If I can get some support from the universities…"

"Is that likely?"

I caught a frustrated look from Mum. "I don't know, Lily." She softened and placed her hand on my arm. "Try not to think about it. The only thing you have to focus on for now is school."

"School?"

The word stuck in my throat. I hadn't thought it through exactly, but with all the uncertainty about whether or not we were staying, I'd started to imagine that I could skip the whole new school thing.

"Why not? That's half the reason we came here."

"But I haven't really settled in yet," I protested.

"And hiding in our cabin is the best way to do that, is it?" She glanced over at the detritus of our obviously-lived-in room, the crisp packets and remaining sweet wrappers. "Dr Balgobin is famous. It's too good an opportunity to miss."

"Famous for what?" I asked.

"Famous for teaching *seven* of last year's Top Twenty Most Influential People according to *Time* magazine, all of whom cite Dr Balgobin as a major force in ... you know, their path to greatness and everything."

"Right."

Mum reached out and touched my cheek – tenderly, regretfully – in a way that reminded me of when I was much younger. "I'm sorry it's not been the smoothest of starts."

I shrugged begrudgingly.

"You'll be OK, though, won't you?"

I nodded slightly, unconvincingly.

"Get some sleep, love," Mum said. "You'll feel better in the morning."

CHAPTER 7

Darkness. Blistering darkness. A darkness that feels like falling. The kind of darkness you don't get topside because it takes five kilometres of ocean to block out the light so completely.

The memory of where I was settled on me as it had the previous morning. I groped to click on the lamp, and a watery yellow glow spilled into the cabin.

It was so *small*!

I wondered if I'd think that every time I woke up from now on. Staring at the walls, I couldn't shake the feeling that they were gradually moving closer, wrapping themselves around me like a shroud, smothering me.

I sat up sharply, my heartbeat a steady *thud-thud* that

seemed to reverberate through my entire body. There was a domed porthole above my bed, but all it did was reflect back my own face in a twisted, purple-grey swirl.

I could feel my reflection watching me.

I got up on to my knees so I could look more closely. I've always thought my face was too small and had too many sharp corners to be pretty. In the reflection, however, it was just blurry fragments, contours, hints of light and dark. I looked like a ghost version of myself. Or not a ghost, but another version, another me, someone I didn't understand.

I winced ... and the reflection winced a fraction of a second later.

Whispery fingers of panic began to stroke the back of my neck, like I'd been having a bad dream and it hadn't quite finished with me yet. The face of a girl like me out there in the ocean, dead, impossible. Then—

So alone...

I leapt up suddenly, stumbling back from the porthole. *What was that?* I'd heard something. No, not heard exactly. *Thought* it. Not even the words, just the feeling. *So alone...* A feeling that was familiar enough to me, especially since all the trouble at school, but which had also come from nowhere, had seemed ... outside.

I moved closer to the porthole, trembling, trying hard to control my breathing.

Nothing. No reflection. Just silt tumbling in a grey haze.

Not possible—?

I stumbled back again, bursting into our main cabin. I flicked on a light and surveyed the tiny space, trying to find some sort of normality. *A cabin, just a cabin*, I told myself. I gulped several lungfuls of air. *Pretend you're in a caravan... A caravan parked in a giant open field*. But my brain and my body knew it wasn't true. It was a caravan all right, but it was a caravan bolted to the ocean floor five kilometres down.

Don't freak out. Don't freak out.

Oh, god, I'm freaking out at the bottom of the ocean.

I shook my head and took another breath. I could feel myself getting calmer. I smothered a wave of hysterical laughter. *Stupid*. Scared of a porthole? This really wasn't cool. I went to the tiny sink and splashed cold water in my face.

The digital clock on the wall read *04:56*. Jet lag.

That must be it.

Jet lag or a Remote Operated Vehicle kicking up silt, messing with the reflectiveness of the window and the water. I considered checking the porthole again, just to be sure, but I didn't want to.

I drew a final, long breath and concentrated on keeping it steady as I exhaled.

Jet lag sucks. With no light down here, the team running Deephaven could have picked any time zone they wanted; "day" is defined only by when they turn up the lighting in the corridors. But to avoid arguments about whether to choose American or Japanese time, they went with the time according to our geographical longitude.

Which made it lunchtime by my body clock.

I looked down and noticed the note next to the kettle for the first time: *Couldn't sleep. Gone to work. Don't be late for school. Mum x*

I read it twice. *Seriously?* On my first day of school?

I flicked on the kettle and did my best to wash one of the mugs from last night in the tiny basin. Mum could be like that sometimes. There's a reason she likes plants. You feed and water a plant, give it sunlight and soil, and it's happy. Mum likes that level of clarity. In her head, all the *mum* stuff was probably done last night and so there was no need for it again today. That's Mum: brisk and businesslike, smart and practical – perfectly evolved for the pointier end of the academic world.

But surely this was different? She knew I was nervous, and yet she'd decided to leave me alone and go to work anyway, *and she didn't even have a real job here!*

I imagined her in the science team's lab, hunched over her laptop and sending strongly worded emails. Or worse, hanging around the lab techs, trying to make herself useful, like the awkward girl in class. Did she really think she could finagle a job here just by looking like she belonged?

Alone in our tiny room, my thoughts swirled. I

shouldn't have come. I should have stayed with Dad. I shouldn't have messed up my life so completely that Mum felt it necessary to bring us here.

I felt like an idiot. I felt like a fraud.

There was a *snick*, and something gave way beneath my fingers. I looked down and realized that I'd pulled the handle off Mum's mug. I held the two pieces, looking at them: a porcelain "C" and a perfect cylinder. I swallowed. I'd done this kind of thing before. Quite a lot, if I'm honest. But I'd promised Mum, and I'd meant it: *a fresh start*. No more breakage. No more *problems*. And here I was, slipping on my second day.

OK, enough procrastination. I had to face this place sooner or later.

I pulled on my flight suit and headed out into the corridor.

I shivered. It was eerily quiet, but also not quiet. Pipes somewhere in the walls tinkled with the sound of the hot water that regulated the temperature. Vents in the ceiling circulated and refreshed the air. It was like being inside the stomach of a sleeping animal, surrounded by the sound of its body's processes.

Just breathe. I could do this. I'd been to new and strange places before… Actually, that wasn't true. Dad didn't exactly do "new and strange". He had to travel a lot for work, but that exhausted him so much he never wanted to go anywhere other than the same holiday cottage in Deal that we'd been visiting every year for as long as I could remember. I'd spent my whole life at the same school, and I'd made exactly one friend in all that time. And she hated me now anyway.

I'd always longed to live an interesting life, to go and see interesting places and do interesting things. But I'd always imagined I'd start a little smaller.

I followed the corridor past regularly spaced cabin doors. Mum and I were lucky. As one of the few families on board, we got a room to ourselves, while most of the staff shared, four to a cabin. I reached the end of our hab unit and stepped over the lip of the bulkhead into the polytunnel. My heart picked up speed as I realized that this was the first time I'd been in a polytunnel on my own. There were no portholes. Just a tube of dull, black polycarbonate. I could feel the uneven surface of the ocean floor beneath me. I touched the wall of the tunnel where it arched over my head and imagined the ocean waiting outside like a predator. What would it be like to be crushed by that much ocean? Would I feel it? Just for a microsecond?

Two more hab units. Three more polytunnels. The layout of Deephaven was confusing. The main rig was set into the rockface, which meant that to get to the canteen from our accommodation I had to first head away from the main rig, take a staircase up a level, and then loop back.

Finally, I got there, stepping over another bulkhead into

the rig's reassuringly sturdy steel shell. The lights were brighter here, still dimmed to remind people that it was technically night-time, but brighter because the main rig was a twenty-four-hour operation. Two of Carter's team were coming the other way, one slightly in front of the other, their shoulders overlapping, which was as close as you could get to walking side-by-side on Deephaven. The first I recognized as Holden, and the next was MacMillan, according to his badge. Holden caught my eye and gave me a look I couldn't quite decode. Resentful? Smug? Superior? They pressed their bodies to the pipework on the walls in a well-practised way, allowing me to pass, then reconvened and resumed their conversation on the far side.

One floor up on the main staircase and I was in the canteen. About twenty people milled about: the blue hard hats and grey flight suits of Ari's operations and maintenance teams, the spotless white flight suits of Carter's installation management team, and two people in green flight suits, designating them as science team members. I hurried into the queue to avoid them in case they knew Mum and wanted to talk to me.

I waited as canteen staff loaded plastic plates with chips and thick slices of gammon. I'd just sat down with my own plate, piled high with chips and ketchup and nothing else, when I caught the flash of an orange flight suit.

"Can I join you?" a voice said.

Orange meant *family*. The same colour as my flight suit,

like an American prison outfit in a bad sitcom. I looked up and saw Jacob standing over me.

"Jet-lagged as well?" he asked, sitting, not waiting for an invite.

I nodded, my heart sinking.

"Excited?"

"Uh – I guess."

I eyed him suspiciously, trying to figure him out. He was ridiculously good looking. Tall and muscular, but not the kind of muscular you get from going to the gym, the kind you get from playing lots of sports, climbing mountains and saving people's pets from burning buildings. At the same time, his face was narrow and serious, almost bookish, as if his overly intense dad was bursting to get out, notebook in hand. It was a bit like when a movie star you know from action movies gets cast as a scientist and it doesn't quite work.

I imagined him as a stay-up-late-doing-his-homework kind of person who then gets up early to practise for whichever "A" team he plays for. The kind of person who would effortlessly break up a fight between two strangers and earnestly explain to them that violence was not the way.

"Look, I think we got off on the wrong foot yesterday," he said. "I get it now, you were trying to be funny … about the light bulbs? Because Ari couldn't possibly know exactly how many there were?"

"Um, yeah." My insides were beginning to shrivel up. "It's OK, it was a lousy joke. Forget it."

"No, no, it's my fault, I should have thought—"

He stabbed his fork into his salad and devoured the green leaves with relish. Of course he would be somebody who made sure he got his five-a-day. I found myself searching for flaws. Was there a hint of arrogance in the way he was looking at me? Nope, not really. Was he being patronizing? Nope.

"I was just a bit wrong-footed, you see," he said, pressing on doggedly. "You'd been sick over quite a lot of people, so I didn't really expect you'd want to talk to anyone—"

Wrong-footed. Nobody our age says wrong-footed.

"Seriously, drop it," I said sharply.

He turned back to his food with a hurt look.

"Look, I'm sorry," I added quickly. "I'm sorry about that. I'm just ... jet-lagged."

He flashed me an Academy-Award-winning grin. "No problem."

"How come I didn't see you at the training centre?" I asked. "Seeing as you're new here as well?"

Jacob looked faintly embarrassed. "Oh, they let us skip the training."

"Seriously?"

"Mum and Dad have been working rigs, solar pontoons and wind farms since I was a baby. They say I was born in a flight suit and a life vest." A flickering, self-conscious smile. "We caught a couple of refresher courses at the seaweed ranch before we came here, but … once you've seen one experimental offshore rig, you've seen them all, right?" He smiled. Modestly. Not fake modesty, real. "Hey, what did Carter want to see you and your mum about?"

"There's no job for her any more," I explained. "We're not staying. We have to go home when the next supply sub comes."

"Oh?" He made a good show of looking genuinely disappointed.

"Maximus Clarke had given her the contract, but … he had an accident."

Jacob nodded gravely. "I heard about that. Except…" He leaned closer, whispering, "I heard it wasn't an accident."

"Huh?"

"They say he lost his mind and took off in a submersible. They reckon he just drove until he ran out of oxygen. It happens sometimes … down here."

He swallowed another forkful of salad, leaving two perfect spheres of dressing at the corners of his mouth. *How do they even get salad down here anyway?*

"Seriously?" I said. "He did it on purpose?"

The thought of Dr Clarke's death *not* being an accident felt like cold water running down my back. The image came quickly, uncomfortably, into my mind. Climbing into the hard innards of a submersible, knowing he wasn't coming back.

"That's what I heard," Jacob said. "A few of the other kids told me about it."

Amongst a head full of images of a doomed Maximus, I managed to note that Jacob had already met the others. Presumably yesterday while I was hiding in our cabin. Presumably they were all best friends by now.

"How do they know?" I asked.

Jacob shrugged. "No sign of a body, I guess. No debris. Plus, they say Maximus was kind of an oddball." He looked thoughtful for a moment, then brightened. "You're still coming to school, though, right? I mean, you have to, it's the law, and besides, Dr Balgobin is—"

"She's famous, yes, I get it," I said.

"Well?"

I nodded reluctantly. I knew I was being sullen and uncommunicative, and I should be making more of an effort, but I've never been very good with people. I don't *mean* to be weird, but things I say just come out wrong.

"Sure." I forced a smile. "Of course I'm coming to school."

Jacob grinned at me. "Hey – it'll be OK. I'll look out for you."

"Look out for me?" I scowled at him. "We're both equally new."

"Sure, but you didn't exactly get off to the best start, did you?"

I frowned more deeply; Jacob looked worried. I could tell he was desperately trying to back-pedal, afraid of upsetting me.

"In what way?" I asked.

"Well … you kind of threw up over a lot of people."

"I said I was sorry about that."

"And there's all that talk about you trying to mess with the fusion reactor. That kind of made some people nervous."

I felt myself flush. This was bad news; Holden must have spread the story around. The first impression everyone would have of me was as the girl who threw up everywhere and then tried to mess with the fusion reactor on her first day. I sighed inwardly; Mum wouldn't be happy about this.

I stood and picked up my tray. "Well … thanks, I guess."

We took our trays to a trolley in the far corner and stashed them. As I did so, I slipped the broken pieces of Mum's mug from my pocket and on to the plate. All the mugs I'd seen in Deephaven so far were identical, and I'd seen a large rack of them near the exit. I plucked a fresh one as we left. At least Mum didn't need to find out that I'd been breaking things already.

"Are you taking that?" Jacob asked, frowning.

"Um – the one in our cabin is broken."

"Oh, right, well, I guess that's OK then." He turned his sunny smile on me again, although there was suspicion in his eyes. "Well, see you in class!"

CHAPTER 8

The training we needed before coming to Deephaven had involved three weeks of theory on an industrial site in Portsmouth, England, and a further six weeks of practical lessons in Newfoundland, Canada.

My memory of that time is a blur. Back-to-back slides and simulations, a lecture hall that smelled of polish and our lecturer's Glacier Mints. And the weather in Newfoundland: a bit like an English summer, except colder, wetter and darker. I didn't think I'd miss it until I came to Deephaven where there is no weather.

Things had been awkward between Mum and me in Portsmouth. We trod carefully around each other, being overly nice. It was like we were in the aftermath of an argument, even though we hadn't really argued since the week after I was suspended.

By the time we got to Newfoundland, things had settled down, but a new paranoia had started to invade my thoughts. Nothing was ever quite right between us. It felt like one of those family holidays where everyone wishes they hadn't come; except I couldn't tell any more if Mum wished *we* hadn't come, or just that *I* hadn't come.

We were the only ones in Newfoundland who were going to Deephaven. That made us a curiosity amongst the trainees destined for more conventional rigs.

"There's a whole science team down there," Mum had enthused over dinner one night to an audience of me and three surly-looking rig workers. "There are world-class teaching facilities, families, everything. It's a new model of working. Fully carbon neutral. Sustainable. Respectful of the local ecology. A true collaboration between science and industry."

A look passed between the three men. The largest – a *roustabout*, he told us, whatever that was – furrowed his brow. "Deephaven? That's where you're going?"

"That's right," Mum said, her smile faltering. "Have you heard of it?"

They nodded slowly. Suddenly nobody looked particularly hungry.

"What's wrong?" Mum asked.

"It's just stories," a thin-faced man said.

"What kind of stories?"

"There's *things* down there," the roustabout said. "Things we haven't seen before."

Mum smiled. "I know. That's what we're going for."

"You don't understand—" the roustabout replied quickly.

"Ignore him," the thin–faced man cut in. "Rig workers are superstitious. That's all."

"It's not superstition!" the roustabout snapped. "It's science."

The third man joined the conversation, a *toolpusher* (apparently): "There were some equipment malfunctions, nothing to worry about. A couple of accidents."

"*Accidents!*" the roustabout scoffed. "Deephaven is too deep, that's what it is. Deeper'n we've gone into the ocean before. Going that deep for that long … it makes people lose their sense."

The thin–faced man looked irritated. "They keep the pressure inside Deephaven at one atmosphere. It's no different from topside."

"I'm not talking about the pressure; there's more to water than *pressure*," the roustabout snapped. "Life begins in amniotic fluid," he continued more softly, "which is basically seawater. Our inner ears evolved from *gills*." He widened his eyes meaningfully. "I knew a woman, a free diver, she said her brain changed when she was that deep underwater. Parts of her woke up. She could *see* the earth's magnetic field."

The thin-faced man snorted.

"It's true," the roustabout insisted. "She *felt* something down there."

Nobody responded for a moment. We watched the toolpusher, anxious to hear his verdict, as if he had the deciding vote.

"Just watch yourselves, OK?" he said at last, choosing his words carefully. "It's probably nothing. But ... there's something *off* about that place."

CHAPTER 9

**LILY FAWCETT: DEEPHAVEN PERSONAL LOG
DAY 3**

They say living on Deephaven is like living in a village. Except it's a village where the nearest shop is seventy-two hours — two boats and a helicopter — away. Where the internet is so slow, they download one newly released movie a week and they watch it together in the canteen on Fridays. It's a village where there is no sky, no wind and no rain (or if there was, it would be salty and it would squash you like a bug). It's a village where everybody wears regulation flight suits and neoprene underwear — industrial-grade super-onesies with Velcro seams and about fifty pockets. A village where, if you ask about anything, they'll just tell you it's a "safety thing".

But when you've got five thousand tonnes of ocean hanging over your head, I'm not sure how fifty pockets, Velcro seams, and flame-retardant underpants are going to help.

Think about it: what kind of person *chooses* to live on an experimental mining rig at the bottom of the ocean? What kind of person chooses to do that with their *family*?

People for whom being an astronaut sounded a little too passé, perhaps? Adventurous types. Brave, confident types who have met other brave, confident types and had brave, confident children. Children who are good and optimistic and outgoing, like Jacob.

Children who don't break things when they get stressed.

Let's face it: school on Deephaven was never going to play well.

I sat, hunched over in my regulation flight suit, while Dr Balgobin introduced me and Jacob to the others.

"We have two newts joining us today," she announced, bright and breezy as a crisp spring morning. "Newts is what we call New Starters, right? New St ... arters? Get it?"

Newts? Cute ... if you're *eight*.

Dr Balgobin was tall, with dark skin and shining black hair that curled around her head like a conch shell. She was slightly younger than Mum and jaw-droppingly beautiful. Her cheeks seemed to glow in the harsh fluorescent lights, reflecting back something warmer and more human; her deep brown eyes held a smile so that when she talked to you it was as if she was *seeing* you, and only you, in a way that nobody else had ever seen you before.

All our lessons would be with her, she explained. There were now eleven children of staff on the rig: six teens in this class and five younger kids in the junior class, taught by Dr Bergel. "But I'm well qualified on all subjects," she added without a hint of pride. "I have a PhD in Applied Mathematics from Princeton, and my Masters in English and Classics is from Durham. We can sort out your preferences for language classes later; I'm fluent in Arabic, Spanish and Mandarin, and I can probably make myself useful in German or Italian at a pinch."

Was she for real? "A PhD *and* a Masters *and* fluent in multiple languages — isn't that taking it a bit far?" I quipped. "What do you do in your spare time? Rescue orphans?"

Dr Balgobin looked aghast. Suddenly the whole class was staring at me, their eyes shifting restlessly between me and Dr Balgobin's hurt expression.

Regret knotted my stomach. *Why did I always do this?* I hadn't exactly meant to say anything out loud, it had just slipped out. In my last school, teachers were fair game, but here the pupils were earnest, hard-working overachievers just like their parents. Of course they adored their teacher!

"Well, in fact, I did spend a few years working in an

orphanage in Bosnia," Dr Balgobin said, faltering slightly. "I hope to go back there someday."

Jacob shot me a desperate look, shaking his head ever so slightly in warning.

I drew a breath. "That's, um, great," I said, back-pedalling. "Really admirable."

Jacob gave me a faint nod.

OK, not my best start. But I'd work through it, I reasoned. I'd keep my head down and after a while people would stop noticing me; that was how it usually worked.

"Right!" Dr Balgobin chirped. "Introductions. Alban, start us off, please. Name and a fun fact about yourself!"

A fun fact? Didn't she know how unbearably painful this was for people our age? For anyone, for that matter. I looked around at the other kids – upright and beaming, eager to unleash their fun facts – and felt a wave of nausea.

"Hi, I'm Alban," said a blue-eyed, athletic-looking boy slightly younger than me. "My fun fact is that my great-great-uncle was Ernest Shackleton, you may have heard of him, he was pretty famous for, like … Antarctica or something."

Shackleton? Probably the most famous British explorer ever? Yes, I'd heard of him.

Another boy stood up next. Tall, slender and serious-looking, about my age I guessed. "I'm Jian," he said. "My fun fact is that I play piano quite well. I performed at Carnegie Hall when I was eight, and I have my own jazz album coming out in the spring."

Quite well? Seriously?! Nothing to feel inferior about there.

I racked my brain for something that would sound OK to these people: *I once watched an entire season of* Strictly Come Dancing *in one sitting?* No, that wouldn't do. Hanna and I once ate a whole pack of Hobnobs and nearly threw up. No, definitely not.

"I'm Ysabel," said a wiry girl with a blond ponytail who looked like she'd just returned from a bracing hike to the top of Mont Blanc. "My fun fact is that I represented Switzerland in the Junior Winter Olympics two years ago." She smiled, pride and self-assurance radiating off her. She glanced in my direction and her brow furrowed slightly. "I hope I get to help orphans one day too."

Junior Winter Olympics? Who even knew that was a thing?

Jacob leapt up next, boy-scout grin and all. His skin was perfect, I noticed, not a hint of acne. He wasn't a boy; he was a perfect CGI simulation of a boy. I wondered what it would be like to look and be so perfect. *Would I be a nicer person if I looked like him?* "My name's Jacob," he said. "My dad's the new Safety Officer on board, and my mum heads up the Pump Inspection team."

"Super important jobs," Dr Balgobin said, amongst approving nods from the class. "But then every job on the rig is important, isn't that right, team?"

Again, everyone nodded and murmured their approval. I heaved inwardly.

"My fun fact," Jacob added quickly, "is that my dad and I once solo sailed from Australia to New Zealand."

The mood changed when the next boy stood up. He was slender and loose-limbed, but he looked less at ease than the rest of the class; his dark eyes seemed inward looking, as if his thoughts were someplace else; he looked more like a shadow than a person, an absence rather than a presence. It reminded me of something Hanna would say sometimes after I asked if she was going to a particular class: *I'll be there in body, if not in spirit.*

"Evan," he said flatly.

I glanced around at the class. Alban suddenly seemed fascinated by the book on his desk. Ysabel was twisting her ponytail like she was wringing out a dishcloth.

"My dad, Maximus, is the Chief Science Officer on Deephaven... Or he was until two weeks ago when he went missing. I'm sorry, that's not much *fun* as facts go."

He sat down again, red-faced. Dr Balgobin placed a comforting hand on his shoulder. "It's OK, Evan." She turned to me brightly. "He won't say it, but Evan's also an off-the-charts genius just like his father. So ... I think that just leaves you, Lily?"

Great. She wanted me to follow *that*? I stood slowly, not knowing what I was going to say even as I opened my mouth.

"I, um … I'm Lily," I found myself saying. "I once put lemonade in my dad's petrol tank, and it made the engine catch fire."

I looked out at the room full of blank faces. Stupid. Stupid. Stupid. The girl who messes with fusion reactors and set fire to her dad's car?

Great, Lily. Just great.

At lunch break, it was all shy smiles and clumsy niceties as we left the classroom.

I followed them into the polytunnel, feeling awkward and outside of things as they chatted about a maths test that was coming up, and what movie was going to be downloaded for that Friday.

"Why did you set fire to your dad's car?" Ysabel asked, turning abruptly to me as we clattered down a prefabricated staircase.

"It was an accident," I mumbled.

"You *accidentally* put lemonade in the petrol tank?"

"No. I mean … it was a joke."

Ysabel blinked. "It's a weird joke."

"Yes," I agreed, feeling flummoxed. "It was."

Ysabel looked at me like I was giving off a bad smell. Behind her, Alban smirked, and Jacob widened his eyes in warning, as if he was urging me to do a better job of not being weird. I missed Hanna. Hanna would have stepped in by now and smoothed things over. She'd have made out the whole thing was just a big, kooky joke for the class's enjoyment: *yay for Lily, she's so out there!* Hanna had a knack for that sort of thing. Fun Hanna, who could get away with things like smuggling her brother's pet snake into class and terrorizing the boys with it. Hanna was my interface. I didn't know how to get along without her.

"So, where are you from?" Alban asked as we arrived in the canteen and collected our noodles and cheese sandwiches for lunch.

"England," I replied.

Alban and Ysabel exchanged a look like they were both rolling their eyes at me.

"Right, I guessed that much. But whereabouts in England?"

"Um – nowhere special."

The canteen was more crowded than I'd seen before. I scanned the various coloured flight suits as they milled around, hoping to spot Mum amongst the green ones.

"Is it a secret?" Alban pressed, leaning his pointy face towards mine.

"No, it's not a secret," I said. "It's just a dumb question."

Alban seemed undeterred. I could tell that he had an agenda of some kind, but I couldn't figure out what it was. My head was starting to pound and the clatter of cutlery seemed way too loud. *I could freak out now*, I thought. I could push my tray and food to the floor and storm off.

That's what I'd normally do, like a little pressure valve popping open inside my head.

But I couldn't. I'd promised Mum, and like Jacob said, I wasn't exactly off to a good start already.

"Does it matter?" I said sharply. "I don't live there any more."

"My family's originally from Vancouver," Jacob offered. "But we've lived all over."

"*Thank you*," Alban said ingratiatingly.

"OK, fine," I said. "I'm from High Wycombe. Happy now?"

"*High Wycombe…*" Alban said, rolling the words slowly in his mouth. He shrugged. "Nope, never heard of it."

CHAPTER 10

Ysabel spent the rest of the afternoon being the first to answer Dr Balgobin's questions and looking smug about it.

Was the failure of the Schlieffen Plan the main reason for the stalemate on the Western Front? Discuss.

Bing! Up went her hand.

Derive an expression to show that the time taken by a proton to travel round a cyclotron is independent of the radius of the path.

Bing! Up went her hand. With every answer, her ponytail bobbed chirpily, and she gave me a sort of self-satisfied smirk, like a corgi sitting on a velvet cushion. Little-Miss-Junior-Winter-Olympics.

By the afternoon break I'd had enough. I peeled away from the group, muttering an excuse under my breath, and headed off to find Mum. I tried to picture the rig schematic to help orient me, but I couldn't find any of the little green embossed signs that indicated which way to go for the science unit. It was like using an underground map to navigate street directions in London. I knew the rig was built in a horseshoe shape around the ridge, the main rig in the centre, the hab units sprawled north and south to either side, like a caravan park that had been built too close to a cliff edge. I knew that the abyssal plain rose steadily to the west, and to the east the level dropped sharply towards the blasted flatland of the telemetry grid. But that knowledge was of little use to me in the twisting, windowless corridors and poorly signposted polytunnels.

I'd just completed a second lap of the main rig and was trying to avoid being spotted by the rest of the class when I ran into Ari.

"Heyyyy, Lily Fawcett." He beamed. "Lost? Canteen's this way."

He gestured towards the canteen, which was right next to us.

"I'm looking for Mum," I said.

"Gotcha." Ari pointed directly above his head. "Two levels up, west polytunnel."

"Of course."

He stopped me before I could skulk away: "How're you holding up?"

I shrugged extravagantly.

Ari punched me on the shoulder. "Atta-girl!"

He turned and practically skipped into the canteen.

Atta-girl? Well ... I guess that makes everything OK, then.

The sounds changed as I walked into the polytunnel. Inside the main rig, everything had a tinny sort of sound – the air conditioning, the quiet hum of the fusion reactor. You stopped noticing it after a while. As soon as you stepped into a polytunnel, though, the high frequencies disappeared and there was a muffled sound instead, like hearing loud music playing from the next room. The west polytunnel ran like a vein along the part of the ridge that led away from the telemetry grid and overhung the trench: two more kilometres straight down, another two thousand tonnes of ocean. I tried not to think about it.

The science lab was at the farthest end of the site, a dedicated hab unit about the size of my old school assembly hall. There were rows of workbenches stacked with test tubes, sinks, flat screens, and serious-looking trays of sample jars. The ceiling was low, as it was in all the hab units, which gave the room a kind of telescopic, zoomed-out feel.

Mum was in the far corner, wearing a white lab coat over her green flight suit and hunched at her laptop just as I knew she would be.

"Lily!" she exclaimed when she saw me. She hugged me

and then called over my shoulder to two of her co-workers. "Joy, Isaac? Come and meet my daughter."

I regarded her suspiciously. She seemed too happy. *Unfairly happy.* In fact, she was beaming, filled with an excited, flighty energy.

Joy bustled over, all smiles and warm-hearted, myopic blinking. She squeezed my hand with her own, pressing a biro into my free hand at the same time. I looked at it for a moment.

"For me?" I asked, nonplussed.

Joy smiled again, nodding slowly. I shot a look at Mum, who gave a short warning shake of her head in reply.

A tall, hollow-cheeked man followed Joy. He had a long, peppery beard, and he gave my hand a slow, mournful shake, his eyes never once leaving the domed porthole behind my head. Something in his eyes irked me. Like he was watching something out there. I glanced over my shoulder, half expecting to see my own face staring back at me, but it was just silt and white light.

"Where were you this morning?" I asked Mum once her colleagues had finished their introductions and retreated back to their workstations.

"I couldn't sleep," Mum answered carefully, her smile faltering.

"I woke up and you were gone."

"I'm sorry," she said. "I shouldn't have left you alone so soon."

I nodded. I was surprised by how irritated I felt. I hadn't meant to come here and give her a hard time, but she was looking so *happy* I could hardly bear it.

"How was school?" she asked.

"Awful."

"I'm sure it wasn't that bad."

"I was thinking," I said, the words coming out in a rush, "seeing as we're only here for a couple of weeks, I thought I could self-study or something instead?"

"But Dr Balgobin is *famous*," Mum protested, her face painted with disappointment.

"So you keep saying."

Mum gave me an appraising look. "Do you really think being cooped up in our cabin is the best thing for you?"

"Yes," I said.

Mum's face tightened; I could tell that she didn't want an argument in front of her colleagues. "The thing is, I think I have a plan that'll let us stay on."

"Oh?"

"It was Joy's idea. It's a long shot, but we've got Maximus's notes. If I can fill in some of the gaps and pull together an application for a grant, even a lousy one, Carter won't be able to send us home until the universities have had a chance to respond."

I didn't say anything. I'd spent all morning telling myself it was going to be OK because we were only here for a couple of weeks. I looked down and started reading from the stack of papers on Mum's desk in order to avoid meeting her eye. There were lots of them, four or five stacks of A4, each as high as a fat hardcover novel, printed in a small, single-spaced font. My gaze fell on the lines nearest to me:

> At the time that turned the heat of the earth, at the time when the light of the sun was subdued, Po dwelt within the breathing space of immensity. The universe was in darkness with water everywhere. The slime established the earth, but beneath that the source of deepest darkness, the depth of darkness...

What?

I frowned at Mum. "Are these Maximus's notes?"

Mum waved a hand dismissively. "They're not all like that."

"What *is* that?" I said. "Po? The breathing space of immensity?"

"It's a Hawaiian poem, parts of it anyway," Joy explained, clearly having eavesdropped. "It's based on our creation story; my mother used to sing it to me when I was little. The *Kumulipo* tells of the three gods: Kāne, Ku and Lono, who pulled themselves from the light-possessing darkness, the Po, to become the darkness-possessing light which formed the earth."

I frowned. "I thought Maximus was studying algae, not Hawaiian religion?"

Mum squirmed under my gaze. "There's plenty of real science in the notes as well."

"And who prints anything out on paper these days?" I added.

"Maximus was a little ... eccentric."

I could tell Mum wasn't telling me everything. I'd spent enough time living with her to know what scientific papers looked like, and this wasn't it. She grabbed a sheaf of notes and started rearranging them, positioning herself so I couldn't read anything more.

I turned away. There was a pressurized tank on the desk nearby which caught my eye instead. It was cylindrical, clear, with heavy moulded seals at the top and the bottom.

"What's this?" I asked.

"Um ... nothing," Mum said guardedly. "Just one of Maximus's samples."

I peered closely at the tank. The liquid inside was silty, slightly grey coloured, and it reminded me of the endless grey bleakness outside that you could see in the spotlights. *This* was the euglenoid? *This* was why we were here?

"It looks like seawater," I said.

"Yes," Mum said. She seemed to be getting flustered now.

"Can you see anything under the microscope?"

"Not ... as such."

"So, it's just seawater?"

Mum pursed her lips. "It'll take a bit of time to unpick

his work, that's all. Maximus was an extremely smart man. He had a plan; we just need to figure out what it was."

I was starting to wonder if she'd thought this through. Did she really think she could extract a plausible research proposal from a bunch of Hawaiian poetry and some old seawater? I peered more closely at the cylinder.

Maybe Maximus had lost his mind just like Jacob said. Maybe his notes were utter nonsense, and maybe Mum was about to mail a pressure jar full of dirty water to the world's most prestigious group of universities in the world.

There were a few tiny sparks of light drifting around the tank, microscopic grains of silt that caught the light as they rose and fell on the convection currents inside.

Resentment boiled inside me. And then something else—

So alone…

Where had that come from? A ball of emotion rose inside me. It caught me by surprise, fierce, overwhelming, almost knocking the wind out of me. I swallowed. The thought of Dad filled my mind. His big, soft hands, his soap and shaving cream smell. *Oh god, I'm going to cry*, I thought. I hadn't cried in months. *Why am I going to cry?* I felt dizzy. I stared at the tank of water, trying to hold myself together. I couldn't breathe. My heart clenched tight like a fist inside my chest. It was like when you dream about someone, and it's so vivid you can still feel them after you wake up. Like when you wake up sobbing and you don't know why.

I was shaking. Suddenly I was thinking about the porthole in my room again. My own reflection watching me. I stared at the water, drawn to it, going *into* it in my mind, and the harder I looked, the more sparks of light I saw.

I tried to back away.

The sparks of light grew in my imagination, twisting and shimmering impossibly. It felt like they were the only light, and if I didn't hold on to them, the darkness would swallow me, and I would *become* the darkness—

Desperately, I lashed out, sweeping the pressure jar on to the floor. It shattered, spraying glass and seawater around my ankles.

"*Lily!* What on earth—?"

"Darling? Are you OK?"

Joy's hand rested on my shoulder, causing me to flinch so hard she took an involuntary step backwards. I stared blankly at her, shaking with the effort of not bursting into tears as the real world drew slowly back into focus.

"I don't want to stay," I said, louder than I'd meant to. "I want to go home."

Mum's look of irritation gave way to worry as she rushed over and put her arm around me.

"I don't *like* it here," I said, pulling away from her. "It *scares* me."

"OK," Mum whispered. "It's OK."

She took my arm, and I allowed myself to be led gently away. I recognized that look; it was her *crisis management* look. It was the look she wore whenever she was dealing with Dad being unreasonable and freaking out about something, or whenever *I* freaked out and caused trouble.

Was I freaking out? I supposed I was.

"I'm sorry, I'll clean it up," I murmured.

"It's fine, I'll do it later," Mum replied stiffly.

She ushered me to the far end of the lab, which had been sectioned off into a kitchenette. There was a table and four chairs, a sink, a kettle and a coffee machine. I sat, my eyes squeezed tight. I listened as Mum boiled the kettle, and then opened my eyes as she sat with a coffee for herself and a milk-powdery tea for me.

"What was that?" she whispered urgently. I couldn't tell if she was worried or angry.

"Nothing. I'm fine."

I thought of Dad, of the day he moved out. *Chill out, Lilypad.* The memory wouldn't leave me alone.

Mum frowned. "Was it deliberate?"

"No, I promise."

The barrage of feelings was beginning to subside. Mostly, now, I just felt like an idiot. I'd promised Mum I would do my best to make this work, and here I was freaking out already, hating on my new class, smashing a sample jar, yelling in front of Mum's colleagues. I had a reputation for letting my emotions get the better of me, and for doing stupid things when they did.

"I want to go home," I said quietly. "This was a mistake."

"We only just got here," Mum said imploringly.

"And it's a *disaster*," I hissed. "Nobody wants us here; Maximus's notes are … are … gibberish, everybody at school is *weird*, and you're just clutching at straws."

"You've got to give it a chance, Lily."

"I have. I don't fit in here."

She didn't need to say it, but I knew what she was thinking: where *do* you fit?

"It's your first day," she said calmly.

"So?"

"We didn't come here lightly, did we? We discussed it. Over and over."

"I know."

I stared into my steaming cup of tea, the lumps of milk powder leaving tiny comet trails of white froth as they floated around the surface.

"You're not going to do anything … silly, are you?" Mum asked.

"No."

"Please."

"I *promise*, OK?"

I wished I felt as confident as I tried to make it sound.

"Maybe I should go home, and you stay here," I said. "I could live with Dad."

Mum blinked. She hadn't expected this. *I* hadn't expected this.

"Is that what you want?" Mum asked.

I tried to read her face. "I don't know. Is it what *you* want?"

Mum pinched her forehead. "Where's this coming from?"

"I … I don't feel right down here…"

Mum shook her head slightly. "Please don't."

"Don't what?" I felt a flash of anger. This wasn't Mum worrying about me, this was Mum worrying about what I was going to *do.*

"We need to make this work, Lily. *You* need to make this work."

"Mum, I'm trying—"

"This is our chance, right? There isn't anywhere else," Mum continued softly. "A fresh start. A chance for me to do something special with my career for once. A chance for you to get focused on your A-levels and get things back on track. You'll need to go to university if you want to get into design—"

"OK, I get it."

I stirred my tea to avoid looking at her. "What about Maximus?" I asked. "They're saying he lost his mind … that he might have done it deliberately."

83

"Don't say things like that," Mum admonished me. "What if his son overheard?"

"I'm *serious*," I insisted, leaning forward. "Look at Isaac. He barely said a word. And Joy? Did she give you a biro as well?"

Mum let out a half-laugh. "They're scientists. We're all a bit odd, you know that."

"What about what they said at the training centre in Newfoundland? All those stories about this place, about what happens when you come down this deep."

"Just stories; a bunch of idiots trying to scare us." Mum looked irritated now.

I took a breath. I wasn't sure what I was trying to say, but whatever it was, she didn't understand. I knew she didn't trust me any more. She didn't understand why I'd done what I'd done at school, so in her mind she had no way of knowing what I might do next. But the *worst* thing about what had happened was that *I* didn't trust me either. "What if I can't make it work? What if you're right and I mess up again?"

Mum's face tightened. She leaned forward too, her eyes cold and serious: "You can't," she whispered. "You can't break things here, Lily. Do you understand?"

Something in the heaviness of her voice made me look up. "Yes, of course."

"There's something I haven't told you," she went on. "Our situation is ... more delicate than it was meant to be."

"I don't understand."

"Carter can't find out about what happened at your last school. Or any of the other incidents. OK?"

I shook my head slightly. "But they must know. We filled out the clearance forms."

Mum was silent.

"Didn't you?" I asked.

She didn't meet my eyes. "I may have omitted a few details."

I gasped in shock. "You *lied* on our application form?"

Mum shook her head quickly, but she wasn't denying it. "Maximus covered for me, that's all. Signed off on some of the paperwork as a favour to an old friend. But now that he's gone, I don't know what's going to turn up."

It made sense: I'd known she was on edge about things working out down here, but this explained why she was *so* on edge. I let out a hard laugh. Mum who had always been so serious, such a stickler for the rules.

"I can't believe you'd do something like that," I whispered sharply.

I looked around at the lab. Nobody was paying any attention, but suddenly everything seemed hostile. I'd felt from the beginning that I didn't fit here, but now I had proof. In fact, being here was probably illegal, or in breach of some very serious contracts. I felt stupid for not realizing it sooner: how was it that I, with my terrible track record, had been accepted into what was probably the most exclusive school on the planet? Eleven families. That was all. Ernest Shackleton's great-great-nephew. A Junior Winter Olympian. And me.

I shuddered. "What were you thinking?"

"It'll be fine," Mum said firmly. She took a slow breath and touched her hair, smoothing it into place. "We needed a fresh start, didn't we? And … and I thought you'd be different once we got down here."

CHAPTER 11

I thought you'd be different down here. That didn't feel good. Was that what she wanted? A fresh start, a fresh daughter. Except now we were stuck down here with invalid paperwork, and if I couldn't keep up my end of the bargain, Mum would be in all sorts of trouble.

Dinner time. I steeled myself as I walked into the canteen. The noise and the smells and the people. If we were staying, I *had* to get used to this place.

And I didn't want to be alone. What had happened in the lab with the pressure jar had scared me. *What was that? Jet lag? Stress?* It hadn't *felt* like that.

My head swam. It was like the sea was pressing against

the walls of my thoughts — like a nagging toothache, a persistent weight.

The other kids aren't so bad, I chided myself. A little uptight compared to regular kids, but that was hardly surprising. Jacob was nice enough; he was making an effort. Alban was a bit scary, but at least you knew where you stood with him. Jazz pianist Jian was … just one of those awkward kids, probably quite a lot like Dad now I thought about it. Ysabel … well, I couldn't exactly imagine warming to her, but she wasn't the first self-loving, judgemental, overachieving brat I'd had to deal with.

I found the four of them seated at a table together, all on their phones, each eating with one hand and scrolling with the other. Our connection to the outside world relied on a series of UAC (Underwater Acoustic Communication) beacons, so it was slow, and basically useless for anything other than messaging and the weekly movie. Within Deephaven, however, the wifi was as good as anywhere, and there were loads of shared internal newsfeeds, books and games in the local servers to choose from. Jacob glanced at me when I approached, and then returned to his screen. *At least he looked up*, I thought.

"Where's Evan?" I asked. "Doesn't he eat with you?"

"You know he lost his dad, don't you?" Ysabel said, her eyes flicking to me briefly.

"Um … *yes*."

She gave me an irritated shake of her head. "Well. He's going through a lot. It's best for you to stay out of his way."

"Fine. I only asked—"

I stopped; she didn't look like she was listening anyway.

I stared at my food. Pasta and tomato sauce. There were other choices, but I had gone with the comfort option. It tasted strange, kind of chemical-y, but musty as well. Jian had selected steak, chips and peas, and was working his way around his plate: he'd just finished his peas and started on his steak, and presumably he'd move on to the chips next.

"How do they even get the food down here?" I wondered aloud, hoping to start a conversation. "It must take a lot to feed this many people. Do we grow it?"

Alban snorted. "*Grow* it?"

"I just meant—"

"Ocean temperature down here is roughly one degree Celsius," Jian said, his eyes still glued to his screen. "It's a natural fridge. They sink a new supply container every other week and the ROVs connect a polytunnel."

ROVs – Remotely Operated Vehicles, I reminded myself. I still couldn't understand why they didn't just use regular names for things.

"Once it's offloaded, we drop the weights and let it resurface," Jian continued, his head thrust forward at his screen. "Then we use the same harvesting pipeline we use for the polymetallic material to transfer the reclaimed weights back to the mainland."

Conversation extinguished. I stared at my food. "Gotcha. Thanks."

"Don't eat sushi on the second or last Friday of the month," Jian added seriously, although it seemed like he was giving the advice to his phone, not to me.

I could feel my own phone pressed against my flight suit pocket, but I resisted the urge to take it out. Taking it out would mean finding out whether or not Dad or Hanna had sent me a message, and I wasn't up for any more disappointment right now.

Alban let out a bark of laughter at whatever was happening on his phone, and a moment later Ysabel, Jacob and Jian threw up their arms in dismay. There was a flurry of chatter and brisk congratulations. I realized they'd been playing a game together.

"Another?" Ysabel said.

"What are you playing?" I asked.

But they were already absorbed in another round. Only Jacob looked up. "It's called Cephalopod," he said. "Evan created it. It's *amazing*."

I waited a polite moment for somebody to offer to include me.

No dice.

"Can I play?" I eventually asked.

"It's better with four," Alban replied.

I glared at them, anger bubbling inside me. Did they know how awful they were being? Or were they just being themselves?

I could feel my hands tingling with the urge to break something. I could shout. I could smash a plate. At least then they'd see me; at least they'd know I *existed*.

I clenched my fists. I couldn't. Mum would never forgive me. Apparently, we'd come to the bottom of the ocean to escape the old me and, it turned out, we'd come on some extremely suspect paperwork. I couldn't screw it up.

"We can make it work," Jacob finally said. "Here."

He gestured with his phone, and I felt my own phone buzz in my pocket as it accepted the local connection. I took it out and started the install.

No messages from Dad or Hanna. I tried not to think about it. I also tried not to think about how Jacob knew all about the game and seemed completely at ease with the group even though he'd arrived here at exactly the same time as me.

Then the game was ready, and my screen was a mass of swirling colours: a breathing, pulsing swathe of dark purples and greens, like coloured sands caught up in a tornado.

"I don't know what I'm doing," I said.

"You draw," Jacob explained. "And our drawings interact with each other."

"Interact how?"

"You'll see."

I tapped the screen and watched dark clouds of colour ripple outwards. They became caught up with the other colours and swept aside as the scene panned wildly upwards. I jabbed the screen to catch it, and immediately more waves of colour intersected and broke into complex interference patterns.

"You have to go with the flow more," Jacob advised.

"Some people think cephalopods, like squid and cuttlefish, are actually the remnants of an alien species," Jian mused without looking up.

"There's no scientific evidence for that," Alban replied shortly.

Jian dragged his eyes from his screen for a moment to give him an incredulous look. "Creatures that can communicate via high-resolution screens fifty million years before television was invented? That doesn't sound a little alien to you?"

"Ridiculous," Alban scoffed.

"Well, the Hawaiians thought they were special," Jian continued with calm authority. "They saw the squid as the last descendent of Kāne and Po."

I looked up. "You know about Kāne and Po?"

"*The darkness at the beginning of the world*," Jian said, his face glowing in the light from the screen. "*And it realized it was alone, and that realization became the light, the Kāne.*"

"Hey – watch out!" Alban interrupted.

I was still prodding, frustrated, at the screen. The colours drew together, and when I tapped them, they exploded into a shower of light, that then swept off to the side. Whatever the others were seeing, I clearly wasn't. *I'm supposed to be good at this stuff,* I thought. User interfaces. Visual cues. This was my thing.

But this wasn't like a system design, this was more like a conversation in colour and shape, and I was never great at making small talk.

"Careful," Jacob warned.

"Careful of what?" I cried, exasperated.

Alban tutted under his breath. The screen was panning wildly now, and I could sense the growing frustration in the others. Enough. I flipped my screen over and let it slap heavily on to the table. The others looked quizzically at me, my anger inexplicable to them.

"It's better with four," Alban said again.

Our cabin was empty, and it felt just as small as ever. Vinyl walls. Formica storage units. It was like living in a Wendy house – the kind of thing you can buy from Argos with a plastic sink and oven, the kind of thing that gets picked up by the first stiff breeze and smashed into the nearest fence.

There was no sign of Mum. She'd be working on her funding application, I presumed, firing out emails and wrangling drafts of different supporting documents. It was her happy place.

The cabin crowded around me. I looked guiltily at the mugs in the sink. How many had I broken and replaced so far? Five? Six? I'd lost count.

No, I couldn't do this; no more mugs. I shut myself in my bed–cupboard and closed my eyes instead. If I lay very still, I could ignore the stifling presence of the walls around me, the baleful porthole above my head. I imagined myself as a cat, curled up on a shelf in an airing cupboard.

The mattress wobbled beneath me in that contrary way that air beds do, like it was trying to shove me off. I wriggled, wishing for sleep. If I were asleep, I wouldn't have to think about the ocean, looming above me. The limitless darkness outside.

I sighed. Sleep wasn't coming, not yet.

I took out my phone and pulled up the last message from Dad, sent two days before we came here: *Hi, Lilypad! Have a safe journey. Super busy with work this week. Will text soon. Love Dad X.* That was over a week ago. No check-in to see how I was doing, nothing. He just couldn't see how big a deal this was for me, how much I needed another text from him. I should have hated him for it, but I couldn't. He did his best. The thought of him felt like a hole inside my chest, like I could imagine him into the cabin if I thought just a little harder.

I'm going to miss you.

I drew a sharp breath and held it.

The thought came into my head from nowhere, clear and crisp. It was my thought, but it didn't feel entirely my own.

I was beginning to tremble.

And then the memory came, as still and vivid as if it were carved out of black marble: dinner at the local curry house, just the two of us, the smell of spices and floor polish—

"I'm going to miss you," I said.

Dad nodded, carefully dipping a poppadom into a dish of chutney. "I'll miss you too."

I waited, knowing there wouldn't be anything more. "Will you be OK?"

Dad examined his poppadom. "I'm fine. I like my flat."

I knew there wasn't going to be any great moment of connection; Dad didn't do that kind of thing. But all the same, I wanted more.

I watched his long, gentle fingers break his poppadom along precise geometric lines. I fought back the urge to cry. This was our last night before I left for the training centre. Surely he could give me more than this.

"Hey, what about him?" I asked, sniffing, collecting myself. I pointed to the youngish couple eating nearby.

Dad brightened, twisting in his seat to see. "Dashboard of an Audi A6. Trying to be flashy, but kind of dated," he said. He turned back to me, more animated now that he was on safer ground. "And the woman he's with?"

"iPhone SE," I replied. "Not as straightforward as she thinks she is."

Dad smiled. This was his favourite game: *what user interface are they?*

"What about those two?" I asked, pointing to two middle-aged men in suits, who'd both mashed their poppadoms into gooey fragments.

"Bosch power drill and mini-screwdriver," Dad said without a moment's hesitation. "But the boss is actually the mini-screwdriver, and he knows it."

I grinned. Dad was the kind of person who couldn't tell if you were angry at him or if you'd stubbed your toe, but he could totally nail someone with a technology metaphor in a blink.

His expression turned serious. I could see he was making an effort to look directly at me. "You know I'm not very good at texting and all that stuff, Lily," he said.

"Are you seriously making your excuses in advance this time?" I replied.

"Mum said I had to be upfront with you."

I fought back my irritation. "I think I'd rather think you *might* text me."

Dad sighed. "It doesn't mean I don't love you. I'm just… You know what I'm like."

He was trying, and that had to count for something,

but the words didn't come naturally to him. It was like he was playing the piano with the sound off.

"You could try harder," I said.

"I will. It's just … I've got a big job. I'm going to be distracted."

"I know."

Dad was much worse when he had a job. He said it was because he had to get his head into the mind of the computer in order to design the interface for it. He said there wasn't room for much else after that, even for the people he loved. Mum said it was because he had his head so far up his own arse he ought to join a circus.

"Are you glad I'm going with Mum?" I asked. "Not staying here with you?"

Dad didn't answer at first. It wasn't a fair question because there was no answer that I wanted to hear. Under the table, I bent the head of my fork back so far the tines pressed into my palm.

"I'd have loved to have you with me, Lily, if I thought we could make it work."

Not an answer.

"But you don't think we could make it work?" I pressed.

"I didn't say that."

I bent the fork back the other way, easier this time.

"It's fine," I said, biting back an unruly urge to cry. "It'll be an experience. A fresh start."

Dad looked relieved. "That's my Lilypad!"

Under the table, the now-jagged edge of the fork's broken neck bit into my fingers.

I gasped as I resurfaced from the memory. I was sweating. That wasn't just a regular memory. That was a dream. Or something else. I didn't want to think about it. I checked to see if Hanna had texted instead; maybe I had somehow missed a notification.

Nothing.

I'd been friends with Hanna since I'd upended a pot of poster paint on her head when I was three. Hanna was herself, always and for ever, and that's why people loved her. And for some reason she liked *me*. More importantly, she understood me, made allowances for me. When I showed up at her sixteenth birthday party in jeans and a T-shirt (everybody else was wearing formal party clothes, as per the invite), Hanna was the one who disappeared upstairs and returned a moment later in jeans and a T-shirt, declaring it a casual party after all. When I freaked out in class the week after Dad moved out, and I had to go and hide in the toilet for a while, Hanna was the one who told the headmaster, Mr Davis, that I had premenstrual pains so everyone would leave us alone.

But I'd ruined it. "It's better we don't speak to each other any more," she had said. "I don't want to carry on pretending everything's fine when it's not."

I'd have been OK with pretending.

I re-read my last text message to her: *They're making us wear orange flight suits and the pasta sauce tastes like verrucas.*

I'd thought she might have sent a smiley, at least.

I put the phone away. I ached to go home, except home didn't exist any more.

Maybe it had never existed.

I ached for the absence of an ache.

I'm going to miss you.

My heart fluttered and turned.

I was going to lose my mind down here if I wasn't careful.

I was starting to feel fidgety, breathless. *This* feeling, at least, was familiar. No more invasive memories, but the feeling that leads to smashed cups and broken forks, and oh so much worse. The feeling that's like standing on the edge of a cliff and knowing you're going to jump even if you don't want to. Like there's a cage full of monkeys right in the centre of your chest howling to be let out. I squirmed on my bed, and it bounced, buoyantly, trying to push me off. I was going to break something – I couldn't help that now – but at least I could make it something small, something quiet and private.

I let my hand slide down the side of the mattress, my fingers making a noise like tiny, distant screams against the polyester-PVC fabric. They stopped when they came to a small protrusion. A valve.

I didn't have to think about it. I pinched with my thumb and forefinger and twisted as hard as I could. The twisted plastic bit my fingers, and for a moment all my energy and swarming thoughts seemed to travel down my arm and congregate in the pain. *Hrnnnghh!* I twisted the other way. It was all still there: the shame, and the regret, and the anger, and the guilt. But at least now it wasn't in my head or my chest any more. *Hrrrrrnnnn!* I twisted and twisted. First one way. Then the other. Then: *Pop! Szzzzz…*

I stared at the ceiling as the air rushed out of the mattress and the hard steel bars of the bottom of the bed touched and then pressed into my back.

I let out a long, irritable sigh.

That was going to be uncomfortable, wasn't it.

CHAPTER 12

Lessons at Deephaven were weird. They were like that feeling of getting tangled up in bedsheets – disorientating and frustrating. Dr Balgobin didn't teach to a curriculum like at my old school. She liked to have *conversations* with us; she wanted us to *spot the connections* between different subjects. One minute we were discussing *Frankenstein* as one of our English Literature texts, the next we were discussing the impact of storytelling on the evolution of the human brain and the development of psychosocial interaction. I scrambled in my notebooks, confused about whether this was history or geography, or something else entirely.

The other kids seemed used to it. Alban, Jian, and Jacob moved between textbooks in a businesslike way, cross-checking and making notes. Evan worked quietly without any textbooks, seeming, somehow, both utterly confident about the work and yet also distant. Ysabel continued to thrust her hand in the air at every opportunity, occasionally looking in my direction like she was pressing home the point that she was clearly ever so much better than me.

Then the weekend came, and it stretched before me like a chasm, nothing but a group of kids who didn't like me and a whole rig filled with breakable things.

I woke early on Saturday. I'd have slept in if I could have, but the tail end of jet lag wrenched me from my bed-cupboard at 07:20.

No Mum. Of course.

Just me. And the ocean watching me through the portholes, like it was waiting to see what I'd do next.

I stared at the grey vinyl walls of our cabin for as long as I could bear. Then I washed in the small shower that we shared with the other cabins in our hab unit and took the long route to the canteen.

It was crowded, and there was an altercation going on when I arrived. Joy was standing with her arms straight down by her sides and her fists clenched, facing Carter.

"It's blatant intimidation, that's what it is!" she squawked.

"There have been irregularities," Carter explained, unflappable and immaculate in his suit jacket even this early on a weekend. "I'm responsible for the rig, and I've implemented this system as a means to hold us all to account."

Nobody else seemed particularly interested in the stand-off. The queue for food continued to inch forward, people moved between ketchup and cutlery stand and the tables. A few glanced at Joy or Carter, but I got the sense that this sort of thing had happened many times before.

"You've *padlocked* the stationery cupboard," Joy said shrilly. "What exactly do you think we're doing with all the biros, Carter? eBay is a long way away!"

"Let's just *try* the new system," Carter replied.

"There aren't even any *purples*!" Joy cried, almost whining.

Carter raised his hands in a gesture that showed them to be empty. Sympathetic, yet unmoving. The fact that he alone seemed to be exempt from the flight suit requirement was more conspicuous than ever.

"You wouldn't have got away with this when Maximus was here," Joy said.

"You can speak to Holden whenever you need anything," Carter replied.

Joy huffed loudly, but she was already striding off. "I see through you, Carter," she called over her shoulder. "I know what you're trying to do." She turned and wagged her finger at him. "You think there's a power vacuum since Maximus disappeared, and you're going to take advantage of it!"

I was standing in the doorway, and Joy almost walked into me. She stopped and leaned closer, speaking in a loud whisper that everyone in the canteen could clearly hear: "I hope your mum finds something. Maximus was the only one with the balls to stop Carter blasting the whole east ridge. Money is the only thing that matters to him. Money. Quotas. With Maximus gone, he'll take his chance, you'll see." She looked sneeringly at Carter, raising her voice again: "There's something down there, Carter! You know there is. You can't just pretend there isn't."

Isaac appeared behind her, following obediently. I hadn't noticed him before. He paused as he passed me, his eyes fixed intently on mine, and yet, somehow, always searching for the nearest porthole. "Memory works differently down here," he said in a warning tone. "You know that, I can tell. You have to watch your step."

Ice water froze against my back. *What?* I started to say something in response, but Isaac had already moved on, muttering quietly to himself. I bolted for the nearest table and then stopped. Alban was already sitting there. He froze with a spoonful of cereal poised in front of his mouth. We watched each other like wild cats who've accidentally run into each other in neutral territory. Which was better: sit or run?

I forced a smile, sitting. "What was all that about?"

Alban shrugged. "Business versus science. Progress versus navel gazing."

"Huh?"

Alban sighed and laid down his spoon. He unscrewed the cap from the salt shaker and placed the cap and shaker on the table in front of him. "Carter represents the Consortium," he said, tapping the shaker on the table. "He's on the hook for making this place profitable. But we only get a licence to mine because an independent science team oversees the whole thing." He took the cap and placed it on top of the shaker. "The International Seabed Authority laid that out in law decades ago," he added. "Carter and the Consortium hate the science team because they think the scientists get in the way of their quotas." He upended the salt shaker and watched the grains trickle out on to the table. "And the science team hate Carter because they know he'll pave this place over and turn it into a multi-storey car park if he gets half a chance." Without moving the shaker, Alban twisted off the cap and let the whole shaker's worth of salt scatter on to the table. "Economic gain and progress versus scientific advancement and preserving the ecosystem, blah blah. Didn't you listen to anything at the training centre?"

Blah, blah...? I thought of Mum and felt irritated on her behalf.

"You're on the side of progress, I suppose?" I said, using my hand to clear the patch of table nearest to me.

Alban grinned. "Actually, my dad teaches the junior class and my mum's an ROV pilot for the sampling crew.

Technically, I'm science." He raised his spoon, laden with sugared hoops of grain. "But really, I'm just here for the food."

I turned back to my breakfast and shuffled damp scrambled eggs around in order to escape looking at Alban. He made me nervous. He had the air of somebody who'd harvest your internal organs and sell them on the internet if you gave him half a chance.

He is talking to me, though, I thought. This was pretty much the most conversation I'd had since my first day.

"Any plans for the weekend?" he asked casually.

I shrugged. "What do people even do around here?"

"We'll probably play a bit more Cephalopod later."

"Thanks, I'll pass."

Alban nodded. "It's better with four."

"Is there really nothing else to do?"

"I'm sure if you asked Jian he'd show you his silt collection."

"Silt? Seriously?"

"There's a lot of science in silt… And not that much else to do," Alban admitted, straight-faced, so I didn't know if he was making fun of me or not. "Whatever," he added. "Just don't get into any trouble."

I glanced up and found him watching me, waiting for my reaction.

"What do you mean by that?" I asked.

"Nothing. What *should* I mean?"

I froze. I could tell from his tone that he knew something. He was baiting me.

"I looked you up," he said at last. "I like to do a bit of background research on new starters. It cost me a whole month's bandwidth allowance, but it was worth it. It's amazing what you can find on the internet."

I pushed my eggs away, icy fingers spreading across my spine. "That's why you were so keen to find out where I lived, wasn't it?" I said.

"It's easier to cross-check with an address," Alban replied unapologetically.

There's still a chance he's bluffing, I thought. I gave him my most hostile stare. "Well? Anything juicy?"

Alban's face split into a look of delight. "Besides the one that made the local newspapers?" he said salaciously. "I mean, how did you and your mum even get clearance to live here after that? Deephaven is usually so picky." He stopped, his eyes widening with sudden realization. "Unless … they don't know, do they?"

My stomach heaved. There it was. Found out already. For a moment he looked almost panicked, as if the thing he'd discovered was just a little too large even for him. Then his expression changed. I watched an idea begin to crystallize inside his head.

"It's bound to come out sooner or later," he said.

"No," I said firmly. "Nobody needs to know. Maximus sorted it for us."

"But Maximus isn't here."

"Please, Alban, you can't tell anyone. Mum's job is really important to her."

My mind raced with a thousand thoughts. How could I fix this? How could I make this right? Of all people, why did it have to be Alban? His face swung back and forth through a catalogue of emotions. It was difficult to gauge his age – sometimes he looked younger, sometimes he seemed much older. At last, he hardened, conviction settling into his eyes.

"You know, rather than waiting for the inevitable, you could at least do some good while you're here."

"What?"

"What do you know about the ERS system?" he asked, feigning innocence.

I glanced at the button on the nearby wall with the little sign directly beneath it. "Emergency Reactor Scram," I said. "What about it?"

"Do you know what happens if you push one of those buttons?"

"More or less," I answered cautiously.

"It ejects the plasma core, dumps the whole thing into the ocean. The rig would drop into emergency power. No harvesting. Lockdown protocols. No EVAs, no output for at least a month."

"So?" I asked, my pulse quickening.

"Joy's right; Carter's going to take his chance and blast

the east ridge before Maximus's replacement can stop him. It's why he kept Maximus's disappearance quiet, why your mum didn't find out until she got here."

"Why are you telling me this?"

"Because if *you* pressed the ERS, it would all stop. You'd stop Carter from being able to survey and blast the east ridge, stop him from doing something irreparable down here."

I swallowed, staring at him in disbelief, feeling for a moment as if I might choke and throw up all over him. "Are you serious? You want me to push the ERS?"

Alban nodded slowly. His initial shock had passed, and he eyed me the way a praying mantis eyes a beetle. "Think about it," he said. "You're nothing but a liability right now. If somebody were to say something ... if your background were to leak for some reason, there would be an investigation. It would blow back on your mum; that's what you're most afraid of, isn't it? But if you hit the ERS, that's a three-billion-dollar silt-storm right there. That's instant dismissal. *No questions asked.*"

"Are you *blackmailing* me?"

Alban frowned, but I could see that he liked the idea. "I'm enabling a public service. Helping you to do a good thing."

I stood slowly, a little shakily. My mind raced. Was this a prank? Was this really happening? Looking at him, I had no way to be sure. Something else had begun to whisper inside my head as well: *what if he has a point?* If I hit the ERS, Carter would freak, and I'd be gone. *No questions asked.* Nobody would care if Mum had skipped a few forms if I was already being sent home. She'd be able to stay, guilt-free, which was what she wanted after all. I'd go home, and this whole mess would be behind me. She'd be in the clear.

"Thank you, Alban," I said, almost sincerely. "I'll think about it."

I roamed the rig in a daze, unnerved by Alban's suggestion. Press the ERS? That was about the worst thing you could do on Deephaven. Mum would never forgive me, even if it did stop Carter blasting where he wasn't supposed to. But would Alban really tell Carter what I'd done at my old school if I didn't do what he said? I didn't know. One thing he was definitely right about was that if he did, Mum would be in all sorts of trouble, the kind of trouble that makes getting a new job impossible. I thought about how much it had cost to train us and bring us here, and whether they'd want their money back if they found out that I should never have been allowed here in the first place. It was bad. Worse than bad.

The sound of the rig hissed continuously in my ears. It was hard to get your head around this place, like turning over a rock and finding a mass of swarming woodlice. There were always people scurrying about, busy with their tasks. Four hundred and seventy-two CRABs roamed the telemetry grid. Fifteen "Cucumbers" – long, tracked transport vehicles – took the polymetallic nodules to the processing units. A hundred and fifty people worked continually in rotating shifts: operating, maintaining and repairing the equipment; connecting, offloading and refloating the food supply units; monitoring and adjusting the fusion reactor; doing the laundry; unblocking the toilets. Everyone with a job and a purpose and a point and a legitimate reason for being here ... except me.

I'd just stepped into the west polytunnel when Ysabel appeared at the other end. She was in her running kit. Tall, lithe, perfect. Her ponytail bobbed gleefully as she bounded towards me. Was it possible to hate a ponytail? Well, I did.

She paused. Removed one of her AirPods. "Oh, hi," she said. She was sweating, her face flushed.

"Hi," I replied, thrown that she had even stopped to talk to me. "Out for a run?"

"Um, obviously." Ysabel squinted, like she was trying to make sense of me.

I forced a smile. "Nice weather for it."

She flinched and gave her head an offended little shake, like she thought I was making fun of her. I wasn't. I was only trying to be friendly; I just wasn't very good at it. She replaced her AirPod and started to jog past me. Then she stopped suddenly.

"Why are you so *mean* to me?" she asked.

I stared at her in shock. "Me?"

Her chest was rising and falling more rapidly than could be explained by her running, and there were tears in her eyes. "I really thought we might become friends, you know."

"*What?*"

"Oh, forget it."

She ran off, her feet clumping dully against the polycarbonate and then clanging as she stepped into the main rig. I stood for a long time, listening to the clanging as it faded away and disappeared into the hiss of the rig.

Seriously? I thought back to class, all the self-satisfied looks, all that eye rolling. Was that her version of being friendly? It was possible, now I thought about it. Like maybe she was trying to impress me, or inviting me to take things less seriously?

I pressed the heels of my palms to my eyes and drew a long breath.

God, I was rubbish at this.

I stormed on, my thoughts clenched tight. I could feel them smouldering, gathering closer, threatening to overwhelm me. I needed a distraction. I had to find a way to get out of my own head.

Mum, I thought suddenly. If she wanted me to be different down here, then she could help.

I found her in her usual spot in the lab. Ari was sitting

with her, drinking tea, chatting. I hesitated, listening to their conversation. "She'll settle in," he was saying. "Everyone wobbles a bit when they first get here."

I didn't wait to hear Mum's reply. I fixed my brightest smile and swept into the room. "Hi, Mum, hi, Ari," I said as breezily as I could.

"Heyyy, Lily Fawcett!" Ari responded, seeming surprised but still genuinely, unreasonably delighted to see me. "How're you doing?"

"I want to help," I said, looking directly at Mum.

Mum looked confused. "I'm sorry?"

"You said you had to sort through Maximus's notes. I can help."

Mum shook her head tightly. "Lily, I appreciate the offer, but it's highly technical research. You might miss something."

"Mum, I'm not useless. I've seen them, remember? They're gibberish. If you really think there's some real science in there, you'll need my help to pick it out."

Ari laughed. "That sounds like Maximus. All spit and fire, less into the paperwork side of things."

"It would be too easy for you to miss something," Mum repeated.

"Please, Mum."

The crack in my voice caught her. I knew what she was thinking: she was thinking that I might do something stupid and destructive if she didn't find something else for me to do. She was probably right. But she still couldn't bring herself to do it. The awful truth of it was that she didn't trust me.

She started to shake her head—

"Or," Ari cut in loudly, flashing a wink in my direction, "I could take her over to see the rig schematic. She's got a knack for this stuff, and I could use another pair of eyes on the fusion reactor."

Mum's face flashed terror signals. "The what—?"

"Fusion reactor." Ari beamed blithely. "It's been jumpy all week. I may as well let Lily take a look; nobody else has the foggiest what's going on."

Mum's eyes narrowed. I could see her trying to decide if Ari was being serious or not, and then deciding that she couldn't take the risk. "No!" she shot back. "No, you're right," she continued more levelly. "I think... I think Lily will be really helpful in the lab ... with me."

CHAPTER 13

The weekend passed in a flurry of paperwork. We requested scissors and a roll of Sellotape from Holden, and (after filling out two entirely unnecessary forms) used them to cut and paste and rearrange Maximus's notes, reassembling the most cogent segments like we were conducting some kind of police investigation.

It felt like revising for the worst GCSE topic in the world, but it was better than being left on my own to brood. By Sunday night my head buzzed with Maximus's stories of deep darkness and the light hidden within it.

I lifted a delicate, taped–together sheet and read aloud:

"In the beginning there was nothing but Po – the endless black chaos. Then Kāne, sensing that he was separate from the Po, pulled himself free of Po by an act of sheer will. Kāne created the light to push back Po ... and he began by saying these words – that he might cease remaining inactive: 'Darkness! Become a light-possessing darkness. Light! Become a darkness-possessing light.'"

"It's beautiful," Mum said.

"It's not science," I replied.

Mum smiled, her exhausted eyes crinkling with amusement. She was curled up on the armchair in our tiny cabin. "He was an interesting man," she said. "I wish you could have met him."

I lifted another sheet:

"At first the lowly zoophytes and corals, followed by worms and shellfish, each type being declared to conquer and destroy its predecessor. Algae, followed by seaweeds and rushes. As type follows type, the accumulating slime of their decay raises the land above the waters, in which, as spectator of all, swims the octopus, the lone survivor from an earlier world."

Mum let out a snort of laughter. I sat back, smiling, enjoying the fact that she seemed more relaxed than she'd been since we arrived. Relaxed, or resigned, I wondered.

"Mum? What are we doing here?" I sighed.

She turned serious. "What do you mean?"

"We don't belong here. We're not experimental deep-sea-rig people."

Mum watched me for a long moment. The dim bulbs in the ceiling made perfect white stars in her eyes. "Maybe we are who we choose to be."

I woke the next morning feeling heavier, as if my jet lag had found its second wind and was winning the battle for my eyeballs. My dreams had been fitful, terrifying. Flashes of turquoise and a sense of being watched. I didn't feel right. I wanted to talk to Mum about it, but it had been so nice working together, feeling almost normal for once, that I was afraid to ruin things again.

There was nothing to do except play along. Chips and sausages in the crammed canteen for breakfast; incomprehensible, meandering lessons from Dr Balgobin. Knowing looks from Alban; cold stares from Ysabel; indifference from the others.

At break time on Wednesday, I followed the group back to the main rig, expecting the usual routine of sitting in silence while everyone else played Cephalopod. Instead, I found that Jacob had organized a football match between the junior and senior classes. A hollow feeling opened up inside me. *Football?* As if Deephaven could get any worse.

I tagged along anyway, reluctant to be on my own and with nothing better to do. The Recreation level was one floor down from the canteen and the largest uninterrupted space on the rig. It smelled of seaweed and sweaty rubber, but after the confines of everywhere else I felt giddy with its relative vastness. There was an entire five-a-side pitch, a big plastic bin filled with soft footballs, and a corner that had been sectioned off to form a gym.

"Come *on*," Jacob cajoled me. "It's *five-a-side*; we need another player."

"Thanks," I said. "But I can't play."

"It's easy. You just kick the ball. You'd be doing us a favour."

I could see the confusion in his face; his conviction was that sport heals all, and there was clearly something wrong with a person who refused to play. I could imagine him building morale with regular kick arounds on the solar pontoons.

"No, really," I said. "I'm clumsy. I'll spoil the game for everyone."

"If she doesn't want to play, that's OK," Ysabel said, making it perfectly clear that she'd prefer it if I didn't play.

"Plus, they're juniors," Alban said, shrugging. "So, it's kind of fair that we have fewer on our team." He shot me a look, and his eyes darted towards the ERS on the wall.

"I'm sure Lily has more important things to do with her time anyway."

I tensed, willing my face not to let him see how much he was getting to me. I deposited myself at the edge of the pitch and drew out my phone. I stared dumbly at it. Nothing from Dad. Nothing from Hanna. The heaviness inside me grew heavier. Another chance missed. Another piece of ordinary social interaction I wasn't a part of. *We are who we choose to be*, Mum had said. But I couldn't exactly *choose* to be good at football, could I?

Working with Mum on the notes had been a nice distraction, I thought, but it didn't change the hard facts. I didn't belong here. Someone who belonged here would be good at football; they'd be good at a whole heap of things I wasn't good at. I watched Ysabel and Jacob laughing as they fought for possession of the ball. They'd been sitting next to each other at dinner all week; they were so obviously going to become a thing, and we were all so obviously going to have to watch it play out.

My eyes drifted to the ERS. It would be easy to talk myself into it. Why not? Every moment I stayed here I increased the chances of Mum getting found out and landing in a whole world of trouble. Even if Alban was just bluffing, he was right: it would come out sooner or later. If I pushed the ERS I'd be sent home, *no questions asked*. Embarrassing for Mum, sure, but she'd be off the hook. And it wasn't as if she'd really wanted me here anyway.

As unlikely as it seemed, it was possible that Alban was being straight with me and hitting the ERS really would stop Carter destroying whatever it was Maximus had been researching. Nobody would ever know it, but perhaps hitting the ERS was the single best thing I could do to help Mum and everyone else down here?

My fingers itched suddenly with the desire to push the ERS. It was the same feeling I got when I broke something, but deeper, more purposeful. Let's face it, I wasn't exactly coping down here. If I didn't do something soon, I'd probably freak out anyway, and then I might end up doing something even worse.

It was a button after all, the simplest interface in the world. It *wanted to be pushed.*

I stood, a little unsteadily, and started walking towards the ERS. Have you ever done something you know you'll regret but gone ahead and done it anyway? *Do not push this button except in extreme emergency.*

I'm not going to push it, I thought. *I just want a closer look…*

"Hey, new girl!"

I froze. Evan was sitting nearby, a tablet held loosely in one hand. He'd been a dark, uncomfortable presence since I'd arrived. A mystery, set apart from the others just as I was. The boy who'd lost his dad; the boy who was here on his own. He was tall, quite skinny, but his arms had tight knots of ligament under the skin, and his eyes had an unwavering intensity that made it hard not to look away.

"You mean me?" I asked.

Evan lifted an eyebrow. "How many new girls are there on the rig? Anyway, what were you *thinking?*"

I glanced anxiously at the ERS. *How did he know? Is it that obvious?*

"I wasn't really going to—"

"Holden's a muppet," he went on. "But I'd still rather *he* ran the highly unstable fusion reactor than you. You didn't really think you could operate that thing, did you?"

It took me a moment to realize what he was talking about. The fusion reactor on my first day. It felt like a lifetime ago. "You heard about that?"

"Anyway, I'd rather you didn't do it again," Evan continued, ignoring me. "Carter's already trying to send me topside, so I don't need you making us all look like a liability."

He dropped his head back to his tablet, his face hidden behind a mop of brown hair. Anger rose in me, a desire to do something outrageous. In my mind's eye, I turned and slammed my hand into the ERS. The lights flickered and died, emergency lighting, chaos. That would show him, wouldn't it?

Is that liability enough for you?

I felt my heart hammering in my chest. I took a breath and held it.

The feeling passed.

Maybe he had a point.

I plonked myself down next to him. "Duly chastised," I said curtly.

He glanced up, and I thought I caught a whisper of a smile on his face. "For what it's worth, Ari told me you saved us from a pretty nasty blackout. It was a good catch."

I blinked, surprised by the unexpected compliment. I felt my face flush instantly, and I held back the smile that wanted to grow on my lips. "Oh. Thanks."

Evan raised one shoulder in a lazy shrug. "Don't let it go to your head."

I watched him closely. There was something appealing about his face, with his full lips and his sharp, enquiring eyes − if you overlooked the fact that he was a bit scary. "They told me to stay away from you," I said.

"That was thoughtful of them."

"Why are you still here?" I asked, blurting out the words before I could stop myself. "I mean ... don't you *want* to go home?"

"This *is* home." Evan gave me a tired look. "Dad and I moved here when I was eight. He pretty much built this place from scratch."

"Don't you have anyone else topside?"

"No," he said. "Mum died when I was three."

On the football pitch, Alban had accidentally knocked over one of the juniors and was helping him to his feet. Ysabel caught my eye and gave me an irritable, questioning look, like she thought I was talking to Evan just to annoy her. *Whatever,* I thought.

Evan was hard to read. He was intense, as if he had a thousand thoughts for every one of yours, but he wasn't about to share any of them. It was intimidating but oddly comforting as well. He had a sense of being *outside,* which appealed to me. The sense that if I told him that I felt all alone, even when I was surrounded by other people, he'd understand.

At least, I didn't feel like I was about to mess up with him, like I did with everyone else down here.

I stared at the ERS. The idea of pushing it seemed a million miles away now. *Had I really considered it?* I felt giddy with my near miss.

"Don't you like football?" I asked, gesturing towards the pitch.

"Love it," Evan replied, sincerely.

"Oh…?"

He glanced up and caught me watching him. "But there's no point trying to play since Dad disappeared," he explained. "They're all so freaked out about it they won't tackle me. It's like they think letting me score a goal is the best way to make me feel better."

"Wow," I said, feeling awful. "That's pretty messed up."

"The grown-ups are worse. Half of them run away when I walk in the room. Ari gets so nervous he practically tears his beard off."

I smiled. For all his bleakness there was a wry, playful edge to him.

"Do you think you'll be sticking around?" he asked. "I heard a rumour you were leaving."

I shook my head. "Carter says Mum doesn't have a job down here without your dad. She's trying to pick up his research, trying to get a grant—"

Evan snorted. "How's that working out for her?"

"Not great," I admitted.

I swallowed uneasily. Did he know what a state his dad's notes were in? Did he know what people were saying about Maximus having lost his mind?

"The notes in the lab won't do her any good," he said after a moment. "They're mostly fake. Dad wrote them to mess with Carter's head."

The words hit me like an iceberg. I sat up. "Fake? Why?"

Evan drew his shoulders inwards and fixed his eyes on me. "The rig isn't the happy-clappy collaboration between science and industry they like to make out in the brochure. We need the metals down here. They power our computers. They power our batteries. They power our fusion generators. The idea was to use limited mining licences to fund research down here. The Consortium mines, the science team oversees what's happening and figures out more effective ways to mine without damaging the ecosystem."

"Yeah, I heard."

"But the Consortium thinks it's not fast enough. It's like being a farmer. You can fill the land with fertilizer and get three times the crop this year but nothing next year. Or you can go slower, do it in a way that means the soil stays your friend. Carter would have dredged the whole trench by now; he would have laid ANFO bombs along the east ridge and destroyed anything that might or might not have been down here, and he'd have come back with a bumper crop of polymetallic nodules and then moved on to the next trench. And he'd have kept going until he ran out of trenches. But Dad had a better idea. He invented the telemetry grid and the CRABs, which are quieter and don't produce a sediment plume. Carter hates it because production and profits are lower, but the ecosystem down here keeps running, so it's sustainable. Do you see?"

"Sure. But why did your dad make fake notes?"

"Dad had put a moratorium on extending the telemetry grid while he completed his research, but Carter was trying to overturn it. It was important that Carter didn't know how close Dad was to a real discovery. Too close, and Carter would convince the Consortium to act immediately; they'd burn political capital to get the east ridge blasted if they knew a discovery was going to come soon that could block them for ever. Too far, and Carter would force Dad's hand by claiming that the research was at a dead end."

My head spun. "So, what happens now?"

"With Dad gone, Carter will take his chance. He can't overturn the moratorium right now, but if he just goes ahead and blasts the east ridge, he'll probably get away with it."

I thought about Alban again. The ERS. *If you press the ERS it will all stop.*

"But Mum can stop him," I said. "If we could find your dad's real notes and pick up his research, we could…"

Evan shook his head. "I don't know where they are."

I blinked. A flash of irritation. Was that it? Mr *off-the-charts* genius and that was all he had? "How can you not know?" I asked. "Have you tried looking?"

"*I don't know,*" Evan snapped. His face was flushed. He took in a single, fierce breath through his nose. I could see him struggling with himself, fighting the urge to cry or shout or something. "I looked, OK? I looked and looked. There's nothing. And if I knew where they were I'd be all over them." He stared piercingly at me. "Not because of the ridge, or Dad's research, or Carter. Because they're *mine*. He would have wanted me to have them. He would have wanted me to know why he—" He stopped. His jaw clenched and unclenched. Then he stood, his long, athletic body unravelling in stages like a complicated deck chair. "I have to go," he said.

CHAPTER 14

I spent my evenings in the lab now, working on Maximus's notes with Mum. Fake or not, I was afraid that if I stopped working on them, there would be nothing to stop me pushing the ERS and having done with it.

In hindsight, the fact that Maximus's notes were printed and stored in a big filing cabinet in the lab should have been a dead giveaway that they weren't real. Nobody used paper these days, except maybe Joy, whom I'd watched bite the nibs off three biros and fill a notebook and a half with intricate doodles in the past week alone.

I'd had an idea that the notes might be in code, that the text might reference something in some way that would reveal the real notes. But it was a stupid idea. I'd started

Googling the text, and I'd found that most sections were cut and pasted directly from Wikipedia. There was one page which looked to have been torn and stuck in from our Geography textbook:

> The term "abyssal plain" refers to a flat region of the ocean floor, usually at the base of a continental rise, where slope is less than 1:1000. It represents the deepest and flattest part of the ocean floor, lying between 4000 and 6000 m deep in the U.S. Atlantic Margin. Lying unattached to the ocean floor in this region are billions of tonnes of polymetallic nodules – potato-sized deposits containing rich concentrations of cobalt, nickel, copper and manganese.

So where were the real notes? Joy had given Mum access to his computer system, so if there was anything on there she'd have found it. His cabin was the only other obvious choice, but Evan said he'd looked, and based on his reaction, I was sure he'd been thorough.

Mum had given up on Maximus's notes and devoted her efforts to creating her own research proposal instead. Her latest: *A Proposal for the Extraction of Human-Grade Food from Phytodetritus.*

"They don't even need to be that good," she explained, typing furiously. "Now that I'm here, even a small grant will give me leave to stay. We can delay things, at least."

"You know what phytodetritus is, don't you?" Joy said.

"Kind of," Mum answered defensively.

"Fish poo," Joy said. "Mostly fish poo."

I went back to the cabinet and retrieved another file. This one didn't contain the usual sheaf of closely typed paper, however. It contained a tablet computer.

Excitement tightened in my chest: why put a tablet computer in a filing cabinet? I looked up, trembling with anticipation, half expecting the others to have gathered around. Isaac was gazing out of the portholes again, muttering to himself. Joy was doodling. They must once have been great scientists to have secured a place on Deephaven, but something had happened to them since they got here. They seemed lost, their heads filled with other things. I returned to my desk and powered on the tablet. It took a moment ... but then it died. No battery. I rifled impatiently through the twisted cabling behind the desk for a charger.

"Everything all right, Lily?" Mum asked absently.

"Yeah, sure," I said. "Just ... out of power."

This time the tablet booted up. I waited, my breath hot in my throat. It was probably nothing. But wouldn't it be amazing if it was something? If I could find the real notes, we might be able to make a case to stop Carter blasting the east ridge, and that might even be enough for the universities to give Mum a new contract of her own.

Something began to load slowly. It was nearly there...

It was … *Cephalopod*.

That stupid game the other kids were obsessed with. I ground my teeth in irritation. I tried to go back to the home screen, but the tablet was locked to Cephalopod and nothing else. The colours twisted, beautiful and unnerving at the same time. I dabbed the screen and the colours curled and prickled in response to my touch. Nobody else was online. It meant I had a bit more time to try and understand what was going on, at least.

My dad says good interfaces make themselves understood. You learn by doing.

I tapped the screen a few more times. The colours drew together and formed a region of densely glowing light. A ball. Twisting and pulsing on the spot. It was an invitation; the interface *wanted* to be tapped.

I tapped. The ball exploded in a shower of brilliant colour. A successful interaction?

Another ball of light formed nearby. Repetition. Like I was a dog being trained to do a trick.

I tapped again. Again, the ball of light exploded and reformed elsewhere on the screen. The colours were jumping around more vigorously now. The ball of light wanted to be chased. It flitted from point to point, the image slewing wildly in order to bring it into view.

I tapped, and the ball of light disappeared in a shower of colour and reformed nearby. Again and again, and all the time the background of moving colour became more frantic.

But something else was going on, I was sure of it. It *felt* like I was tapping the balls of light, playing a game of tag. But the real game, the real message, was in the background. My hand automatically chased the balls of light, but another part of my brain watched the pattern. The faster I caught the balls, the more frantic the throbbing background became. But *too* fast, and it lost interest, slowed down. The timing ... that was it! I smiled as the realization came to me: it was the pulse. Like when you swing on a swing, and you have to catch the right point in the arc so that your shifting weight adds to your momentum instead of working against it.

I let myself fall into the rhythm, not too fast, not too slow. The interface wanted to show me something, I was sure of it. But what? Maximus must have put this on, I thought, and he'd done it for a reason. *Tap ... tap ... tap ... tap...* Once you knew what to look for, it was a pretty effective lock screen.

Then the image froze, and faded away, and everything changed.

CHAPTER 15

The alarm on my phone wrenched me from sleep the next morning. Time: 04:00.

I blinked in the darkness, my head buzzing with the remains of a dream: the thought of Maximus and his last drive out into the ocean. *I'm falling… I'm alone.*

I crept out of my bed-cupboard as quietly as I could. Mum snored softly from her room. I paused outside her door and listened, reluctant to leave. It was such a novelty to have her here; usually she came back after I was asleep and left before I woke up.

I slipped out and padded along the hab unit and into the polytunnel. Even when it was asleep, the rig felt like it kept one eye open. The air-conditioning vibrated subtly in the walls. The emergency strip lights in the floor woke up automatically and lit a path. I crept through the metal corridors, painfully conscious of the noise of the steel gratings shivering under my feet. I followed the steadily growing buzz of the rig. The noise escalated as I stepped into the canteen.

Around thirty or forty people were eating or chatting energetically, mostly ops at that time. Men and women who'd probably worked their whole lives on or in the sea: salt-weathered faces, broad shoulders, exuberant laughs. I spotted Evan on the far side of the room. Not only was he the only one sitting on his own, the two tables either side of him were empty as well.

"Eating alone?" I said, affecting a casual tone. Alban had told me that he ate at this time to avoid the rest of us.

Evan glanced theatrically to either side of him. "I certainly hope so."

"Well, not any more." I sat, barely containing my excitement. "I found something."

Evan watched me sceptically, but he said nothing.

I placed the tablet on the table and pushed it across so he could see it.

"Cephalopod," he said shortly. "I wrote it. It's better with four, though."

"So people keep telling me," I said. "But Cephalopod's not a game. It's a lock screen. This version is, anyway. It's been modified."

Evan frowned. I'd caught his interest.

"It's in the timing," I went on. "It's quite clever. Like your father *wanted* someone to be able to guess it. But only someone who was looking for it." I preened a little. "Someone exceedingly, exceedingly intelligent."

Evan stared at the screen. "Where did you get this?"

"It was in your dad's filing cabinet."

"Can you show me?"

Tap, tap, tap, tap. I was pretty proficient at it now. The waves of colour grew more vibrant, then flickered and melted away. Evan's eyes opened wider.

What lay behind the Cephalopod colours wasn't Maximus's notes. It was another game. Or maybe not a game – a simulation. It looked like the cockpit of some kind of submersible. Many of the digital displays and readouts were familiar from the standard submersibles they'd taught us about at the training centre, but it was also profoundly different. More sophisticated; more *intense*. It reminded me of the time Dad had taken me to see a fighter jet simulation he was working on. It was his job to make all the hundreds of controls and readouts understandable to somebody who had to make decisions really, really fast. I remember sitting in the cockpit as Dad took off, the simulator shifting on hydraulic pistons to give the illusion of motion.

I remember Dad leaning back nonchalantly. "What now, Lilypad?"

"I don't know how to fly a plane!"

"Look at the controls. What does it want you to do?"

I looked. "This one," I had said. "The flaps need adjusting."

"Good."

"I don't know what flaps are!"

Dad had grinned at me. "A good interface makes itself understood."

In the canteen, Evan was tapping intensely at the display.

"What is it?" I asked.

"It's a simulation of an amphipod launch sequence," he replied.

"Which is…?"

"A new kind of submersible Dad's team was working on. He designed them, and his team topside was building them for him. I was helping."

"Helping how?"

"I wrote this training programme." He shook his head. "I installed every copy. He must have created an extra one and hid it away in the science lab, behind a copy of Cephalopod. But why?"

"Unless it's a message?" I hazarded.

Evan nodded. I watched as he expertly navigated the controls. I'd spent a bunch of time playing with it last night, and I'd figured out the basics: batteries, CO_2 scrubbers, buoyancy, waterlock. I'd blown up a few times, but I could successfully complete the launch sequence now.

Evan completed the sequence and the display turned

green to indicate a successful launch. Then it froze and flicked back to the beginning.

"I tried that," I said.

"It's strange," Evan said. He leaned back, frowning thoughtfully. Then he pushed his food to one side and stood. "Come on. I have an idea."

I followed him as he hurried through the canteen and into the main stairwell, our feet clanging on the metal grating. His face was fixed and serious, lost in thought, but there was an energy to it, a hopefulness I hadn't seen before.

"Where are we going?" I asked.

"The amphipod bay," he answered shortly.

"What's that?"

"We have a few prototype amphipods," Even said. "There must be something he wants me to see down there. It's the only reason he'd put the launch sequence into a loop like that."

We clambered through the pressure door that led to the sub bay. It was bordered by orange and yellow chevrons and the words HAZARD, RESTRICTED AREA.

"Are you sure we're allowed down here?" I whispered, sticking close.

"My dad was the Chief Science Officer, and now he's missing, presumed dead," Evan said, his voice an odd mixture of sadness and salacious pride. "I'm allowed *everywhere*."

We followed the corridor around the corner and past another large sign which read: AUTHORIZED PERSONNEL ONLY. Two burly-looking ROV drivers appeared, their heavy boots clanging on the metal floor. They glanced at us as we approached, and one looked like he was about to challenge us until the other touched his arm and whispered something. They parted, pressing themselves against the walls for us to walk past.

I shivered anxiously. If the command centre was the brains of the installation, this was the lower intestine. It was where the inspection ROVs were launched and retrieved. Where the CRABs docked for maintenance. Everything that came on or went off the rig came from this level.

"Do you want to explain to me what's going on?" I asked.

"For as long as I can remember, Dad told me there's no such thing as a safe submersible excursion, no matter how careful you are. He always knew there was a risk he wouldn't come back, so I know he'd have prepared a message for me just in case." He paused, looking for the right words. "A goodbye. I kept expecting Ari or Dr Balgobin to show up with a letter or something. I searched our entire cabin. Nothing."

"But you think this is his message?"

"Yes. I think he *hid* it here because he knew I'd be the only one who'd realize it was a message."

"Kids!"

My heart dropped as I heard Ari's voice ring out behind us. He hurried down to catch up with us, his feet hammering on the grated floor.

"What's going on?" he asked, a touch breathless.

"Um, I just wanted to give Lily a tour of Dad's lab," Evan said.

"At four in the morning?" Ari said dubiously.

"We, er … we couldn't sleep."

I nodded quickly. "Jet lag, you know what it's like."

Ari scratched his beard unhappily. "You know this is a restricted area, right? You'd better head back up to the main deck." He hesitated, then added feebly, "I can arrange a tour for you both in the morning, if you like?"

I cast Evan a panicked look. He swallowed. There was a haunted look in his eyes that hadn't been there a moment before. "Ari, please," he said. "I don't want to go back to my cabin … not yet. It's just … this place makes me feel closer to Dad."

Ari's mouth pinched. He paled. At last, he sighed in defeat. He leaned forward, his eyes darting left and right: "If anybody asks, I didn't see you, OK?"

We nodded.

"Thank you," Evan said soulfully.

Ari moved off, reluctantly, tapping a thoughtful rhythm on the piping as he went. Evan turned to me, and his face relaxed once more. He offered me a tired smile that was surprisingly triumphant. "You see? Works every time."

CHAPTER 16

We moved on, past two or three more RESTRICTED AREA signs and through a sealed door for which Evan had to key in a lengthy code sequence.

"Did you come down here with your dad a lot?" I asked.

"I'm kind of a genius with this stuff," he said. I glanced at him to check if he was making fun of me, but his face was expressionless. *Not even boasting*, I thought. *Just stating a fact*. "I've been here since I was eight," he went on. "It's not like there was a broad range of hobbies to choose from."

We stopped outside a pair of enormous pressure doors, twice the size of our garage door back home. Evan took a white plastic key card from his pocket and tapped a plate next to it. Instantly, the door began to slide open like a giant rock being rolled aside, accompanied by the loud hiss of hydraulics.

It revealed a large room, as wide and long as the Recreation level but twice as high, and noticeably cleaner and better maintained than everywhere else on this level. Various banks of slick-looking equipment lined the walls, including a row of computer consoles similar to the ones in the command centre. Over on the far wall I could see the outline of an enormous, disembodied manipulator arm, disused and half buried in a mass of wiring and hydraulic pipes.

"Whoa," I breathed.

The floor was open in the centre of the room, revealing a large pool of water that shone and rippled, casting complex, shifting patterns everywhere. Evan tapped a control on the wall, and the pressure door slid shut behind us.

He moved over to the console and began inputting commands on the large, translucent screens. I jumped as a whirring sound kicked in overhead and a rack descended from high in the ceiling. I could hardly make sense of what I was seeing. The machines slung on the rack looked a bit like mechanical shrimp, each one with a black dome at the front like a giant insectoid eye and four slender antennae sprouting from the outer rim. They rocked slightly with the movement of the rack. Their "bodies" were hunched up behind the dome and made from a series of overlapping plates which tapered into a narrow "tail" that hung down towards the back. Eight pairs of legs dangled below each body, the front two solid, polycarbonate claws, the rest looking more like coarse black ropes coated in stiff bristles.

Cilia drive, I thought, like the fine hair–like cilia some sea creatures use to propel themselves. I'd seen them in the *Future Visions* displays at the training centre, but they were not supposed to be anywhere near ready for practical use yet.

"Are they—?" I asked.

"Amphipods," Evan said. "These are the first prototypes."

"They're…"

"Ugly?" Evan suggested, helping me out.

"Repulsive," I agreed.

"Dad got carried away sometimes. He liked to make his designs *'biologically accurate'*." He gave me a weary look. "He thought engineering should learn from biology. To be honest, these turned out better than some."

I took a step closer.

"Did he do the Cucumbers as well?"

"Of course." Evan smiled.

"And the CRABs?"

"Like I said."

Now that my initial surprise had passed, I realized that the domed capsule was a cockpit. Evan tapped another command and the nearest pod popped open. He leaned inside to look, then drew back, trying to hide his disappointment.

"No note?"

He offered me a weak smile. "That would have been too easy, wouldn't it?"

The dark cavity of the pod stood open in front of me. A gel seat and the darkened panels of a set of computer consoles ready to power up. Excitement squeezed inside me. "Can I sit in one?"

Evan wavered, then relented. "Just be careful. Don't touch anything."

I leapt up and settled into the pilot's seat. It was big and comfortable and adjusted automatically to accommodate me. Several sets of servos hummed as the screens moved into position. Two control panels slid closer, and a soft blue glow rippled across them as they sprang into life. It was exactly the same as the simulation. "Did he design the rig schematic as well?" I asked.

Evan smiled again. "Of course."

"I knew it." I breathed in the new-car smell of the console and thought of Dad. "My dad would love this," I said. "He specializes in human-computer interfaces, you know. People think of it as just being a kind of computer programming, but it's not really. It's more like being a translator."

"Mm-hm," Evan murmured. He was absorbed by the

screens now, working at the console below them, typing rapidly, not listening. I could see how badly he wanted to find a message from his dad. But at the same time, I could tell that a part of him *didn't* want to find a message, because finding something would make it real.

"Anything?" I asked.

"If he left anything, it'll be here." He tapped some commands. "This was what he was working on before he disappeared." He tapped the screen and a three-dimensional drawing of the ocean bed appeared on the main display behind him. "This is sonar topography of the ocean floor. You see the rig here? Then the telemetry grid, then the east ridge on the far side of it."

I nodded.

The ragged slope of the abyssal plain was rendered in false-colour contours. I could see where it dropped away to the basin where the CRABs worked, and on the opposite side, the rising level and the much sharper drop-off into the trench. The outline of the rig showed up in clear reds and oranges, an obviously man-made addition to the natural seascape. "He was taking seismic profiles of the ridge, and he found something interesting." Evan hit another key and a red overlay appeared, showing a vast cavern beneath the ocean floor, extending in all directions. "He was convinced it was a sinkhole. A cavity. He called it the Rift."

I blinked, trying to get a sense of the scale. The image

had zoomed out so that the two-kilometre trench on the west side was now little more than a tiny notch, the Rift filling the whole rest of the display.

"That's not possible," I breathed. "That must be much deeper than the deepest part of the ocean."

"He couldn't get a reading from the bottom … but yes. There were resonances that led him to think there might be a thin part of the crust somewhere in the east ridge, a path connecting the ocean to the Rift."

"That's why he was trying to stop Carter from blasting there?"

"The Rift starts a kilometre deeper than where we are now, on the far side of a passageway Dad believed to be somewhere in the east ridge. But he needed the amphipods to get real evidence, and they weren't ready…"

"When he hired Mum, he said he'd found something – a *euglenoid*? Do you think it has anything to do with this?"

Evan shrugged. "It's possible… We're finding new species every day; if there's any kind of outflow from the Rift it could contain all manner of new things."

He fell silent. I could see the disappointment in his face. He was searching and not finding anything. *What must it be like?* I wondered. To have grown up with your dad telling you he might not come back from his next trip but going anyway. My dad travelled for work all the time and he never sent one text, but at least I knew he was coming back.

The nearest I could get was thinking about the day Dad moved out. Standing by the front door and not knowing what to say, the thought of all the white plastic letters from his laptop floating in our pond. I had felt like the Rift then. I had felt like darkness and depth.

Tentatively, I tapped a key on the amphipod control panel. A menu unfolded with further options. It was just like the simulation. *What next?* I thought.

The launch sequence.

There – flashing orange. A row of four numbered buttons had lit up on the OLED display in front of me. I tapped them one after the other. *Tap. Tap. Tap. Tap.*

They'd shown us the basics of submersible operation at the training centre. Batteries. Buoyancy. CO_2 scrubbers. Certain functions are common to everything because everything has to deal with the same challenges of being at the bottom of the ocean. The amphipod was no different, except that it was designed with a flair and elegance that would have made Dad clap his hands with glee.

Dad says using an interface is like having a conversation with the designer. A good designer leaves a little bit of themselves behind. Sitting there in the amphipod, I realized that he was right. It was unnerving, like Maximus was here with me. He was probably a bit like Dad, I thought, but gentler, maybe, more playful. It was like there was a joke always pushing at the corners of the interface, but the joke was just there to reassure you.

Evan was getting more agitated in his search. *It's my fault*, I thought. I'd set him up, given him hope, and I'd been wrong. There were all sorts of reasons why Maximus might have left a tablet in his filing cabinet. All sorts of reasons why he might have put both Cephalopod and the amphipod simulation on there. I imagined he was probably someone with a busy mind, someone always flitting from one thing to the next. I'd been desperate for an answer, and now I'd pulled Evan into the same mess.

My fingers worked automatically through the launch-prep sequence, clicking through acknowledgements and warnings, running the pre-launch diagnostics. A knot of my own anger was beginning to tighten inside me now. My discovery had changed nothing. Everything was as messed up as it had always been.

I didn't belong here; I wasn't wanted. Not by Mum, not topside by Dad. Everyone hated me. I was a liability. I was alone.

Once, for three weeks in a row, I soaked Dad's new mobile phone in the sink and then dried it off so he wouldn't suspect why it wasn't working. He kept taking it back to the shop and persuading them to give him a new one, and I kept breaking it as soon as he got it home.

Why would I do that?

Another time, I boiled his wallet on the hob.

And, at school, I'd done something that my best friend would never forgive me for.

Stop it!

I didn't want to go there. Not now. But I couldn't stop. The memory rushed into my mind, taking my breath away. My shame was like an electric shock. Like a tidal wave. It was like a cage full of monkeys rattling their bars.

So alone...

There was a hiss of hydraulics and I watched in dumb detachment as the gangplank retracted and the clear Perspex cockpit slid around me with a satisfying *hsssss—chuchunk!*

My fingers darted over the controls. They knew what they were doing, working automatically through the pre-launch protocols. A confused feeling rose inside me. *What was happening?* I opened my mouth, but I couldn't speak. *How was I doing this?*

A part of my mind felt at ease, like I had done this a thousand times before.

But no – that wasn't me. I was Lily Fawcett, and ... *I was so, so alone.*

Far off, a mechanical noise started that sounded like grinding teeth. Then more hissing of air. My ears popped as the air pressure inside the cockpit of the amphipod changed. Evan had stopped working on the console and was staring at me now, his mouth a silent "O" of surprise.

A strip of yellow and red lights around the pool had started to blink regularly.

Evan was waving. "Go! Go!" he was yelling.

I felt a flush of pride. Was I doing something right for once?

"Go! Go! Stop!" Evan screamed, waving wildly.

Wait. That wasn't right. Go. Go. *Stop*. That didn't make any sense. People often don't make a lot of sense to me, but that was … troubling. A number was counting down in front of me, but suddenly I felt disorientated. What was I doing? What had I done? Why did my ears keep popping?

"Stop! Stop!"

Realization hit me. An icy slap. Why would I think he was saying *go*…? It would make much more sense if he was saying—

"NOOOO!" Evan screamed.

Overhead, I felt as well as heard the retaining arm detach with a heavy CHU-*CHNK*, and the world dropped out from beneath me.

CHAPTER 17

Oh—Oh—Oh—Oh—Oh—

Water swallowed the amphipod. The murky innards of the pressure tank surrounded me on every side. I was sinking. I was strapped into half a tonne of amphipod and I was *SINKING!* I swiped desperately at the controls. The displays were blinking, but they no longer made any sense. *What have I done?* It was getting darker. The pressure door over the pool had slid shut. *What is wrong with me?*

I. Was. In. So. Much. Trouble.

It was dark. Close. Just a strip of lights to illuminate the sides of the tank. I was sinking too fast. I couldn't breathe. My mind screamed. I was going to hit the bottom, and it was going to *hurt*—

I drew a shuddering breath. Why hadn't I hit the bottom yet? The pool couldn't be *that* big? Then something made me look up – and I wished I hadn't. Deephaven was above me now ... far above me. Nothing but a dark shape, receding quickly.

What was happening?

Everything was happening.

Warning lights flickered and emergency buzzers yelled. The amphipod wasn't happy.

I was SINKING.

What had I done?

I leaned forward and saw only blackness below.

I looked up again: Deephaven disappearing into silty murk.

I scanned the controls. The console looked like a firework display. It looked like a slot machine. It looked like a fairground ride on rocket fuel. *This wasn't a simulation!* OK, calm down. The amphipod needs you to do something, that's all.

I pressed a few of the controls. Nothing seemed to change. The amphipod was still screaming at me.

OK, the amphipod needs you to do *quite a few* things.

I pressed some more controls. If a user interface was supposed to be a conversation with the designer, then Maximus was being distinctly shirty with me right now.

I drew a deep breath and thought of Dad.

Look at the controls. A good interface makes itself understood.

I slowed right down. I stabbed a series of red buttons which were asking to be pressed. I found a gauge that was begging to be adjusted and adjusted it.

The ragged slope of the valley surged towards me. I pushed the control stick forward and swept along with the gradient, the hair-like cilia a blur beneath me. More alerts. More tapping. At the last possible moment, I found the automatic buoyancy control. I hit it and I was suddenly travelling horizontally along the valley bottom.

The rockface flickered past, and the red glow of the telemetry grid loomed up from below. I took a couple of breaths and puffed them out. OK, just throttle down ... throttle down and I'll be OK... Six new displays lit up and none of them were pleased to see me.

My head swam. I gasped, too terrified to catch my breath.

"Ewello – ne..."

"What?" I called. "Who's there?"

"Wellow on – esss uh wellow – on—" A voice crackled in my head.

"Mum? Dad?"

You're supposed to be good with computers, Lily, prove it! I tried to make sense of the squalling displays. Digital readouts and virtual dials, everything changing rapidly. *You can't, can you? You're going to die down here!* The red glow of the telemetry grid rocketed past beneath me. Like falling

151

sideways. Like Apollo 11 in the moon landing. Except Apollo 11 didn't have the east ridge to contend with.

The ridge—

I was in a car crash once. Not a bad one. Hanna's older brother was giving us a lift home; he took a corner too fast and put us in a ditch. I still remember how it felt in the moment before the road dropped away, when we knew we were going to crash but we hadn't yet. I remember being aware of our own momentum, the weight of the car and our own bodies driving us forward. I remember scanning the length of the dashboard, taking in every detail, every spot of dust, every dent and nick in the PVC. And then the sound. The terrible sound. Crunching metal and breaking glass.

The east ridge loomed up ahead of me.

There would be no sound when I crashed. The percussive implosion when the hull breached would swallow everything. They taught us that at the training centre. But there was the same sense of momentum. The sense that you *should* be able to stop, but you know you can't. I wrenched the controls, and the amphipod swept sideways, this way and that. My thoughts seemed to come faster and more tightly. I saw every rise and fall and fold of the rockface. My eyes followed every crevice and overhang. An infinite number of rocks to crash into. In those few seconds, my brain took it all in.

I closed my eyes and waited for the impact—

Which never came.

My stomach lurched horribly as the amphipod changed direction, tilting forwards into a dive. I opened my eyes. Still moving. Surprised not to be dead. But how? My thoughts felt sluggish, overloaded by too many terrifying things all at once. The console of the amphipod was still yelling at me; it looked like somebody had eaten a pack of Skittles and then thrown up over a Christmas tree. But I hadn't crashed.

My brain seemed to watch from a long way away. Rock flashed past me on every side. Stalactites and ragged spears reached out. Where was I? A cave? A passageway? I couldn't have just *driven* into a cave; I'm not that lucky.

The amphipod's collision detection system must have taken over. It followed the curving line of the passage as it angled first left, and then down, down. Like a rollercoaster that never stopped. My breath caught in my throat as another wall of rock reared up in front. I wrenched the controls, and I felt the tail of the amphipod clip something as I slewed past. Then—

Blackness. The cave opened into a new space. Vast. Utterly empty. Just black. Blacker than black. Bright black. My indicators told me that I was still moving, but I could see nothing to confirm the fact. It felt like you could move for ever down here and not hit a thing.

"Tsss un nneellow nnone—"

"What?"

"The yellow one! Press the *yellow* one!" Evan's voice yelled, becoming suddenly clear.

A beam of light strobed across my pod, and I saw the hunched form of another amphipod chasing me. In the centre of a thousand frantic indicators clamouring for my attention, I saw now a single yellow light, pulsing slowly. I pushed it.

And everything stopped.

Evan's amphipod slid to a halt next to me. My heart felt like it had broken loose and was rattling around inside my chest. I heaved a shuddering breath and looked around. Still black. The spotlight from my amphipod cast a grey line of non-shadow ahead of us. My control panels glowed a contented blue.

"What *on Earth* were you thinking?!" Evan shouted furiously.

He scowled at me, his face lit a ghostly orange by the interior lights of his pod.

"I ... um... You came after me?" I said.

Evan blinked, forgetting his anger, and I saw that he was scared, scared for me. "You could have *died*."

I swallowed. "Um – hmm."

"How did you do that?"

"Do what?"

"Launch. You shouldn't have known how to do that, even after the simulation."

"I... I don't know."

We sat in silence for a moment, ak̲ ̲ ̲ ̲
enormity of our situation. The soothi̲ ̲ ̲
dashboard gave the illusion that everyt̲ ̲ ̲ ̲
control, but we both knew it wasn't. We were out her̲ ̲ ̲
alone. We weren't even at the bottom of the ocean any
more, we were … nowhere.

"You came after me," I said again.

I fought an unexpected urge to cry. I felt shocked by
the size of my gratitude: that I wasn't dead; that I wasn't
alone down here.

"What was I supposed to do?"

"Is this your first time actually driving one of these?"
I asked.

"Yes." Sullen.

"You're very good."

"The simulation," he said. "Lots of practice."

I thought for a moment. "The interface is a little
confusing, if I'm honest—" The look on his face stopped
me. He wasn't in the mood for constructive feedback.

I looked down. My breath died in my throat as if the
blackness had swallowed it. The legs of my amphipod
dangled over fathomless nothing. There was no ocean
floor. No telemetry grid. No rocks. Were it not for my
instruments and the gentle tug of gravity, it wouldn't even
be possible to tell which way was up.

"Where are we?" I asked. "More to the point, where's
the bottom?"

"We're in the Rift," Evan breathed. "You drove us into the Rift." His voice was strange, almost in awe. "Dad had been searching for the entrance for months, how did you…?"

"I didn't do anything, I just…"

Realization dawned on his face. "He must have programmed the coordinates into the amphipods. He must have been closer than he let on." He squeezed his eyes shut. "Stupid! I'm so *stupid*! That's what he was trying to tell me: he'd found it, he was just waiting for the amphipods to be ready." He blinked quickly, seeming to come back to himself. "We need to get back to the entrance before we lose our bearings."

He tapped a control and his amphipod started to ascend. I followed. Now that the display was calmer, it looked pretty simple to control. Elegant, just as the rig schematic had been.

I peered around, straining my eyes in every direction. So … we were in the Rift – a massive cave – and we were trapped. This wasn't good. My spotlight picked out the solid wall of rock above our heads. It looked similar to the ocean floor, like a mirror image but more rugged. Vast towers of rock jutted down from the darkness like inverted skyscrapers, enormous crystalline stalactites glittering in the light from our spotlights. There were places where the rock was smooth and rippled, almost like melted plastic, and places where it appeared as though it had been crushed into fierce shards.

"We're really *under* the ocean floor?" I breathed.

Evan nodded.

"I want to go home," I said.

"Me too," Evan replied. "We need to find the passageway."

My throat squeezed tight. Everything was so black. I felt the ocean closing around me. It was like a part of my brain was calling out, hollering in terror, but the sound was so tiny nobody could hear it. "Can we use our instruments? Retrace our steps?"

Evan shook his head. "Mine aren't working. What about yours?"

I checked. "Nothing."

"The ocean floor is above us, so the positioning systems will be all messed up. It's part of the reason Dad hadn't used the amphipods yet."

I could feel myself starting to panic. I gulped a lungful of air. It felt like a band was wrapped around my chest, winding tighter and tighter. It had taken months for Maximus to find a path from the ocean floor to the Rift. Without our instruments there was no reason for it to be any easier to find the path going back the other way.

"Can we radio the rig for help?" I asked.

"Radio doesn't work underwater. We use underwater acoustic communication, UAC – the computer translates our voices into high-pitched sound waves so they can travel through water. That's how we can talk to each other.

But the range is not much better than our voices. You might as well shout for help."

"*HEELPP!!*" I shouted abruptly.

"Lily…" Evan said.

"*HEEEEEELLLP!*"

I felt the sound erupt from my mouth, impossibly loud, and for a moment it wasn't me screaming, it was the whole ocean.

"Lily!" Evan said, louder this time.

"*HEE—*" I fell silent. "Oh, when you said I might as well shout for help, you meant … not to."

"Yes," Evan confirmed. "That's what I meant, Lily."

I drew a slow, shaky breath. I felt better for it, anyway; the screaming had released a knot inside my body.

We scanned our spotlights over the lines of rock, looking for signs of any cleft or gap that might signal the route back to the surface. Or to the bottom. Or whatever.

"It's hopeless," I said. "I'm all turned around. We don't even know which direction we came from."

Evan met my gaze with serious eyes. "We'll find it."

I swallowed. The air felt thick, like it was unwilling to enter my lungs. I checked my battery and oxygen readings. One hour. Not great. Not long enough. But I shouldn't be having difficulty breathing yet.

I was panicking. I needed not to panic.

It would be hours before class started and anyone noticed we were missing. Our best hope was that somebody had spotted us leaving. Or maybe Ari would decide to go back to find us and check the amphipod bay. But even if that happened, what good would it do? There was no way they'd find us down here.

"I'm sorry," I said, my voice cracking. "It's all my fault."

"We'll find a way out," Evan said again. "Look, the compass is down, and we have no inertial log. I think searching in a spiral is our best bet."

We agreed to start from where we were and work outwards, side-by-side, an ever-increasing spiral until we either found something – or ran out of oxygen.

"Get your spotlights into all the folds," he said, his voice struggling to stay level. "It's better to take our time. We can't afford to miss it."

I glanced down through the Perspex, and the blackness beneath me took my breath away again. *Focus*, I whispered to myself. *You need to focus.* An image popped suddenly into my mind: the road outside my old school, Hanna's boyfriend's blue Fiesta parked outside the newsagent's. Why was I thinking about that now?

"Be careful, you're drifting off the line," Evan said.

"Sorry," I muttered thickly.

I shook my head to try and clear my thoughts. Something weird was happening. It felt like something was inside my head, rifling through drawers and turning out cupboards. Memories I hadn't thought about in a long time buzzed inside me, tumbling over each other. The day

159

I put glue in the locks. The day I switched off the freezer. The day Dad left. The day I saw Talha's blue Fiesta—

"Lily…"

I couldn't breathe. I was burning. I was freezing. I was darkness.

Oh, my boy … my boy…

Evan's voice was suddenly urgent, but it felt distant, muffled, like it came from another world. "Lily, you're having a panic attack. Just stay calm, OK—"

So black. So alone. Not words. Maybe this was what dying was like? They say your life flashes before your eyes. But this wasn't just my life. I stared down into the blackness, and I heard another voice in my head. Maximus. *Oh, my boy … my boy…* Sinking, the first crack appearing in the cockpit. *Not rated for this depth. No choice. Now or never.*

I was thinking about how it felt to be alone. Before. After. Images I hardly understood. Thoughts that made me so cold I could hardly bear it.

I'm falling. I'm alone.

And then – darkness.

CHAPTER 18

Darkness. My irregular, galloping heartbeats filled my ears.

"Evan? Evan?"

Calmly: "I'm here."

"Where's everything else?"

"Our amphipod computers just rebooted. We lost the console lights and the spots."

"Is that normal?"

"I don't know."

"It's really dark."

"Are you afraid of the dark?" Evan asked.

"Um … no. I guess not."

"That's good."

"I'm afraid of being stuck in a hidden sinkhole under the ocean floor with less than an hour of oxygen left."

"Yes, that's reasonable," Evan replied, deadpan.

Just then ... I saw something.

A light. Like a match being struck. It flared intensely and then faded out, leaving a streak of purple in my eyes. For a moment my heart leapt because I thought somebody had found us. But after the light faded there was only blackness again.

"Did you see that?" I asked.

"What?"

"A light."

"I didn't see anything."

Then another flare of light.

Then another.

"Tell me you saw that," I said.

"Yes. Yes, I see it!" Evan gasped. "What's going on?"

Another. And another. Purple. No, turquoise. Like a peacock's feather. Or the flash of colour on a kingfisher's tail. Another and another. They were all coming at once now. Fireflies. Embers from a bonfire. The sea was full of them. Full. Like ... for ever. An infinite parallax of turquoise, going on and on. Pulsing, dancing incandescent spasms of light that jumped and spun all around us. Faster and faster.

"What is it?" I breathed.

"Oh ... my," Evan murmured. "It's full of *stars*."

Each dot of light appeared from nowhere and then sparked away, like it was driven by a jet of its own colour. More and more and more of them, filling the sea around us. It was beautiful. It was terrifying. It was like a cathedral roof. It was like the dome of the night sky, but bigger, brighter, closer.

"Are we dying?"

"No," Evan said. Adding, unhelpfully, "Not yet." He shook his head. "It must be some kind of phosphorescent protist."

The purple lights rippled around us, each one small, but together they were so bright we had to squint to keep looking at them. As I watched, I realized that the lights weren't moving randomly. Amongst the flickering, dancing shapes there was a pattern. There was something here that felt familiar. A rhythm. Like a pulse. A natural ebb and flow. An organization that bound the lights together.

Like the pulsating background of Cephalopod.

"Wait – this is it!" I said suddenly.

"What?"

"It's the euglenoid your dad contacted Mum about. He said it was bioluminescent – it glowed – and he said it showed *microbial* intelligence. I don't know what that means, do you?"

"It means it's *smart*," Evan said. "Not each one; each one is just a single cell, but together they act intelligently. But it doesn't make any sense; he'd have told me if he'd seen this, I'm sure he would have."

There was a soft *click*, and our console lights came back on, flooding the screens in front of me. I gasped with relief. Then the spotlights clicked on, and their intense light whited out everything else. Quickly, we dimmed them so we wouldn't lose our night vision. Evan tapped a control on his dashboard and a compartment opened on his amphipod. A spindly robotic arm extended from the abdomen of the amphipod.

"We need a sample of this," he said.

I checked my oxygen. Forty minutes.

"We need to get out of here," I said.

"I know, I know. This won't take a minute."

I stared hard into the twirling patterns, momentarily fascinated by them. There *was* something there. Like a dance, or a rhythm. An order in the chaos. I could almost, but not quite, see it. The way the players in an orchestra will seem to be doing their own thing, but at the same time working together.

"Can you see it?" I asked. "The pattern."

"What pattern?"

Back at the training centre I'd watched a movie about the Humboldt squid. A researcher was using their own laser rig to communicate with it, imitating its own bioluminescent patterns.

Something tugged at the back of my mind, a memory.

Suddenly, the pulsing lights changed. The region directly in front of me grew brighter, drawing the other euglenoids to it. A ball of light formed. Blue-purple-turquoise. A surging sphere coalesced as if all the euglenoids had chosen to phosphoresce together. I looked at Evan and saw him staring back through the dome of his amphipod.

"What's it doing?" he breathed.

"I don't know," I said. "Wait, I want to try something."

I nudged my controller and the amphipod glided towards the light.

"Lily, don't—"

The moment the amphipod touched it, the ball of euglenoid burst into a brilliant display of light, a detonation like a firework exploding all around me, so bright I had to shield my eyes with my hand.

"Wow," Evan remarked. "Just, wow."

A new ball of light appeared, like the first, but a metre or so to the left. Hundreds of points, frantically circling each other. Like a beehive. Like a city. Like a Christmas tree bauble.

"It wants to play," I said, smiling slowly.

Evan shook his head. "That's not possible…"

Excitement trembled in my chest. I moved over to it, manoeuvred the amphipod into it. Instantly, the ball burst into a shower of colour. Evan let out an astonished gasp.

"It's like the game," I said. "Like Cephalopod. Your dad

must have been down here already. He must have played with it, like this, and modified your game to simulate what he saw."

Evan's face tightened. "No way. He'd have told me."

"You're saying it's a coincidence? Your dad's version of the game mimics exactly what's happening here?" I shook my head. "This is what he was so excited about, Evan. This is why he wanted to bring Mum onboard."

I drove into a third ball of colour. More explosions of light. Another ball appeared, further off. I got that one too. And the next. The quicker I got to them, the quicker they reappeared. I laughed.

"See? Smart."

Evan replied after a moment, "They're single-celled creatures. They can't *play games*."

"Not on their own," I said. "But all together … it's just like you said. Like a shoal of fish. Or an ant's nest."

The next ball was further away, almost lost amongst the background of shimmering euglenoid. I moved closer to it. Swatted it. The colours erupted so suddenly I felt my breath catch in my throat.

"Lily, wait – we don't have time for this."

I glanced at my oxygen supply. Thirty minutes. The next ball of light waited. Expectant. Hopeful.

"OK," I said.

Reluctantly, we reformed and tried to pick up where we left off. Inch by painful inch, our spotlights trained on the dark, irregular rock. Except now we were distracted by the constant pulse of the euglenoid around us, crowding us. A ball formed nearby, and I gently knocked against it.

"Lily, don't—"

It popped triumphantly. Now another ball appeared, further off in the same direction. Something strange was happening. My head rang with peculiar thoughts. *Curious creatures...*

"Lily, *please!*" Evan called. "We don't have long."

"I have to see... It might..."

I tagged the next ball, and the one beyond that. Thoughts that were not my own crowded into my mind. *Better get back... Not rated for this depth...*

The light of the euglenoid filled my eyes. It filled my mind. It wanted me to follow. I moved towards it. The lights were hypnotic. A drumbeat. A pulse.

"*Lily!*" Evan shouted.

But he was following me. He had no choice. I was moving fast now. I swatted two more balls. Always they appeared slightly further away, always in the same direction. I moved faster. The lights matched my pace.

I followed. I couldn't *not* follow. *So curious... Wonderful!* The colours burned my eyes. The noise of them brayed inside my head.

"Lily, *please!*" Evan said again. "We're going off track. We'll never get back like this."

I swatted another ball and the afterglow faded slowly. I stopped dead.

"Look," I said.

At first, I couldn't be sure; my eyes were seared with the light of the euglenoid. But then my vision calmed, and I could see it more clearly, scintillating against the uneven underside of the ocean floor.

The passageway back to the surface.

CHAPTER 19

Of all the irresponsible, foolish, *expensive*, dangerous, selfish things, apparently jettisoning yourself into the deep ocean was number one.

The grown-ups practically queued up to yell at us.

We'd arrived back at Deephaven to find the sea swarming with submersibles and ROVs out looking for us, and when we finally burst back into the air and safety in the amphipod bay, we found Ari and his team waiting anxiously.

"Oh … kids…" he groaned, clawing at his beard. "What were you *thinking*?"

He hurried us directly to the command centre, muttering and tutting to himself all the way, and there we found Mum, Dr Balgobin and Carter gathered around Carter's desk.

Mum looked distraught, her face caught between being furious and terrified and relieved all at once. Dr Balgobin gave me a look that seemed so full of regret I immediately wanted to throw myself at her perfect feet and beg forgiveness.

"Have you any idea how much productivity we lost as a result of your actions?" Carter raged. "How many unscheduled submersible hours we just clocked, how many ROV maintenance cycles we'll have to undertake?" His neck was scalding red beneath his immaculate collar. "Have you any idea how much your little adventure cost this organization?" he added. He glared at me. "More than you will *ever* earn, Lily Fawcett."

My head spun. I felt sick. I felt like I was shrinking. The grown-ups were glaring at me so fiercely I felt like I was getting younger and younger by the second. I was ten, no, now I was eight. Pretty soon I'd vanish altogether.

After the first glance, I didn't dare look at Mum again. I'd made her a promise, and now I'd broken it in spectacular style.

I caught Evan's eye instead, and he offered me a stoic smile in return. He was probably angry at me as well; it was my fault that we'd been out there in the first place. But at this point, the boy I'd nearly got killed was the nearest thing I had to a friend.

"I blame myself," Carter continued, in a tone that

implied the complete opposite. "I've been saying all along that a deep-sea rig is not suitable for untrained personnel, let alone children. I shouldn't have let them talk me into allowing a science team on board in the first place."

Dr Balgobin exchanged a worried look with Ari. "The science team is hardly *untrained*. Everyone has followed standard procedures."

"And look what *standard procedures* led to," Carter responded, gesturing at me.

"Nothing like this will *ever* happen again, I guarantee you," Mum said determinedly. She dragged her fingers through her hair, her eyes wild and searching.

"You can't *guarantee* anything." Carter rounded on her. "No more than I can *guarantee* that nothing will go wrong down here, no more than I could *guarantee* poor Maximus's safety." Evan tensed at the mention of his dad. Carter saw it too, but it didn't discourage him. "If I'd stuck to my guns," he said, turning to Evan, "your father would never have been down here. He'd still be alive."

I watched Evan's face, afraid about what he might do in response. *Is that the plan?* I thought suddenly. Did Carter *want* Evan to lose his temper? The more of a scene he could cause, the more he could use our little escapade to put pressure on the science team, the more he could cement support from the Consortium to blast the east ridge.

Evan stood, slowly, calmly, and set the pressure jar on Carter's desk.

"We found proof," he said. "Dad was right. He'd found the Rift, just like he said. It's under the east ridge." He smiled triumphantly. "What's down there ... it's incredible. Entirely new. We're going to be researching it for decades, and the universities will *never* let you near it."

Carter frowned at the pressure jar — a smooth, round glass canister, about the same diameter as a mayonnaise jar but twice as high, with a big rubber seal on either end.

"Your dad lost his mind," he responded coolly. "Everyone knows it. Either that, or he was making up fairy stories to try and obstruct the business of the rig. I'm sorry to be the one to say it, Evan, but your father lost his credibility *years* ago."

I could see Evan's chest rising and falling, his fists clenched. Mum leaned forward, peering at the sample. I felt my own chest tighten in excitement. She'd understand. As soon as she saw what the euglenoid could do, she'd have everything she needed to stop Carter and win her own contract on board Deephaven. Nothing else would matter.

"It's true," I said. "We found the euglenoid Maximus hired Mum to investigate down there. It's bioluminescent, just like he said. And it's ... it's *intelligent*." I heard Evan draw a breath, but I was too excited to stop. "We played a game with it. We played *tag*. And it showed us the way back out of the Rift…"

I trailed off, noticing the looks I was getting. Too late, I realized that I'd gone too far. Evan was looking horrified, willing me to stop. The others were looking disappointed, like they'd thought for a moment we really had found something, but now they knew that it wasn't possible.

"Is this meant to be some kind of joke?" Carter sneered.

Mum shook her head slowly, sadly. "It looks like the other samples in Maximus's lab. We tested them; there's nothing there."

"No, Mum, it's not true—"

"We've wasted enough time on this nonsense." Carter's mouth twisted as he looked at me. "If there are dangerous caves on the east ridge where people could get trapped, it just gives me another reason to blast there and make it safe."

Carter turned to Evan. His tone was gentle, but his eyes were like hard nuggets of iridium: "Evan, I'm sorry. I shouldn't have let you stay down here so long. I was trying to be kind, but I can see now I haven't been fair." He shook his head sadly, theatrically. "I'm putting a case to the committee tonight for you to be relocated. In the absence of any relations, a social worker will find you a good foster home, somewhere topside, somewhere you can be safe." He flashed a patronizing smile that was almost convincing. "You'll get to go to a *normal* school. Have a *normal* life. A rig is no place for a lone child – especially after what you've been through."

Evan's mouth opened. He looked demolished. He stood unsteadily. I wondered what he was going to say. What he was going to do.

"I... I need to sleep," he murmured.

I watched bleakly as Dr Balgobin guided him out. I was desperate for him to look my way, to catch my eye and give me some sign that he would be OK. But he didn't turn.

"We should go too," Mum said after he'd gone.

"Wait," Carter said. "There's something else you should know."

Mum flashed me a warning look. Dr Balgobin and Ari both frowned in anticipation.

"I was notified that you have been making a number of funding applications to the university."

Mum stiffened but said nothing.

"You should know I've been doing my own research," Carter continued, "and I've discovered some troubling information about your daughter."

Mum's eyes opened wide. "I don't—"

"Your daughter was *expelled* from her last school, Dr Fawcett," Carter said, hardly able to contain his delight. "A fact that wasn't disclosed in your application, and one that would certainly have demonstrated her unsuitability for a high-risk environment like this."

Seawater swirled in my stomach. The truth was out. It was finally out.

"Technically, she wasn't expelled," Mum responded tightly.

"Allow me to rephrase: she *would have* been expelled if you hadn't taken the job here and come to an arrangement with the head."

I looked desperately at Ari and Dr Balgobin. I felt bad for disappointing them. I hardly knew them, but both had been inexplicably kind, acting as if they believed in me, liked me, even. Now that look was gone, and its absence burned inside me.

"What's your point, Carter?" Mum asked.

"My point is that I have good grounds for starting legal proceedings against you, Dr Fawcett," he said. He looked both happy and mean at the same time, like he was eating a piece of cake he knew belonged to someone else. "You would be liable for the cost of your training, your time here, and the rescue operation your daughter just triggered."

I watched the blood drain from Mum's face. "The form asked if there had been any disciplinary actions," she said, her voice trembling. "The answer was no. I'm under no obligation to disclose behavioural issues or ... emotional problems."

Emotional problems. That was Mr Paley, my old head's, phrase.

Carter leaned forward menacingly. "Your daughter's *emotional problems* are a danger to everyone on this rig. I'm a reasonable man, Dr Fawcett, and I'm advising you to consider your next move carefully, especially with regard to your attempts to filibuster the review board." He licked his lips. "I will ruin you if I have to, Dr Fawcett; consider this fair warning. There won't be any second chances."

CHAPTER 20

It started with a boy. What a ridiculous thing to start with, but there you go.

Talha was one of those slick, knowing kind of boys. Dark hair, dark eyes, an aura of being somehow more worldly than the rest of us – even though everyone knew his dad just worked as the accountant for the local furniture store.

He's interesting, Hanna had said after she met him at a party I hadn't been invited to.

He was older than us by two years, he drove a car (a

176

Fiesta that looked to be on its last legs), and he was on the management training programme at the local Waitrose.

Hanna had started seeing him. He was her first real boyfriend, and she was every bit as irritating about the whole thing as I'd feared she would be.

"You're with him *all* the time," I said.

"I'm not," Hanna said defensively. "I'm with you now."

"We're at school; you don't have a choice."

"You wouldn't understand. This is different. This is special."

"Oh, *barf*..."

"What's your point?"

"I miss you."

I knew this conversation wouldn't go well. Dad had moved out months ago, but I still felt like I was falling and not hitting the ground. I knew I wasn't being reasonable, but I didn't let that stop me.

"You left me on my own at lunchtime yesterday," I said. "I accidentally smashed a plate and nearly got into a fight with the dinner lady."

Hanna scowled. "You should be able to get lunch without getting into a fight, Lily. That's not *normal*, you know that." I started to protest, but Hanna carried on: "You're too clingy. It's like you think we're still eleven. You're *suffocating* me."

I looked around the quad where we were sitting. A few of the younger kids were playing football; another group was deeply involved in a card game of some kind. There was one boy, I noticed, standing off to the side, alone, his hand working nervously at the wall as he chipped away at the mortar. *I hate break times*, I thought. *It's not fair on the kids who don't know what they're supposed to do.*

"I'm sorry," I said. "I just... I miss Dad."

Hanna sighed theatrically – not the response I wanted. "When are you going to stop whining about your bloody dad?"

"I wasn't whining."

"Yes, you were. My dad left too, you know. He ran off with the Amazon delivery driver; that's much worse."

"Three years ago. And you said you get free Amazon Prime now, which is great."

"Jesus, Lily, that was a joke, obviously!"

"Why are you being so mean?"

"You're *attention-seeking*."

"I'm not."

"Then why do you do it?"

"Do what?"

Hanna let her head fall back in frustration. "What do you think? *Accidentally* smashing plates? All the ... breaking things!"

"I don't—"

Tears rushed into my eyes. I sensed danger because this part was new. Hanna had always been the one who guided me through the confusing battlefield of secondary school. She was the only one who was there for me when Dad left. She told me off when I was being an idiot. She consoled me when I cried. People couldn't understand why she hadn't ditched me years ago. But we had never, ever talked about me breaking things. I had always figured she knew, but she didn't mention it, and I was grateful for that. As if not mentioning it was her way of accepting it, letting me know that it was OK.

"What did you break this week, huh?" she went on meanly. "How about the interactive whiteboard in the English room that suddenly doesn't work? And *somebody* broke the nibs off all the pens. Was that you, by any chance, Lily?"

"Stop, please stop…"

"How about the punctured basketballs in the sports hall? And the blocked toilets? How about the glue in the fifth-form lockers?"

I frowned. "Wait – no, I didn't do that one."

Hanna was glaring at me now. Didn't she know she was my only friend? Didn't she know that without her I'd fall apart, and then *anything* might happen?

She stood up. "You're a *freak*, Lily. I'm done with it."

I watched her leave. *A freak.* Was that what I was?

For the rest of the day, I walked around school with my skin hanging off. I was a gory mess, but nobody seemed to notice. It wasn't fair that I could be so torn up inside and still look perfectly normal on the outside.

That evening, I saw Talha's car pull up outside school, and I watched him dart into the newsagent's for cigarettes.

Asshole. I dumped my can of lemonade in his petrol tank, and I felt a lot better for it. I don't know why I felt better, I just did.

I always did. For a while, at least.

I'd done this before, to Dad's car, and his car had caught fire in the driveway. It was a small, manageable fire that was quickly put out. A small, manageable moment in which the universe listened to me for once. If I'd thought anything at that moment, it was that the same thing would happen to Talha's car.

Except this time the car didn't catch fire in the driveway. It caught fire on the motorway, and when Talha pulled on to the hard shoulder – freaking out most likely, going too fast – he rolled the car into the ditch.

He broke his wrist, and Hanna broke two of her ribs and lost a tooth, and everyone agreed that it could have been much, much worse.

They figured out it was me right away. The newsagent had seen me, but I'd have confessed even if he hadn't. In the movies, the bad guy cuts the brake cable on the hero's car, and you get to watch the hero fight for control as their runaway convertible careers down a winding mountain road. I was the bad guy in this movie.

It didn't matter that I hadn't really meant to hurt anybody. I could see it in the looks of the police officers

180

who came to our door. I could see it in the looks of everyone around school, and Mum, and even Dad: they didn't understand me. I was an alien to them. That was what had scared them the most.

CHAPTER 21

Mum stalked up and down our tiny cabin, her face incandescent with rage.

"What were you thinking?"

"I—"

"How could you?" Her voice was high and thin; her eyes pleaded for understanding.

"Mum, I didn't mean—"

"You *promised*."

"I know, but I—"

"I don't want to hear it." She lifted her hands and held her head. "I don't know what to do with you, Lily. I honestly don't."

Tears pushed at the backs of my eyes. My thoughts

squirmed. Computers have undo buttons: you mess something up on a computer, and it's just *CONTROL-Z*. Boom! Problem solved. I needed one of those buttons.

"What's going to happen now?" I asked in a small voice.

"Well, we're finished. Carter knows everything. So, what's going to happen is that we're going to pack our bags and leave as soon as the next supply sub gets here, just like Carter wanted from the start."

"He's just trying to get rid of us so he can blast the east ridge."

"Yes," Mum snapped. "And thanks to you he's succeeded."

Later, I lay in my room, my face hot and my heart still beating fast. The hard slats of the bed made my back ache. I took out my phone and looked at it: no messages. Nothing. Not from Dad. Not from Hanna. I wanted to cry, but I couldn't. I hadn't cried since Dad left. I'd wanted to many times, but the tears turned inwards instead and nothing came.

"I don't understand you," Hanna had said to me.

Her lip was still so swollen and packed with dressings that she could hardly speak. The stitches on her lip would likely leave a scar, I'd been told, and it would be a few months before her mouth had healed enough to consider replacing the tooth.

"I'm sorry…"

"We had an argument, Lily. Just a silly argument. You could have killed me."

"I know."

"Why? Why do you do it? Can you explain it for me, at least?"

But I couldn't. I couldn't then, and I can't now.

Looking up at the ceiling, alone in my tiny bedroom, my thoughts trampling over each other – this was exactly the kind of situation where I usually broke something. The desire to create breakage tingled in my arms and legs, like a spring that had been squeezed too tight, like that cage full of monkeys squashed into my chest, desperate to get out. If I let them out, they'd smash and smash. But at least the breakage would be outside, not inside me.

What should it be? What should take the blame? I considered the horrific, textured, beige, vinyl walls and imagined hacking at them with the table lamp.

I felt the weight of the pressure jar in my pocket. I'd taken it on impulse when we left Carter's command centre; nobody had cared. I took it out now: grey silt; lifeless. Of course it was. Nothing could survive this deep. Maybe Evan and I had dreamed the whole thing after all. A shared hallucination. Evan had wanted to believe in the Rift as much as I did. We'd been frightened, ready to believe anything.

Did you see that?

What?

A light.

Yes! Oh my ... it's full of stars.

I kneeled up on my bed with the pressure jar in my hand and looked around the room.

Stupid... Loser... Screw-up... Freak... the monkeys whispered.

I caught sight of the porthole. My whispery reflection watched me. I was an idiot for coming here, for thinking I could fit in with these exceptional people. A flash of convulsive anger squeezed tight inside me, and I raised the pressure jar over my head and slammed it on to the glass.

CLLUNNKKK—!

The impact shook my arm painfully. The sound seemed to reverberate through the walls of the rig. I drew my arm back and punched the pressure jar as hard as I could into the porthole.

CHHUUNNKKK!

It was a good thing Mum had gone back to the lab.

CHAHUN-KKK!

It hurt my hand, but it was a good pain. It was a loosening and a tightening at the same time, a shifting of feeling from my head into my body. Dimly, through the rage, I knew that if the porthole cracked, five thousand tonnes of seawater would rip me to shreds. I didn't mind. Part of me actually wanted it. To be smashed, to be torn apart. It was just how I already felt anyway; I'd like for other people to see it too, that way they might understand for once—

So alone…

I wanted the jar to smash. I wanted the universe to see me, to understand me.

When glass shatters, it's like an outward breath, a sigh. All the feelings that were caught up inside come out with the fragments.

Cllunn—cllunn—cllunnkk—clunnn-kk—!

My arm throbbed.

Alone. So alone.

A limitless isolation. The feeling of waiting upstairs and listening to Mum and Dad fight downstairs. Mum: a pinched forehead and the feeling that we ground her down. Dad: confused blinking and, *Chill out, Lilypad.* Once, when I was little, I'd fallen and scraped my knee, and I remember realizing for the first time that he just didn't understand … he didn't understand that all I needed was a hug.

I raised the pressure jar behind my head and felt my whole body tense as I prepared to thrust forward with all my—

Light!

Sparks of beautiful blue-turquoise shimmered into view, dancing and spitting and swirling around the jar just as they had in the Rift. I stared at them for a moment, sweating from my exertions.

I gulped air. It was real. *It was real.*

Or else I really had lost my mind.

"What are you?" I murmured.

It didn't reply. Of course it didn't. The lights darted erratically back and forth, pulsing with the same almost-imperceptible rhythm as I'd seen in the Rift.

"Why now?" I asked. "Was it the banging? Or something else?"

The colours turned and folded into themselves: rhythmic, shifting.

"Great," I murmured. "Now I'm talking to algae."

I pressed my hand against the glass, and the patterns shifted towards it, drawn like iron-filings to a magnet. "Incredible," I breathed.

I couldn't wait to show Evan. *This will change everything,* I thought. Mum would be able to study the euglenoid just like Maximus had wanted. She'd prove that it was something new, petition the universities to let her stay on. Even if I still had to go home because of my excursion in the amphipod, it didn't matter. At least I would have done something right for once.

Then something odd happened. A shift. A disconnection. *Snap.*

Like a switch, or a cotton thread snapping. The lights vanished.

My mind had moved to Mum, and home, and I'd felt something vanish from inside my head.

I stared at the lifeless jar in disbelief. "Seriously? Are you actually kidding me?"

I slammed the pressure jar against the porthole.

Clunnk!

Nothing.

Clunnk!

Nothing.

Cllunnkk! Clnnn-kk!

Nothing.

My chest heaved. Already, the flash of hopefulness and relief I'd felt when I'd seen the light had drained away, leaving nothing but black and cold inside me...

A shudder rose up, a great burning thunderstorm. A crashing torrent. I felt small and worthless and like I had no control or value in the world. I hurled the pressure jar at the far wall as hard as I could. It clanged against the vinyl, cracking a chunk of the wall covering and exposing a satisfying slice of bare metal beneath. The jar hit the floor and rolled slightly. A crack opened along one side and the aluminosilicate case fizzed furiously as it tried to seal the leak. Inside, the grey liquid was still and dark.

"Good riddance," I muttered at the silent jar.

CHAPTER 22

**LILY FAWCETT: DEEPHAVEN PERSONAL LOG
DAY 14**

I have a head full of things I'm not keen to think about. I remember the first time I broke something. I was very little. I remember waiting upstairs, scared of the sound of my parents arguing downstairs. I wanted to go down, but I knew they wouldn't like it. I remember taking Mum's earrings and dropping them into the toilet, watching them roll down the inside of the bowl like a slow-motion landslide. I remember Mum's furious, dismayed face, and Dad's uncomprehending look.

It's like having a giant spider in the corner of your mind. It's so ugly that just looking at it makes you feel sick. But you can't ignore it once you know it's there.

I went to class the next morning as normal, hoping to see Evan, but there was no sign of him. The others ignored me, lost in their books, or pretending to be.

Dr Balgobin didn't mention what had happened. She just smiled as warmly as ever. She was so lovely. But as soon as everybody had sat down, she announced the beginning of a new special topic: rig safety!

The class sighed and put away their copies of *Twenty Thousand Leagues Under the Sea* (which they'd been enjoying immensely, of course) and instead passed around copies of *A Working Manual for Rig Safety and Procedure*.

Ysabel flashed me a resentful look. They all knew it was Carter's idea, his way of making a point, but it was still my fault. *Nuts to you*, I thought. Little-Miss-Junior-Winter-Olympics could glare at me all she wanted, I didn't care.

"Lesson one," Alban declared with a loud sigh as he opened his book. "How not to blast yourself into the ocean."

Ha, ha.

I stuck up my hand.

"Yes, Lily?" said Dr Balgobin gently.

"Where's Evan?"

"He needs rest," she said, avoiding my eyes.

"Is he going to be sent topside like Carter said?"

"The Consortium is arranging foster care for him. He'll take the next sub."

*

The weekend passed in a haze of Mum avoiding me, and me avoiding everyone else. Mum stayed mostly in the science lab, writing emails, enquiring about teaching jobs. She knew there was no chance of staying here now.

I kept to our cabin as much as possible. Evan didn't respond to my messages. I was sure he hated me for getting him into so much trouble he couldn't stay here any more. I stared at my reflection-less, hazy porthole and wished that I could take a sub and drive off into the hadopelagic wastes just as Maximus had done. But it was impossible, so I snapped the handles off the mugs in our cabin instead, and then went promptly to the canteen for two more and snapped the handles off those as well.

Whenever I left my cabin, I caught the resentful looks of the other residents. *There goes the troublemaker*, I felt them thinking. *She has … emotional problems. Better keep your eye on that one.*

Everywhere I looked, my eyes fell on an ERS button. Waiting, just waiting to be pressed. If I was leaving anyway, I should do it, right? My final act could be to scupper Carter's plans to blast the east ridge. No one would know, but *I'd* know; I'd have at least something to be proud of myself for.

Sunday evening I found myself outside Evan's cabin. I paused, my hand hovering near the door. *What am I doing?* Surely if he'd wanted to see me, he'd have answered my messages.

I knocked.

He didn't answer at first.

I pressed my face to the rigid plastic door and called in: "Evan, open up. I need to talk to you."

Nothing. Then there was a sound inside, like somebody had slid a pile of papers off their knee and was sitting quietly, listening.

"I know you're in there, Evan. *Please.*"

Another sound.

Then the door clicked open, and Evan stood facing me. He looked strained, his face pale. He wore a grey T-shirt and regulation neoprene underwear that revealed long, sinewy legs. He let the door swing open and stepped back inside. His cabin was identical to ours, except it was a wreck. The foldaway desk had been half wrenched from the wall. The drawers and cupboard doors lay open, their contents strewn over the floor.

"Um … sorry about the mess," he muttered, picking his way back to his armchair.

"What happened?"

"I kind of, um, smashed the place up a bit after our meeting with Carter."

He flashed me a self-conscious smile. The sink in the kitchenette looked to be mostly filled with broken crockery; curled pieces of broken glass lay scattered around the floor nearby.

"I know that feeling," I muttered, surveying the breakage.

"Really?" Evan said, his voice flat. He gave me a tired look. "You know how it feels to be told your dad is missing at the bottom of the ocean, do you?"

I felt my face turn red. "I'm sorry, I didn't mean…" I took a breath before my anger made me say something stupid. "You're right, I don't know how any of that feels. I just meant … I know how it feels to want to break things sometimes." He nodded, and I swallowed to try and stop my voice cracking. "We need to talk."

"About what?"

"About what happened down there. Was it real? Did we imagine it?"

"Honestly, I don't know." He gave me a cheerless smile. "There's no evidence for what we saw. That sample is dead, just like the others. I thought because it had come directly from the Rift it would be different, but…"

I thought of the jar, still lying on my cabin floor somewhere. He wouldn't believe me if I told him I'd seen it glow again. And even if he did, what good would it do? I'd tried everything. Either I'd imagined it, or the sample had died right there in my cabin, and what I'd seen were just its last moments.

"I guess it can't survive the transition on to the rig," Evan continued. "If there really was anything there at all."

"There has to be something we can do."

Evan shrugged. He picked up his tablet and began tapping idly at the screen like he'd forgotten I was there.

I waited. I could see the flickering shapes of the amphipod simulation over his shoulder as he worked through the launch sequence. CO_2. Battery. Buoyancy. When it was complete, and the simulated amphipod was ready to launch, the sequence froze and snapped back to the beginning.

The memory of my own amphipod launch rose up in my mind: a sick, shaky feeling.

Evan looked up. "Why did you come here, Lily?"

"I wanted to tell you I'm sorry," I said.

"Please don't."

"I *am*."

Evan sighed. "I know how this goes. You apologize. I'm grumpy and resentful. Then I relent, and we agree that it's OK, really, that I'm going to be sent topside, that maybe I'll have a perfectly nice life there after all and it won't matter that I never found out what happened to my dad... Is that what you want to hear?"

"No."

Evan's eyes were raw. "Dad never got over Mum dying, you know. He used to say that we came here because it was the only place on earth he didn't keep expecting to see her. But I don't feel that way about Dad. I want to stay here *because* it's the only place I can imagine him. I can still smell him; I can still *feel* him; he's part of the rig. How am I supposed to leave him behind and go topside?"

I shook my head. I had nothing.

"I... I like you," I said. "I wish we could have been friends."

Evan nodded, a wry smile. "Yeah, I wish we could have been friends too."

A tight feeling squeezed my stomach, and I was surprised to find myself wondering if I really meant *friends*, or if I meant something else, and wondering at the same time whether he really meant *just* friends or something else.

"Maybe once we get topside, we could—"

"Don't."

"OK."

We fell silent. He was right. I didn't even know which continent he was from. His accent, after so long on Deephaven, was from everywhere. What were we going to do, become pen pals?

"Did you find anything else in the simulation? His message?" I asked.

Evan shook his head, eyes still on the screen. "There's nothing there. He wanted me to find the Rift. He didn't care about anything else."

"That can't be true."

I knew I should leave; he clearly didn't want me there. I watched him work at the simulation, his brow furrowed in concentration. The scientist's son who wrote simulations of his dad's inventions, the boy who threw himself into the deep ocean just to rescue me. In a different world, if

I hadn't screwed things up so badly, we could definitely have been more than friends.

I watched his hands glide over the shifting dials and displays. Something was niggling at the corners of my mind. I knew something was wrong with what I was seeing, but I couldn't put my finger on it.

"Do that bit again," I said. "Whatever you just did there."

Evan gave me a sceptical look but hit reset and ran through the sequence from the beginning.

"There!" I said. "What's that?"

Evan studied it for a moment. "I don't know. Some kind of readout."

"But what's it reading? What are those numbers for?"

Evan shook his head slightly. "I don't remember..."

The numbers on the display danced erratically, randomly, but they always cycled back in a repeating pattern. That didn't make any sense. There was no real *physical* value that would behave like that – water pressure? Velocity? None of it fitted with the way the number was changing. But that wasn't the strangest part.

"That display isn't in the real amphipod," I said. "Your dad must have modified your simulation as well."

Evan squinted at the numbers. "Are you sure?"

I nodded.

"Why would he add another display?"

We sat, watching the meaningless numbers cycle.

Suddenly, Evan sat up, a small gasp coming to his lips. "It's an encryption key."

"A what?"

Evan was already moving. He stumbled on a bunched-up pile of flight suits, almost fell, righted himself. "It'll be on his laptop." He dug out a laptop from amongst a pile of ring binders. "This might be it," he said tightly.

He balanced the laptop awkwardly on his knee and started keying the sequence in. His eyes flicked quickly between the tablet and his laptop as he copied the numbers. I picked my way over the messy floor and stood behind him.

"Well?" I asked.

"I… I don't know…"

He finished the sequence. The screen stuttered for a moment.

Then Maximus's face appeared.

Close-up on-screen. The resemblance to Evan was striking now I knew him better. The same angular features. That sharp, questioning look in his dark eyes. I recognized the room as well. It was *this* room. The kitchenette. The door into the bathroom. But before Evan had smashed it, before his world had broken apart.

I placed my hand on Evan's shoulder. I could feel it rising and falling rapidly.

"Are you OK?" I asked.

He turned his head and stared at me. "This is it."

CHAPTER 23

This is Dr Maximus Clarke with a message for Evan Clarke.

    Oh, my boy ... my boy... If you're seeing this, then something has gone wrong. I never meant for this to happen.

    I am so, so sorry... I need you to understand why I did what I am about to do.

The image of Maximus leaned forward, his eyes blazing.

Evan — I found it! Seismic profiles have revealed a lesion in the east ridge. Just as I suspected, thermal imagery has confirmed a higher water temperature compatible with increased hydrostatic heating. If the Rift is down there, this is where it'll be connected. And if my modelling is correct, the combination of warmer water, high pressure, and nutrient-rich sediment should make it a promising environment for ... well, we'll see, won't we?

I've programmed the coordinates into the amphipods, but they're not ready yet, and I'm running out of time. Carter is putting pressure on the universities to release the moratorium, so I need something concrete, and soon.

I'm sorry I've kept this from you. The truth is, I know you're not going to like what comes next. I've decided to conduct an initial survey in a regular submersible. The Rift begins a further kilometre below the ocean bed, beyond the official operating capacity of the submersibles. But I think I can increase the internal pressure of the submersible and breathe hydreliox. I can reinforce the outer hull long enough to validate my theories ... I hope. I know it's a risk.

But we are scientists, Evan; what are we here for, if not this?

Evan pressed pause. I realized I was still holding on to his shoulder. I was about to take my hand away when he reached up and covered it with his own. I tensed, my hand growing warm under his.

"The submersibles are barely rated for *this* depth," Evan murmured. "*Another kilometre?* He knew it was too deep."

Evan hit a key and the video resumed. It stuttered briefly. Then Maximus was back, but he'd changed. His hair was dishevelled, his stubble a little darker.

I've seen it! It's magnificent, Evan. So much more than I'd ever imagined! I wish I could tell you about it, my boy. Believe me,

I'm half wild with the desire to tell you. But if I told you, you would ask me not to go back, and I would have to listen to you, wouldn't I? So ... there we are.

The fact is ... I must go back.

What I have found is utterly remarkable. A species of bioluminescent euglenoid, far more active and more densely integrated than anything seen before. Intelligence like you wouldn't believe. It's hard to accept, but I swear it's true: we played together! A game of tag. I'm not even sure now if I taught it, or if it taught me. Game play? Structured interaction? And it's learning so fast. I believe the euglenoid to be functionally equivalent if not superior to chimpanzees. Can you imagine? Their intelligence must come from their collective interaction, a kind of distributed brain.

You know as well as I do that this is a revolution in our understanding of the world. Evan, this will change everything!

But I fear that in my excitement, I have made a terrible mistake. I shared my initial findings with Carter in the hope that I could persuade him to delay his plans to blast the east ridge. Sadly, I think it had the opposite effect. I'm sure he's hastening his preparations. I had hoped that I could submit my samples to the university and provide proof that this is a significant find. But for reasons I can't explain, the samples have all become inert as soon as I brought them on to the rig.

Evan was shaking his head, his eyes red and furious. He squeezed my hand more tightly.

"Stupid, stupid, stupid…" he muttered. "I should have known… I should have noticed…"

Maximus went on.

My video recordings are inconclusive. The submersible cameras just don't have the contrast we need. I'm missing something, I know I am. I need to go deeper; it's the only way. It's hard to explain, but I feel compelled. I can't risk waiting until the amphipods are ready. If Carter blasts the east ridge, then the passageway will be closed and the euglenoid lost for ever. We may never find another. I have decided to make one more survey. I will reinforce the hull and increase my target depth. I expect the prevalence of euglenoid to increase with depth, and I hope that I can capture more conclusive footage.

I'm sorry, Evan. If you're seeing this, then my gamble didn't pay off. It's OK to be angry, I know you will be. I've made arrangements with Ari and Dr Balgobin in the event that something goes wrong. It won't be straightforward, but if you want to stay you can. I think they can swing it for you. I hope, in time, you'll understand why I can't risk letting this discovery be lost to the world.

This is science, Evan. This is what we came here for. This is what we exist for.

So … fingers crossed then, eh?

The image of Maximus reached forwards, out of frame, and the video froze. Evan tapped the keyboard, but there was nothing more.

"Evan … I'm so sorry," I said at last.

Evan didn't move. His jaw clenched and unclenched. I bent forward and wrapped my arms awkwardly around his shoulders. I felt him lean back, pressing his weight against me, his body shaking against my own.

We stayed like that for a long time.

At long last, Evan stopped shuddering. I let go and shuffled back to my armchair, feeling self-conscious. I waited for him to say something. When he didn't speak, I said, "We have to show Mum." I made my voice as gentle as possible. "She'll pick up his research. It's what she came here for as well."

"No," Evan replied firmly.

"Why not?" I asked.

"If Dad couldn't convince Carter, then your mum won't be able to."

"She can try."

"She'll just make him move more quickly."

"Then what?"

"We'll go back ourselves. Get the evidence Dad was after."

I would have laughed except he wasn't smiling. "You're not serious?"

Evan shifted in his seat. "The amphipods are new; nobody is trained for them. It'll take weeks to certify a pilot, and even then Carter wouldn't sanction a trip out to the Rift. We're the only ones who can do it. The amphipods can go deeper than the submersibles; we won't have the problem Dad had."

"And do what? The euglenoid doesn't survive on the rig."

"We'll take better recordings."

I felt myself beginning to panic. He meant it. Of course he did. There was a kind of logic to it. But there was desperation as well.

"No," I said. "You're not thinking straight. I can't... *You* can't."

"Lily, *listen* to me—"

The thought of the Rift had set my heart twisting and lurching in my chest. I felt sick. The memory of nothing but falling, falling, falling. I felt it reach up inside my head, more terrifying than I'd have thought possible. *So ... so ... alone.*

"It's too dangerous," I said, my voice shaking. "We nearly got lost in there."

"It'll be better this time," Evan said, trying his best to convince me and knowing at the same time that I was a long, long way from being convinced. "We know what we're doing. We'll stay close to the passageway."

"No. We explain the situation and persuade someone else to go down there. We can show them how the amphipod works. There are professional sub pilots who'll pick it up in no time—"

"They'll lose their jobs and Carter will blast the ridge before we can convince anybody. We have to go now. Today."

"This is stupid."

"We're both going topside anyway," Evan said. "What do we have to lose?"

"We nearly *died*!"

There was a look in Evan's eyes that I recognized from his father on the video – determined, focused, reckless. He drew a long, slow breath. "Fine. I'll go on my own. You can't stop me."

"Evan – please don't."

I stared at him. There was no doubt he meant it. He wouldn't wait; the minute I stepped out of here he was going to get dressed and head down to the amphipod bay.

The question was, was he going alone or was I going with him?

I bit my cheek. "OK," I said.

"Seriously?"

Evan seemed worried now, but relieved at the same time.

"You came after me, I can't let you go on your own, can I?"

Evan beamed. "Are you sure?"

I nodded.

"But we need to wait until later tonight," I said. "I'm supposed to be having dinner with Mum; she'll get suspicious if I'm not there. She'll be back in the lab by nine."

"Nine," Evan said, struggling to contain his excitement now. "It's a date."

CHAPTER 24

I headed directly for the ops room after I left Evan, my stomach churning.

Ops was set apart from the main rig, near to the reactor and the battery units, and I knew I'd find Ari there. I paused outside for a moment and peeked around the bulkhead door. Ari was laughing, chatting to a colleague with a mug of coffee in his hand. A tug of emotion hooked my insides. It looked cosy in there, appealing but out of reach. Not being a people person doesn't mean you don't envy people who are. It was like standing outside a restaurant in the rain and looking in through a well-lit window.

"That you, Lily?" Ari called, spotting me.

I ducked behind the bulkhead and pressed myself against the cold metal wall, wishing I hadn't come. This was a mistake. Evan was going to hate me for it.

Ari's face appeared, his smile blazing like I was his long-lost best friend. "Heyyy, Lily Fawcett," he said. "You wanna come sit for a while?"

"Um … yeah. Thanks."

I followed him inside. The desk was piled high with big, beige computer screens, the bulky, old-fashioned kind. The work surface was stained from many years of coffee rings, and there was something that might have been Marmite on the keyboard. This wasn't the flashy tech of the command centre; this was the practical, hardwearing kind of tech that does the real work. On the screen, however, was the same schematic as I'd seen in the command centre – the same interwoven colours, the beating heart and pulsing neurons of the rig.

I caught a brief exchange of looks between Ari and his colleague. Like all of Ari's team, she had a capable, no-nonsense look about her, her long brown hair neatly tied back in a bun, her face hard and lined. Her eyes, however, sparkled with warmth and intelligence. She flashed me an understanding smile as she slipped away.

"Where the magic happens," Ari said, gesturing lazily around the chaotic ops room. "I'd offer you a cup of tea, but…" He indicated the handle-less mug. "Catering seems to be having some issues with the crockery at the moment."

I looked away, embarrassed. "You know it's me breaking them, don't you?"

"It's my job to know what happens on this rig."

"Sorry," I muttered. "It's ... it's kind of a habit."

"So...? How're you settling in?" Ari asked absurdly.

I felt myself smile; the question was so incongruous. "Everyone hates me," I said.

"Apart from that?" Ari grinned.

Sometimes I wondered what went on in that big, optimistic brain of his.

"It's my fault Evan is going to be sent home."

"Apart from *that*?" Ari said.

"I'm scared he's going to do something stupid."

Ari's face became more serious. I took a deep breath. If I was going to betray Evan, I should do it now and get it over with.

It's for his own good, I thought. I was so used to being the one who screwed everything up, it felt odd to be doing the right thing for once. Odd, and also terrible.

"He's planning to take an amphipod and go back to the Rift," I said.

Ari's eyes widened. "Why the blazes would he do that?"

"He thinks he can find proof about his dad's research and stop Carter from blasting the east ridge."

Ari whistled softly, a sonorous sigh. "Oh, the poor boy. Losing both parents; it's been too much for him. I'll talk to him."

"He won't listen."

Ari gave a short laugh. "I never let that stop me."

"You need to *do* something," I said, my voice coming out more loudly than I'd intended. "He's not thinking straight. He's going to do it. He's going tonight."

"OK … I hear you." Ari held up a calming hand. He turned to his computer and tapped a few keys. "There. Your friend is safe."

"What?" I hadn't expected it to be *that* easy. "What did you do?"

"I removed his access to the amphipod bay. He won't be able to get in without a valid key card. I'll let everyone know not to let him borrow theirs. Discreetly."

"Oh."

I sat back, feeling a bit sick. How would Evan react when he found out he no longer had access to his dad's lab? I considered meeting him at nine anyway, going through the pantomime of being surprised when his key card didn't work. But I couldn't face it. Better that he knew it was me. Better that I was honest with him.

I turned to the screen to avoid Ari's penetrating look. The rig schematic showed the operation of the rig in multiple bands of colour.

I watched the ebb and flow of data represented by the schematic as it shuttled through the Central Control Network. The fusion reactor cycled up and down as the power usage across the rig shifted and the fail-safes directed electricity to wherever it was needed most. It was like watching an enormous animal, breathing slowly, turning over in its sleep.

"Beautiful, isn't she?" Ari remarked.

"Yes."

"I don't even see the numbers any more," he continued. "The pictures are just there to let me know what kind of mood she's in."

"How is she today?"

Ari drew a slow breath and shook his head. "She's been jumpy for the past few days actually. I don't know what's going on."

Once he'd said it, I could see what he meant. The user interface looked … uncomfortable. Like a dog who couldn't get settled in its basket. Like the rig was having a bad dream. Red threads showed the power distribution, but there were hotspots, areas where systems were overheating and the fail-safes were rerouting power to the wrong places. Ari spotted one in the same moment I did and tapped the screen. Power relays switched, the power rerouted. But as soon as that hotspot had settled, another blossomed elsewhere.

"That shouldn't happen," Ari muttered.

"Is it safe?" I asked.

Ari laughed shortly. "We're five kilometres under the surface of the ocean, Lily, and we're living on top of a fusion reactor." He flashed me a wicked smile. "We're fine. We have thousands of fail-safes to cut the power if there's a problem; you just have to keep on top of things, that's all. This is … it's just normal stuff. Rigs have bad days, just like people."

"Here," I said, pointing. "You missed one."

Ari tapped the control. "You've got the knack, that's for sure."

I fought back a grin, hoping that the glow I felt inside wasn't showing too much on my face. "It makes more sense to me than people, anyway."

Ari shrugged. "Don't be so hard on yourself, Lily. Most people down here are pretty tightly wired; it comes with the job." He gave me an appraising look, and I fidgeted uncomfortably. "You're not as different from the others as you think," he continued. "Your breakage is on the outside, that's all. A lot of people keep it inside."

I thought about Mum and Dad, how they'd smashed up our family again and again until it couldn't be put back together.

"I feel so angry all the time," I said.

Ari tapped some more commands. I felt the rig shudder as he adjusted the plasma flow in the main core and the eddy fields tugged at the hull. "You've got a touch of the sea snakes, that's all."

"Sea snakes?"

"Squirming, angry things that wriggle around in your chest so bad you need to find a way out for them."

"I think of them as monkeys. Like a cage full of monkeys."

Ari nodded. "Same difference. We all get them. People are too wrapped up in themselves to see what's going on for other people, that's the trouble. We need to look *outward*, not inward, do you see? And while you're at it, stop thinking about the *thing* you did and start thinking about the *feeling* you had. What's behind it all?" He broke off as a series of lights lit up on the rig schematic. He tapped a sequence of commands that dumped some of the fusion plasma to cool things down. "Full of sea snakes today," he muttered. "If I spend my day trying to wrestle them all back into their box, they'll just come out again later, and it'll be worse when they do. I might as well let them roam a bit. See what they're about. It doesn't help being scared of them." He sat back and gave me a wise look. "Understanding is the first step to acceptance, Lily."

"That's smart." I smiled. "Who said that?"

Ari grinned mischievously. "Albus Dumbledore." He turned back to the schematic. "That's what I like about you scientists: all you want to do is understand. You know that understanding comes first." He tapped the screen. Shook his head slowly. "That one's fixed itself. Damnedest thing."

"Why is ops all the way out here, not in the command centre?" I asked.

"I prefer it out here. Out here you can *feel* the reactor; it's the only way to know what's really going on. Carter and his people can sit in their fancy office and call it what they like so long as they stay out of my way."

"You ought to be running this place," I said. "Not Carter."

"That's not how it works," Ari replied. "It's Carter's show. He handpicks his team."

"But Holden's not even very good, is he?"

Ari barked with laughter. "I said he handpicks them, I didn't say he picks them because they're any *good*." He leaned closer, conspiratorially. "He picks them because they're *obedient*."

CHAPTER 25

**LILY FAWCETT: DEEPHAVEN PERSONAL LOG
DAY 17**

I used to dream that I was falling. Now, I dream that I'm sinking.

It's worse.

I dreamed of the Rift that night. Of black and falling and emptiness and cold. Even when I woke, the feeling pressed against the inside of my skull, like it was a part of me, like it could swallow me whole if it wanted to.

Something was wrong with my brain. It didn't feel like my own any more. The walls were closing around me, and I could feel every inch of the twisted piping and conduits, every gram of the five thousand tonnes of water squeezing the rig.

The email was waiting for me the next morning when I woke up: the supply sub would be here in two days. Me, Mum and Evan would be on it. Part of me felt relieved at how soon it would arrive: I could last two days down here with everyone hating me and something wrong with my brain. Probably.

I knew that Mum was already at the lab. She said she had some leads for jobs, places we might go next. She said *we*, but I'd decided that I wasn't going with her. I'd go back to Dad's instead. After that … I didn't know what I'd do.

I put my phone down and rolled out of bed. My foot touched something cold and heavy, and I bent down to pick it up. The pressure jar of euglenoid. Silty water. I resisted the urge to sling it at the porthole again. The crack from when I'd last thrown it was still visible, the embedded air-reactive sealant in the aluminosilicate case now dried into a tightly knitted scar.

A thought scratched at the back of my mind. It *had* glowed. It hadn't been my imagination. So, what had triggered it? I thought back to the moment I'd seen it glow. I'd been so angry. My head had been so full.

Something Ari had said came back to me: *don't think about the thing you did, think about the feeling you had*. What if I—

The naked white stubs where the keys used to be on Dad's laptop.

Hanna's face as she limped painfully towards me with broken ribs.

Mum's earrings rolling over and over at the bottom of the toilet.

These were things I never thought about normally. I formed the thoughts carefully in my mind, doing my best to recall every detail.

Mum shouting at Dad so hard her face looked like it was boiling.

Dad's confused look: chill out, Lilypad, it's fine.

No, no, no! It's not fine, Dad. You're leaving and it's absolutely not fine.

The memories came so easily. I remembered what Isaac had said to me that day in the canteen. *Memory works differently down here...* He was right. Memories I'd kept pushed down for months, years, forced themselves into my thoughts.

There—

Cold, claustrophobic fear crept over me. Yes. I could feel it inside my head now. If I held my mind just right, I could almost touch it. A curiosity. A watchful question.

I stared at the jar. It was glowing. The euglenoid activated, pulsing and drifting. Not dead. Beautiful blue-turquoise embers, rising and falling. I placed my hand on the aluminosilicate and the colours of the euglenoid shifted towards it. There was something else too. I could feel it pressing against my skull. An uncanny feeling. Black. Alone. Not words. *Feelings.* All that black. Comforting black. No – terrifying black.

Maximus!

Not rated for this depth.

Anxious.

No choice. Now or never.

Images I hardly understood.

Oh, my boy … my boy…

I dropped the pressure jar and backed away. My heart hammered in my chest. My hip caught against the folding desk, and I stumbled and fell. I hit the ground heavily. My hand rose to my mouth. I wanted to scream, but I couldn't find the air.

It's inside my head!

Rubbish. Not possible. I'd lost my mind. I was sick. I had to be.

I could feel it, a steady pressure. Not just in the jar, but outside in the ocean as well, and in the Rift. A gossamer-thin thread permeating the water, permeating the rig, connecting it all.

The euglenoid didn't have words. Its interface was feelings. It had found its way into my head, and it was poking around in there, feeling what I felt.

I sat for a long time where I'd fallen, too scared to move. Too repulsed to reach forward and touch the jar. *It's inside my head.* A perfectly rounded weight. A black marble.

I forced myself to think logically. The jar must be just a tiny part of the intelligence. There was no way there was enough euglenoid there to approximate something that could *think*. It had to be connected to the rest of itself somehow, connected to something … vast. I tried to reach out with my mind – out to the rig, to the sea around it, to the Rift, to the perfectly rounded weight inside my mind.

There – a hungry movement, like a shadow shifting inside my brain. Pressure welled up in my throat. I wanted to cry so badly it felt like a silent scream trapped in my throat. *I've been alone for so long…* My words. But not my feelings. The bluish-turquoise aura shimmered and twisted.

"Hello, you," I murmured shakily.

The glow moved. It twitched uneasily in my mind, the way a butterfly will snap shut if you touch its wing.

If I could show this to Mum, she'd have all the evidence she needed.

The lights guttered and began to fade.

"No, wait – please—"

The thread stretched taut. I took a breath and reached out again. It wanted something. Memories. It moved towards them inside my head. Memories I usually kept pushed way down, memories I didn't want to have. *OK…* I thought. *You can have this one.*

Consciously, with effort, I formed the memory of Mum's tomato planter in my mind. I'd doused the bamboo poles in lighter fluid from the barbecue and watched the flames devour it. Mum had told me to rebuild it as a punishment.

But then she'd joined me. We worked on it together. We were so proud of ourselves. We brought our lunch outside and sat and admired it while we ate.

So much light!

Feelings, not words.

"Sun," I said to no one in particular. "That's sun."

More.

The pressure jar glowed more brightly, like a light bulb in the moment before it blows. I drew a breath and let it out in a long, quivering sigh. I nodded slowly.

OK, I get it now. I know what I need to do.

CHAPTER 26

The metal gratings clattered merrily under my feet as I rushed to the lab, the weight of the pressure jar in my flight suit pocket banging against my thigh with every step.

I needed to find Mum. You can't always tell what will get a scientist excited; Mum once didn't sleep for two days because she'd found a new variety of fava bean on eBay. But the world's deepest living organism? One that could interact...? *Play tag? Share feelings...*

It was like finding life on Mars.

Actually, no.

This was *much bigger* than finding life on Mars.

I could feel it still there in my mind. A timid presence, a slight pressure. I could hold it, and in doing so I could keep the euglenoid in the pressure jar active. I could *prove* what Maximus had discovered and what Evan and I had been saying, and it would change *everything*.

It would be the biggest scientific discovery ... *ever*!

My thoughts fizzed with the idea of it. I could already see the look on Mum's face. For once, I hadn't broken something. I'd *discovered* something—

"Class is this way," a voice called accusingly.

I stopped. I was just crossing the polytunnel that connected the edu unit to the main rig, but Alban and the others stood in my way.

"You're going the wrong way," Alban said, clarifying himself.

His blue eyes flickered over me like he was cataloguing my faults.

"Um ... I need to go see Mum."

I sensed the danger immediately. The pack closing ranks against the outsider. The swift, understanding glances that passed between them. *Why do people always do this to each other?* That instinct to draw together, to strengthen their own bonds by identifying and punishing the outsider. *Why am I always the outsider?* It had been the same at school after I hurt Hanna and Talha. The school united in hating me for what I'd done.

"I don't think you should be roaming around the rig on your own," Alban said.

"It's not safe," Ysabel agreed.

Don't rise to them, I thought. I could feel the weight of the euglenoid in my pocket. *Show them?* I wondered. I recoiled at the idea. A wave of feeling, not entirely my own: how fragile the euglenoid was, how fragile my connection to it.

"You don't have to worry," I said, struggling to keep calm. "I'm leaving the day after tomorrow."

"You can still cause a lot of damage in two days," Alban remarked.

A jet of irritation. *Don't do this.*

"What? You want to *arrest* me?" I snapped.

I revised my estimate of Alban's age. He was definitely younger than the rest, maybe only just in the senior year. He was a little boy trying to cause trouble to make himself feel less small. All that crap about the ERS was just kid's stuff, I realized. I was stupid for ever letting it get to me.

"What you did was so irresponsible," Ysabel said.

"It was an accident," I replied weakly.

Self-righteous Ysabel. What was her problem?

"There are fifteen subsystems on an average submersible, I'm sure amphipods are no different," Jian observed. "It's hard to imagine how you activated all of them in the correct sequence by accident."

Tightening. Tightening. The feeling clenched around my throat. Did they think they were better than me? Did they think I didn't count because I didn't play jazz piano?

"We're just trying to understand what happened," Jacob said.

"Yes, thank you for that, Captain America," I snarled.

"Evan won't survive topside," Ysabel cut in now, her voice tight, not playing like Alban was, genuinely upset. "He's lived down here his whole life. He won't know how to…"

"I know!" I shouted in response. "Do you think I don't *know*?"

The thought of Evan was overwhelming. Where was he? He probably hated me more than anyone. And Ysabel was right, it *was* my fault. He could have stayed if it wasn't for me; Ari and Dr Balgobin could have made it work for him.

The pressure jar of euglenoid seemed to grow heavier in my pocket.

"I need to see Mum," I said thickly.

I started to push past them, stepping through the bulkhead that separated the polytunnel from the main rig.

"You're not going to do anything silly, are you?" Alban said.

Walk away. Just walk away.

The meanness in his voice stung me. The fact that the others were going along with it. They didn't know me. They thought they did, but they didn't.

I turned. *Oh no, Lily … not this … please don't…*

"*Asshole!*" I shouted.

The sound came from nowhere, taking me by surprise as much as it took everyone else by surprise. I stepped closer to Alban and slammed my hand against the steel bulkhead, glaring at him. "Is that what you want?" I spat.

Alban's eyes opened wide; he stared at the place where my hand had slammed into the wall right next to the ERS. I was taller than he was, I realized. How come I'd never noticed that before?

"Did you tell them?" I continued, my voice loud and angry. "Did you tell them that you've been blackmailing me? Did you tell Carter what I did to get me in trouble?"

I lifted my hand and slammed it down again. Harder. Closer. Alban's face turned white. I lifted my hand again and slammed it repeatedly against the steel.

SLAM. SLAM. SLAM. SLAM!

"You can't blackmail me any more!" I shouted.

SLAM. SLAM!

"I can do what I like now. Do you see?"

Humiliation, guilt, anger – all rose up inside me. *Why am I like this?* Thoughts and memories buzzed in my head. Thoughts I hadn't allowed myself to think in a long time.

I always ended up doing stuff like this. Like the time Mum and Dad were fighting in the car, so I leaned forward and let off the handbrake.

Or the time I gouged a line of plaster out of the wall in our living room.

Or the time I put the remote control for the television in the microwave.

Danger that I didn't fully understand flashed in my mind.

"Lily, Lily, it's OK, just calm down." Jacob's reasonable, overly grown-up voice sounded like it was a million miles away.

My head spun. Everyone was staring at me. I could feel their hostility, their fear. It was just like school: Lily, the outsider. Lily, the atrocity.

No, no, no, a part of my brain cried. *Not this, not now.*

I felt like I was outside the rig, looking in through a porthole. I could see the others, their lips moving, but I couldn't hear them. All I could think about was the ERS.

SLAM. SLAM. SLAM!

Rapid. Like artillery fire walking to its target.

Really? Was I going to do it?

"Lily...?" Jacob said, pleading. "Lily, please stop."

I stopped. Breathing hard. They looked terrified. I felt awful. I let out a ragged sigh. "I'm fine," I breathed more calmly. "I'm sorry."

Then the feeling rushed up inside me. A feeling like lava. A feeling like monkeys. And something else as well. A feeling that was black and cold, and vast, and very lonely.

SLAM!

CHAPTER 27

The sirens started low, like a growl, and wound up and up until it felt like the whole rig was howling in pain. Then the lights went out.

Red emergency lights, more sirens, a shadowy rushing here and there. And my four classmates staring at me through the dimness, appalled.

There was a good deal of running around from Ari's ops team, and a dash to the emergency muster point in the canteen.

Then, a tense hour later, Carter summoned us to the command centre to tell our stories.

Mum stood silently, refusing to meet my eye. Jian, Alban, Jacob and Ysabel gathered round with their parents, everyone astonished by the taboo that had been broken, keen to unpack what had happened for the official records.

"We were arguing," Ysabel said. "About the trouble last week."

"And then she got angry and pushed the ERS," Alban said.

Carter nodded, satisfied. "Everyone saw this?"

There was a moment's hesitation, a shadow of doubt.

"I didn't actually *see* her push it," Jacob put in, always the nice guy, always looking for a way to make everything better if he could.

"But you could tell she was thinking about it," Alban said.

"She was definitely thinking about it," Jian agreed.

"Thinking?" Carter said suspiciously. "Or doing?"

Alban frowned, less convinced than he'd thought he was. "Who else could it have been?"

"I need clear eyewitness testimony to press charges," Carter persisted.

"She was hitting the wall," Ysabel said, a little uncertain. "She definitely looked like she was *going* to push it."

I said nothing. There was nothing I could say that would make any difference anyway. But here's the thing: I *didn't* push it. At least … I didn't think I had.

It's blurry.

Not that it mattered. Everyone thought it was me. Let's face it, *I* would think it was me if I were them.

The others filed out, leaving me and Mum alone with Carter and his technical team.

"I want your daughter confined to her cabin until the sub gets here," Carter pronounced sombrely. "We'll have to bill the university for the unscheduled egress, of course. I'll be recommending to the Consortium that they press charges against you for breach of contract."

Mum's face twisted in anguish. "Carter, please. We're already leaving; there's no need—"

"You knowingly brought somebody on board with a history of criminal damage and reckless endangerment. A history you wilfully omitted from your application forms," Carter said. He opened his palms in a gesture of defeat. "And let's be honest … *somebody* has to take the rap for all this lost productivity. It may as well be you … and Maximus."

"Maximus?" Mum asked, bewildered. "What does he have to do with it?"

Carter looked pleased with himself, and I realized with a start how perfectly I'd given him exactly what he wanted. "Maximus had a lot of influence, Dr Fawcett; he's pretty much the only reason the science team lasted down here as long as it did." A muscle quivered in his jawline. "Now that I can demonstrate that he was complicit in your fraudulent application, and I can show the impact that crime has had on the rig, I can make a case for having the whole team removed." He smiled at me. "Congratulations, Miss Fawcett. You've changed the face of deep-sea mining for ever!"

We filed silently back into the elevator and up to the canteen. The rig was still on emergency power, but with the incident resolved, most people had returned to their regular posts. There was just a handful of people in the canteen, choosing from the meagre selection of freeze-dried emergency rations.

Ari appeared, running to catch up with us. "Hey!" he called. He rubbed his beard anxiously. "Carter told me what he's planning. How're you both? Are you OK?"

I exchanged a look with Mum.

"We're so sorry, Ari," Mum said.

Ari tried his best to offer us a reassuring smile, but even he couldn't quite manage it. "Come on, you two … I'll make you a cuppa. Dr Balgobin is in the ops room. She has something she wants to run past you."

Mum hesitated. "I have to take Lily back to our cabin."

"I won't tell the boss if you won't," Ari said. He winked. "Now, do you want that cuppa or not?"

He led us through the polytunnels to the ops room. I realized as soon as we got there how much I really *did* want that cuppa. The reassuring peacefulness of the ops room, Ari's non-judgemental calm.

I thought of Evan. "Will the locks to the amphipod bay still be active?" I asked.

Ari gave me a reassuring nod. "All taken care of."

I breathed a sigh of relief. At least Evan was safe. At least that was something I'd done right.

It was surprisingly quiet in the ops room. Just Dr Balgobin sitting over a desk, illuminated by a single emergency lantern next to her. Most of the screens were off; just a handful still glowed starkly in the dimness, showing the rig schematic as it worked through its various reboot procedures. I understood what Ari meant about preferring it out here now, away from the main rig and nearer to the reactor. All the fraught bustle and drama of the rig seemed like a distant dream. It was just us out here in the middle of the ocean, and the schematic, and the reactor – the beating heart of the rig.

"I gave the rest of the team a few hours off," Ari explained. "There's not much to do while the reactor runs through its safety checks."

Dr Balgobin looked up. "Dr Fawcett," she said, seemingly relieved to see her. "Carter told me about the science team being disbanded. You must be devastated."

"It's my fault," Mum muttered, still sounding shell-shocked. "I should have kept a closer eye on her."

She crumpled into a chair and rubbed her temples. I sat nearby, feeling awkward, wanting to be near but not too near the others. I'd been numb since our visit with

Carter, but now the full awfulness was beginning to burn through. I had no idea if pressing the ERS would stop Carter from blasting the east ridge as Alban had said, but even if it did, it wouldn't make up for the loss of the science team. I'd thought after I caused Hanna to get hurt that I'd finally done the worst thing I could possibly imagine doing. But this was different.

I tried to touch the euglenoid in my mind, to activate the sample in my pocket, but it was hiding from me. It had retreated, as if scared off by the shockwave of the plasma ejection. I could still feel the hollow patch in my head where it had been.

Mum turned to me suddenly. "I give up, Lily." Her lips moved silently for a few moments, her words lost to emotion. "I think … I think I really give up on you. I'm beaten. You've beaten me, OK?"

"Mum, please—" I said.

"Why do you *do* it? Is it to hurt me? Is it because you blame me for Dad?"

"*No...*"

"Because you haven't just hurt me this time. You've hurt *everyone*."

"I know—"

"By getting the team sent home you've hurt *science*."

"I *know*—"

"You've hurt *humanity*."

Wow. OK. Dimly, I wondered how long you had

to be grounded in order to make up for hurting all of humanity.

Ari stepped in and placed a steadying hand on Mum's shoulder.

"I'm sorry," Mum said, fighting back tears. "I'm just ... I'm so, so sorry."

"It's OK, Ruth," Ari said. "We'll figure it out."

He placed a cup of tea on the desk next to her and another next to me.

"It occurred to me that there might be something in Maximus's notes," Dr Balgobin said. "I know it's a long shot, but if we could demonstrate the seed of some novel research, we could pitch for a small team to remain and continue to enforce the moratorium."

Mum shook her head. "I've been working on them for weeks. It's all nonsense. Cut and paste from the internet mostly. Some poetry. Joy told me some of it was from Hawaiian religious texts."

Dr Balgobin seemed unperturbed. "Some of it, yes," she agreed. "But some of it..." She held up one of the sheets of paper to read from. "'*It was darkness and light intermixed, but it didn't know it was alive until we played together.*'" Dr Balgobin smiled at our blank looks. "It may sound like it, but that's *not* part of the *Kumulipo*."

Mum frowned. She was intrigued but not convinced. "It's still not science either."

"And this," Dr Balgobin went on. "'*It misses me when

231

I'm gone. It wants me to go back, and I'm afraid if I don't it will get upset with us."

I sat up, my heart beating more quickly. Was Maximus's real research amongst his reams of nonsensical notes after all? After we'd found his message, I'd expected to find his research on his laptop as well, hidden by the same encryption key. But there had been nothing.

"There's a pattern," Dr Balgobin went on. "I think I've got the measure of it. Look, this is the next section: *'The samples are not dead, I am sure of it, but they are inert. I lack a way to activate them. When I go to it, I feel it reach out to me… I think it likes me.'"*

"He's right," I said, my voice tight in my throat.

Mum and Dr Balgobin turned to look at me.

"I figured it out. I was coming to tell you before…"

I thrust my hand into my flight suit pocket and took out the pressure jar. Dr Balgobin, Mum and Ari all looked. Nothing. Silty grey water.

"Lily, I don't know what you're doing, but …" Mum began.

"I'm *serious*," I insisted. "I learned how to activate it. It needs … a connection or something. A feeling. Watch."

I stared at the jar, the silty fragments drifting lazily around in tiny, invisible convection currents. I closed my eyes and tried to concentrate. To summon the memories.

The police standing sternly at our door.

Mr Paley when he called me and Mum into his office.

Nothing. I could tell there was nothing there. When I opened my eyes, the others were watching me. Mum didn't look angry any more, she looked worried.

"We should get you back to the cabin," she said. "It's been a long day."

"No, you have to listen."

"Lily, *please*."

I opened my mouth, but no words came out. There was nothing to say, no reason she should listen to me.

"Could you show me some more of Maximus's notes?" Dr Balgobin said to Mum, cutting through our stand-off. "I think between us we might have a chance of extracting his real research."

Mum nodded. "Yes, that would be…" She trailed off, her face tightening. "I'm sorry. I need to stay with Lily."

Mum pressed her hand to her forehead. Irritable. Resigned. Lily, the inconveniently large luggage. Lily, the liability.

"Mum, I'll be fine," I said. "You should go."

Mum shook her head. "You know I can't leave you on your own right now."

She was right. If I went back to the cabin on my own now, I'd break something. I'd break *everything*.

"She can stay with me." Ari flashed me one of his great beaming smiles, like all was fine and dandy in the world. "I'll keep an eye on her." He gave me a questioning look. "If that's OK with you, Lily?"

My gratitude swelled up inside my throat like a balloon. *Who was this man?* Ari the good-natured Chief Operations Officer. Ari who had no need to care one jot about me, but who could so effortlessly fix a situation that had felt unfixable a moment ago.

"Yes. I'd like that," I said, trying to hide how happy the idea made me.

Mum looked doubtful. "Won't Carter object?"

Ari snorted ruefully. "He's too busy thinking he's won. I can handle him."

"Would you mind?" Mum asked.

"Not at all," Ari said. He pointed towards the same Marmite-and-coffee-stained desk as I'd sat at last time. "I could use the help keeping an eye on the fusion reactor."

Mum stood, then stopped, a frown clouding her face. "Ari?"

"Yes, Ruth?"

"Don't let her touch anything."

"Make yourself at home," Ari said after they'd gone.

"Aren't you angry at me like everyone else?" I asked.

Ari shrugged. "I'm sure you've got your reasons."

"I didn't push the button," I said. "You've got to believe me. Something is wrong with this whole place. I'm… I'm scared."

Ari gave my shoulder a consolatory squeeze. "It's OK, Lily," he said. "Just take it easy for a while." He turned to the schematic and tapped a few keys. "The reactor's still cycling up, but this bit is mostly automated. Everything will feel a bit happier once we get the main lights back on, right?" He pulled up another screen. "Here. Keep an eye on the coolant flow, will you?"

A flashing light on the far side of the room caught his attention, and he slipped away to deal with it. I slumped into the sagging office chair. The ops room was empty except for me and Ari. The rig schematic looked fractured, like somebody had randomly carved slices through it. Some bits looked normal, other bits were blank spaces where the subsystems waited their turn to be powered up and rebooted. It would be like this for days, I thought. Tense, uneasy days living on battery power and no Friday movie. I was glad I wasn't going to have to stand it for long.

I give up, Lily... That's what Mum had said. It felt so final. But it was what people did, wasn't it? Mum and Dad had given up on each other. And now Mum had given up on me. A memory came to me, pushing its way into my mind: when I was really little, I used to tell myself that Mum and Dad *had* to love each other because there was no way they'd put up with each other if they didn't.

I wanted to go home; my heart ached for it. Except I wasn't sure where home was any more. Home wasn't just our old house. It was feeling safe, feeling loved, feeling *normal*. I wasn't sure how I'd ever feel that again.

I stared at the silty liquid inside the pressure jar. If I

could activate it again and show Mum, maybe we could still change things. But whatever fragile connection I'd felt before, it was gone. It didn't matter how hard I stared at the passing flashes of silt, there was nothing.

I watched the schematic, my mind wandering. The scrubbers flickered as they refreshed their firmware. The fusion generator produced a steady 0.2 megawatts, rising uniformly as its plasma accumulators filled. The sub bay waterlock was offline and scheduled to be rebooted in four hours. Below the main rig, the display showed four hundred and seventy-two CRABs as pinpricks of red light moving around the valley. Still running on battery power for now, I imagined them sifting through the rubble of the ocean bed like crusty old beachcombers, picking out glistening clumps of rock to take back to the main rig.

It all seemed so remote, so alone, so unlikely. I didn't get it until we came down here. It was too easy to forget about all this when you were topside, to take your TVs and cars and central heating for granted. You had to see it for yourself before you really understood the trade-off you were making. All that activity, all that *industry*.

I looked back at the pressure jar. Were the grains of silt more visible than before? I could almost feel it there. Watchful. Anxious. I squeezed my eyes tight shut and reached out ... almost ... but nothing.

"Lily."

The voice from behind made me jump. I spun around, slipping the pressure jar into my pocket at the same time.

Evan was standing behind me, his eyes serious. "Hey."

"Um – hey."

What is he doing here? Had he come to yell at me like everyone else? Did he want to tell me how disappointed he was with me as well?

"I'm – I'm sorry," I said.

I could see Evan wrestling with himself, whatever he had bottled up inside him fighting to get out. I'd gotten him thrown off the rig, his home; I'd stopped him doing the one thing he thought might save him.

"I didn't believe it at first," he said. "I kept texting you. It was only when you didn't answer that I realized it must have been you."

"I couldn't let you go."

I braced myself. I was tired of being yelled at.

"I know you thought you were doing the right thing." Evan sighed as he sat down. Not what I was expecting.

"I did," I said carefully.

"Do you know what irritates me the most?"

"No?"

He looked at me. "You were probably right."

"Oh." I felt a little deflated. I'd been working myself up for another fight.

"I wasn't thinking straight. It was a stupid idea."

We sat in silence for a moment, neither one of us

sure where to go next. Had he just forgiven me? No, it wasn't that exactly. He understood, that was all. Whether he agreed or not, he understood, so by the rules of his internal logic there was no need for forgiveness. I watched his dark, thoughtful eyes as they scanned the schematic. *Off-the-charts genius*, Dr Balgobin had said. He must be, I thought.

"I didn't hit the emergency reactor scram," I said.

"I know," Evan replied, unfazed.

I sat up. "What?"

Evan allowed himself a small, oddly shy smile. "The glass wasn't broken."

I let out a gasp of surprise. How come I'd never thought to check? How come *nobody* had thought to check? "Why didn't you say anything?" I asked.

"I only just checked. But I knew you wouldn't do something like that."

I smiled. *I* didn't know I wouldn't do something like that. What made him think he could be so sure?

"So, what happened?" I asked.

Evan shook his head. "I don't know. A glitch, maybe?"

"A *glitch*?"

My mind raced with the possibilities. *The ERS gets triggered right when I'm threatening to push it?* That was too much of a coincidence. I was missing something, I knew it. But what? Had somebody framed me? Was it sabotage?

"What do we do?" I asked.

"I don't think there's anything we *can* do," Evan said. "Carter doesn't really care who triggered the ERS; he's going to use it as an excuse to get rid of you, me and the science team. He's got exactly what he wanted."

The reality of it hit me suddenly: I was really leaving. The day after tomorrow I'd be on a sub, then I'd be back on the surface, then I'd be on a boat, in an aeroplane, landing at Heathrow... By the time I stopped moving this place would be a distant memory.

I felt myself beginning to tremble. I didn't want to go. I especially didn't want to go *like this*. A panicky, tight feeling closed around me. Something was happening.

It was back inside my head. That wall of black. I tried to push the thought away, but it wouldn't stop. It was coming closer. More urgent, more fearful. Something was different. The blackness. I couldn't stop it. Needles of fear dropped one by one down my spine.

So, so alone...

"Lily?"

The tone in Evan's voice pulled me from my thoughts and made me look up.

"Lily, what are you doing?"

"What do you mean? I'm not doing anything—"

Evan looked panicked. "What are you doing to the CRABs, Lily?"

Fear had drained the colour from his face. The CRABs were going offline, I saw now, their indicator lights winking out, one after the other, a swathe of black sweeping towards us.

"It's not me," I said.

A display showed how many of the CRABs were left. It was dropping fast: four hundred and fifteen. Three hundred and eighty-four.

"Ari!" Evan called. Two hundred and fourteen. One hundred and ninety-two. "Ari!"

Ari came over. His eyes widened. "What did you do, Lily?"

"Nothing!" I cried. "I didn't do anything!"

Ari tapped a few keys.

Forty-seven.

"Please, you've got to believe me. I don't know what—"

"Yes, OK, Lily," Ari snapped, still typing.

Eighteen.

"Oh, that's not good," he muttered.

From somewhere outside, a rolling noise like thunder echoed around the walls. "What's that?" I gasped.

"Plasma core is becoming unstable," Ari said. "The eddy fields from the containment field are shaking the steel hull."

The lights flickered. Ari tapped a few controls. A vibration shivered beneath us, the way it feels when a train passes under your feet.

"That's really not good," Ari muttered.

"What's not good?" Evan asked.

Ari didn't answer. He was checking displays on his dashboard, tapping controls. Every sensor, every subsystem, every servo and valve and relay was going wild. The fusion generator was spiking. One point five megawatts and climbing. The plasma containment field wasn't strong enough and the system was dumping excess power into every other system to prevent an overload. I watched as the rig desperately tried to compensate for the influx of unwanted energy. Fail-safes shunted power around, but systems overloaded where the current spiked, and the problem cascaded through to the next set of systems. A chain reaction, gathering speed.

"Look at that," Evan said, his voice hollow with shock. "The amphipod bay. The waterlocks are opening."

"Somebody's taking out the amphipods?" I asked, bewildered.

He pointed to an indicator. "They're on remote."

"So, who's driving them?"

"No one. No one has access." He looked at me. "Scrubbers are overclocking as well, and the ROVs have powered up."

"The power's surging. It's like somebody's turning on all the lights."

Great swathes of the rig were lighting up, while at the same time other parts were going dark as trip switches overloaded. But it was the pattern that scared me the most. It wasn't random. It was like there was something in there. Something big and scared and blind, blundering through the rig's systems like a wild animal. I watched it move towards the battery stations, the fail-safes snapping shut in such a way that I could almost *see* the thing sweep across the rig. I could hear it too, an inhuman noise, a dark, rumbling resonance deep within the rig's foundations.

I jabbed my finger at the screen and diverted power to the cooling system just in time to balance out the wave of current. Warning lights flickered, stabilized.

"Good catch," Evan murmured.

Ari nodded approvingly. "Keep it up, Lily! You might save us yet." He pressed his finger to the comm-unit in his ear. "Ari to Carter. Carter, do you copy?"

Nothing. A wave of black strobed across the rig schematic. The lights flickered. I hit a sequence of fail-safes to make sure we kept power to the life support and the containment fields.

"Ari to Reactor Room, come in?"

Nothing. A cold finger of fear pressed against my spine.

"Ari to Rig Controls… Anyone—?"

CHAPTER 28

Blackout.

An astonishing darkness, so black it took my breath away.

I jumped when Evan's hand closed around my own.

"It's OK," he whispered. "Ari will sort it out."

"What's happening?" I whispered back.

"I'm not sure. Nothing should be able to knock out the backup grid like that."

I listened to the rustling sound of Ari moving about and the growing whine of the reactor. "Stay where you are, kids. We wouldn't want you to – *Ouch!*" There was a hollow crack as he bumped into something and hissed in pain. "– walk into anything, now, would we?" His sound moved over towards the far wall. "The fail-safes must be jammed." There was another muted hiss of pain. "Of course, if somebody had thought to put a dab of luminous paint on the button, they could have saved us a whole load of trouble."

I squeezed my eyes shut so I could pretend it wasn't so dark. My heart pounded in my ears.

So dark... So alone...

"There!" Ari declared.

A series of electrical clicks signalled the relays snapping into place. A slightly dimmer version of the emergency lights flickered into action. Ari waited while the schematic rebooted. It came up red. Lights blinking frantically. He rubbed his beard. "Hmm. Yeah. Not good."

"What?" I asked anxiously.

Ari flicked a switch and tapped a few commands. "Worth a try..."

"*What?*" I insisted.

Something shifted inside my head – a darting, fretful movement. Panic ripped through me. Raw, visceral, not entirely my own.

"Stop!" I gasped. "Whatever you're doing, you're scaring it!"

Ari and Evan turned to me, their surprised expressions visible even in the dim light. I swallowed and tried to clear my head. My mouth felt thick, alien.

"You need to shut down the reactor," I said.

"We only just got her fired up again," Ari protested.

My head strained with thoughts that made no sense.

Power rushed through the grid like hot lead and the euglenoid bucked and twisted in my mind. "There's too much power," I said, struggling to explain the confused sensations in my body. "If the fail-safes push the power back to the reactor, the accelerators will overload—"

"There's no need to worry, Lily," Ari said, patiently but dismissively. "I know what I'm doing."

There was a sharp *crack!* as one of the monitors behind us burst in a flare of orange. I yelped in surprise. Ari and Evan glanced at each other. I scanned the rig schematic more closely. A festival of lights. One by one, the rig systems were overloading, tripping out faster than the fail-safes could compensate.

"Please, trust me," I begged. "Hit the ERS. We have to shut it off *now*."

"Just give me a minute, Lily—" Ari held up his hand. "Do you hear that?"

Evan nodded.

I became aware of the noise a moment later. A heavy sound from somewhere far below us, like an aeroplane engine starting up. A trembling sensation beneath our feet.

"Dammit, she's right," Ari breathed.

"Shut it off! *Now!*"

Ari reached for the ERS panel and slammed it with his open hand. The glass cracked beneath his palm.

Nothing. The noise grew louder.

He slammed it again.

A third time.

Nothing.

"Too late…" he murmured. He cursed bitterly and turned to us. "Listen, kids. We're right next to the plasma core here. If the field breaches, it's going to throw us halfway to Japan, do you understand?"

We nodded.

"We need to get out and seal this section off, OK? We need to do it quickly. Do you remember your training?"

Evan nodded solemnly.

I stared in panic. "Training? What training?"

"OK, then," Ari continued, not hearing me, "we're going to take the polytunnel back to the main rig. We're not going to stop. I lead the way, and you follow *right* behind. We're going to stick *really* close together, do you hear? We're *not* going to allow ourselves to get separated *under any circumstances.*"

I nodded. Stick together, I liked the sound of that.

The overloading reactor was emitting a high, keening noise now. The power was cycling up, like a tightening spring, and any moment now there would be nowhere else for the energy to go; the field would rupture, and the shockwave would rip the rig apart like a tin can.

"I'm scared," I whispered.

"It's OK," Evan said. "We'll be safe once we get back to the main rig."

Ari turned and strode into the polytunnel. I hesitated

for just a second, so scared that my legs couldn't decide which one should move first. Then I followed—

Then—

I was somewhere. Somewhere I didn't expect to be.

Bed. Half asleep. I was having a bad dream, something about the rig.

Lily! Get up! Get up – now!!

My mind swam queasily. That was Evan's voice. What was Evan doing in my room? I felt self-conscious. What if I'd been drooling in my sleep?

LILY!

An alarm of some kind. *Whooopp-whop, whoooopp-whop.* Why was I *wet*?

I tried to open my eyes, but the pain in my head was like a tonne weight holding them closed. Was I late for class? No, that couldn't be it. Carter was sending us home; there would be no more classes. No more Ysabel, Alban, Jacob or Jian. Or Evan, brooding in the corner. I was surprised by how sad the thought made me feel.

"We have to *go!*" Evan shouted. "We have to *go now!*"

My eyes snapped open, and the real world rushed back. My head throbbed and I was shivering so badly I could hardly feel my arms.

There had been an explosion. One of the battery units must have blown out. Monitors and consoles were strewn over the floor, scorched and blinded. Water poured in through some unseen seam and swirled around the desks. The pressure door to the polytunnel had shut, and Ari was on the far side, hammering frantically on the glass.

"Lily? Are you hearing me?" Evan shouted.

"Y-Yes, I hear you."

"We can take the other polytunnel past the edu unit. We don't have much time. We've got to go, do you understand?"

"What about Ari?" I asked. Ari's face was red, and tears poured down his cheeks as he pounded on the Perspex of the pressure door.

Evan caught my shoulder. "Ari's not the one in danger, Lily."

His words cut through my confusion like a knife. Suddenly, the full force of the emergency sirens filled my ears and the hiss of the water coming in through the cracked porthole was not a hiss any more but a roaring torrent. Ari was gesturing towards the pressure door at the far side of the ops room.

I scrambled to my feet, stumbling over the half-submerged debris. Evan dragged me after him. It was only a few metres to the door but, like a bad dream, I didn't seem to be getting any closer. Ice-cold water bit through my trainers and rushed up my legs. *Three metres. Two metres.* The ocean wanted to kill me. I could almost smell its hunger. *One metre—*

I stepped over the bulkhead into the polytunnel, relief

flooding through me. But Evan had stumbled; he was still inside.

"*Evan! Come on!*"

Water swirled around the bulkhead.

Evan lunged towards me. He was going to make it. But at the same moment, a relay clicked shut and the pressure door began to slide.

"*Run!*" I screamed.

Evan hurled himself at the door. I stared blindly at the emergency override panel. A mass of buttons and a coded keypad. Not a chance.

Block it, I thought. Use something to block it.

I reached into my pocket and felt my hand close on a cold, oblong object. My phone. I reached up and slipped it edgewise into the gap before I knew what I was doing. The door shut against it. The screen popped instantly. The metal case bulged. But it held. It held.

Evan's face appeared in the gap. "Here—" He thrust his white key card out to me. "Use this!"

Water spilled over the lip of the bulkhead. I saw it then on the cracked phone screen – two notifications. Dad and Hanna. They'd texted!

"Lily!" Evan shouted. "Quickly!"

Snapping back to reality—

I took the card. It nearly slipped from my numb fingers. I tapped. The door fell backwards with a hiss and Evan half fell, half swam through the bulkhead along with a wave of water.

"Go! Go!" he screamed, scrambling to his feet.

We splashed along the polytunnel, the icy water billowing around us. The pressure door ahead marked the junction between two further polytunnels. We ducked through. A moment later the whooping alarm sounded as the door detected the rising water and slammed shut.

The last pressure door, the one that connected us to the main rig, was just up ahead. "We're nearly there!" Evan yelled, putting on an extra spurt of speed.

My lungs burned from the effort and the saltwater, and my wet clothes felt like lead weights tied to my arms and legs. All I could see was the door ahead and the bulkhead that led back into the main rig and safety.

We were so nearly there; we were going to make it— *CRRA-AAK!*

The floor shuddered under the force of a secondary explosion. A freezing torrent thundered through a burst seam overhead and knocked me to the ground. The world swirled around me. Ice water rushed into my mouth.

I hauled myself to my feet. Staggered. Reached out to steady myself. I thought of Mum – was she searching for me, lost and frightened too? I pushed the thought away.

Beside me, Evan was on his knees in the water. I dragged him upright.

But we were too slow. The door settled into the bulkhead and sealed tight.

We were dead.

CHAPTER 29

We were so dead.

The pressure doors either side of us were sealed to protect the rest of the rig, but frigid water was pouring into the polytunnel so fast it was already up to my waist. My legs throbbed with the cold; my body shook.

Evan patted frantically at the many pockets and pouches of his flight suit: "Where is it?" he breathed. "I had a spare… Dammit – why so many pockets?"

I stared dully at him. Surely he knew it was hopeless? He ripped something from his pocket and thrust it at me. "Here! Put this on," he said.

He handed me a piece of folded plastic, a kind of beige

hood like the cheap cagoules they used to make us wear on outings at primary school.

"Are you serious?" I yelled over the noise of the water and creaking polytunnel. "There are five thousand tonnes of water behind that wall, what good is this going to do?"

"*Put it on!*" Evan begged.

I slipped on the hood, not having the heart to argue with him any further. It had tassels that clipped around my neck and an extra-long brim at the back like a fisherman's sou'wester. Evan pulled out a second hood for himself. We looked ridiculous.

"You're making us wear hats?" I said, hysteria rising. "We're going to die, and *this* is what you're worried about?"

Evan opened his mouth to say something, but in the same instant there was a sharp *thack!* like a gun going off, loud even over the throbbing water, as one of the bolts in the door popped out of its hole and splashed into the currents below.

Then—

Everything happened.

The water hit me in the same instant as I saw it. The tunnel crumpled into itself, the tiny nanotubes of polycarbonate shattered and shredded in one implosive crush. A vicious swirl of water and twisted metal lifted me off my feet and spun me around. The impact wrenched my neck brutally to the side. I was driven backwards, propelled by wicked currents that curled and foamed. *I was dying. I was actually dying.*

But still it wouldn't end. I felt myself pulled down and out and out. Out into the tumbling and open ocean.

Why am I not dead?

Something beige-brown caught my eye. Something that didn't belong. The shape whizzed past my field of vision.

A whirlpool of shattered polycarbonate and debris followed. Glimpses of the rig and the ripped-up ends of the polytunnel flapped in the currents. A feeling like being torn apart. *Maybe this is dying,* I thought. *Maybe it just takes longer than people think.*

A moment later – there it was again. Small and beige, orbiting in the same swirling currents as me. The beige-brown shape came past again, slower this time. My breath rattled in my chest – *in … out … in … out* – I couldn't make it slow down. I was alive. I was still alive. *But how?*

Now the shape drifted to a stop in front of me. A beige rugby ball, a giant inflatable onesie made from congealing memory foam. Small ciliate thrusters trembled on the upper arms as it fought to match my speed and rotation in the currents. It came closer, and I noticed a tiny, illuminated porthole moulded into the foam. Evan's face stared at me from inside – white, terrified, determined. *Some kind of survival suit,* I thought.

Wait – now I understood: I was in a survival suit too. I could feel the memory foam tightening around me.

Evan floated directly in front of me so we were chest to chest. His suit had stumpy arms and legs that ended in four hooked claws at the front and what looked like tiny suction cups at the back. My own suit, I guessed, was the same. He reached forward and hooked his suit's claws on to my shoulders. He pressed his helmet against mine so that we stared face to face. *Calm down*, his steady eyes told me. *You're safe.* I fixed my eyes on his. I took several slow lungfuls of air.

I can't move! I screamed.

My own voice reverberated around me, but Evan shook his head. I watched his lips: *No sound.*

Now that my breathing was beginning to calm, I could hear the resonant knocking and clanging of the shattered rig settling around us, but our voices, I presumed, were too quiet to carry through both suits. Evan's lips parted in a smile that was probably meant to be reassuring. *Another fine mess you got me into*, his eyes said.

I smiled back, an unexpected warmth spreading through me. Even in the dimness of his helmet lights I could see every pore and line of his face, the flecks of colour in his dark eyes. If it wasn't for two layers of aluminosilicate and memory foam, and the murderous ocean all around us, this would be … intimate.

A slight sideways pressure rocked me. Evan was slowing

us down, helping us come to a steady hover. I didn't want to look away. Locked together like this, seeing nothing but his determined expression, I felt safer than I'd felt since I arrived.

But I had to see what had happened to the rig.

I reached forward with my fingers within my suit and felt a small thumbstick with my right hand and a row of microswitches with my left. I tapped a microswitch, and a small heads-up display appeared in front of me. Buoyancy, battery, O_2, velocity. I pressed the thumbstick and felt myself move away from Evan.

Maximus's team must have designed these for emergencies. The weight of the ocean was too heavy down here for a regular diving suit, but somehow they'd compressed the entire pressure-compensating unit into those flimsy-looking sou'westers.

A noise nearby made me turn, and I saw that the implosion had ripped the polytunnel away from the rig. Shredded suspension cables still wheeled around us, drifting slowly through the water like tangled hair. Beyond that, I could just see the rest of the site through the silt that had been stirred up. Several hab units had been pulled from their mountings, their polytunnels cracked and shredded; still others remained attached, rocking wildly, like they were caught in a storm.

I looked at Evan and saw that his eyes were wide with shock. They'd warned us about this at the training centre:

the fusion reactor relied on electromagnets to contain the plasma, but it was possible for those fields to destabilize, collapse and escape into the surrounding area. Massive electromagnetic fields and a rig made of steel – you didn't need a physics degree to know that that was a thoroughly terrible thing. *The eddy fields would rip us out of the ground like a daisy*, Ari had warned us on our first day.

But the fail-safes should have tripped out and shut down the reactor, and if they didn't work, that's what the ERS buttons were for. And even if nobody had been able to get to an ERS, the system should have burnt itself out by now.

Something was keeping the reactor running, the untethered electromagnetic storm pulling and pulling at the weakened rig infrastructure.

My stomach twisted. The edu unit stood alone, detached from the rest of the rig, its polytunnel shredded. *The others are in there*, I thought. Trapped. Shaken back and forth by the relentless eddy fields.

Suddenly, one of the thick steel cables that anchored the unit to the rock detached. It flung itself upwards and curled back on itself in a fierce whiplash, made ghostly and unnerving by the resistance of the water slowing everything down. Then another went the same way, and another.

The release of tension as the bolts gave way caused the cables to rear up like cobras and thrash through the water, clanging against each other. Another failed, and another, and another. I stared at Evan, but there was nothing we could do. Faster and faster, the remaining cables gave way as they were forced to take on more and more weight. Then, as the full weight of the edu unit began to rest on the bolts and beams beneath it, they too began to buckle and fold, until at last they collapsed in on themselves like cardboard, and the whole unit began to slide.

Oh, no, no, no, no...

I tried to scream, but no sound would come out. I could see Evan shouting something, his expression wretched within the silent bubble of his survival suit. We watched helplessly as a cloud of billowing silt rose around the sliding edu unit. Then it reached the edge and dropped, tilting forward into the valley. The last glimpse I saw was it hitting an outcrop of rock, lifting and beginning to roll. I imagined Jacob, Ysabel and the others thrown around inside. A twisting, pounding, tumbling snowball filled with people. Falling. Falling.

Think. Think. Think. Think.

There had to be something I could do. They'd slide down the valley until something stopped them; if nothing got in their way, they'd fall right down to the telemetry grid. They couldn't survive that.

I scanned my heads-up display. My battery was down to eighty per cent already. The suits weren't designed to be piloted around; they were wait-to-be-rescued units; if I went after the others I'd drain the battery almost immediately.

I looked at Evan.

It was hopeless. I'd probably die. But at that moment, something else had gripped me. I needed to do something, anything; I needed to help. Or try to, at least.

I thumbed the controller inside my suit and started to drop.

I saw the flash of comprehension in Evan's eyes as he realized what I was doing. He reached out with a stubby claw and hooked it around an emergency grab point on my arm. I wriggled to get away, but Evan clung on, shaking his head, begging me to stop. But I'd made up my mind. I pressed the thumbstick and my ciliate drives yanked me backwards and away from him.

I dropped. And the rig, and Evan, vanished above me.

CHAPTER 30

It wasn't like piloting an amphipod. The amphipod had floodlights, gel seats and air-con. It was designed to be a bubble of technology between the pilot and the ocean.

The survival suits were different. They were dark and cold and flimsy in comparison. My wet clothes pressed against my body, chafing at the seams and cold against my back. My teeth chattered.

Darkness closed around me as the emergency lights and the burning battery unit of the rig above me slipped beyond the ridge. I pressed my head forward and stared down into the black below. The telemetry grid was out, and with it the row of floodlights that usually marked its perimeter. The only light was from the edu unit, wedged against a rocky outcrop about halfway down the slope. They'd got lucky. If the outcrop hadn't stopped them, they'd have kept going all the way to the telemetry grid.

I kept my eyes fixed on the edu unit, adjusting my buoyancy to slow my descent. I watched the battery indicator tick down steadily. *I am going to die*, I thought. *I am going to die trying to save Ernest Shackleton's great-great nephew and Little-Miss-Junior-Winter-Olympics.*

This was really stupid.

But something had hardened inside me. I was done being a liability. I was done being a freak. I was done living in a world where *not messing up* was the best I could hope for.

The lights from the edu unit stuttered and died. A choke escaped my mouth. There was nothing now, no light, nothing. Just black and falling.

My helmet light picked out the dim outline of the structure in the same instant that I slammed into it.

I slid, winded, my momentum carrying me along the angled roof. I twisted, scrambling for something to hold on to. The clawed hands of the survival suit scraped, but they had nothing to grip. The suckers caught and then popped off in a series of disheartening *mwop-mwop-mwop-mwop* sounds that reverberated through the lining of my suit.

At the last moment, the raised edge where my faceplate was moulded into my suit caught on an access handle and brought me to a jarring halt. I clung on, hanging by my chin.

I drew a shivery breath.

Not the greatest rescue bid in history.

I reached forward inside my suit for the thumbstick. There were a million ways to get this wrong. I nudged it briefly, and the ciliate drives whirred, churning the seawater around me and pushing me up. I scrambled to safety on the top of the edu unit, praying that I didn't overshoot and fall off the opposite side. Between the silt and the weak lights on the survival suit, I could hardly see a thing. My heart pounded with each beat, and each breath sounded like a hurricane in my ears. *Get a grip.*

OK, now what? I leaned closer to the surface of the edu unit and could just make out the moulded lip of the dock point. They'd explained it to us at the training centre: all hab units had multiple emergency dock points that made it possible to dock with a submersible or polytunnel and escape without being exposed to the high pressure outside. But now that I was here, a new thought had dawned on me: the dock point on the edu unit was no use unless my survival suit had a connector that was compatible with it.

My breath tightened; these suits weren't designed for this. They probably didn't even have connectors. I twisted my body around, hoping to catch a glimpse of a connector. On my chest? On my back? There was nothing, just the smooth balloon-like curve of the memory foam. I tried the microswitches – nothing. I pressed my hands to the dock point on the edu unit, hoping that my proximity would trigger some kind of automated docking system. But nothing. Of course, these suits were meant to be towed into a sub bay; there was no need and no room to install dock point connectors.

I felt the panic rising inside me. I'd made a terrible mistake.

Then something knocked into me, nudging me sideways. I tried to turn, but I couldn't see what it was. A moment later, a small beige beach ball with pudgy arms and legs appeared in front of me – Evan!

I shook my head in disbelief. He'd come after me again, despite knowing that it was a stupid gesture. I shot him a furious look, which for some reason made him smile.

He was saying something. I dabbed the thumbstick and moved closer. Our faceplates clunked together.

... re—tal conne—tor...

I shook my head. *What?*

... rec— connector—...

I nodded. *Yes. Yes.* We needed the connector. *Where?* I mouthed.

A look of frustration. He formed the words carefully, exaggerating the movements of his lips:

... rec—al connector...

What?!

... Rec—tal conn—ec—or...

Evan backed away from me, his foam-clad legs dragging lightly on the surface of the edu unit. When he was over a dock point, he sat, drawing up his legs and allowing himself to drift slowly downwards. The connector protruded from his backside, a moulded ridge of foam designed to dock with the edu unit.

Ohhh: rectal connector!

It latched on, and a startled look came over Evan's face in the moment before he was sucked into the edu unit.

CHAPTER 31

It felt like being flushed down a toilet, falling and being pulled, and a slight twist. The memory foam of my survival suit released and ejected me down and backwards through the airlock like a snake shedding its skin. I landed heavily in a shower of icy water and took a moment to orientate myself. We were in Dr Balgobin's tiny office just off the main classroom.

And someone was screaming.

Evan was next to me, pulling himself to his feet.

"Why did you come after me?" I asked. My voice was sharper than I'd intended.

He looked apologetic. "I wasn't sure you'd find the rectal connector."

"Rectal connector?" I said, resisting a smile.

"I told my dad not to call it that," Evan replied. "But he said it was accurate."

I shook my head. "Well, we're *both* trapped now. We're stuck down here, you know that, right?"

Evan shrugged. "What are friends for?"

Suddenly, I was holding him. I wasn't exactly sure when I'd decided to, or how I'd crossed the small space between us, but my arms were tight around him, and I'd pressed my face into his neck. I felt his arms close around me as he hugged me back. He was damp and cold, a bit clammy, and a noise escaped me that was either a laugh or a sob, I couldn't tell.

"What are you doing here?" a voice said in surprise.

Alban was standing in the doorway, his brow furrowed. His hand was frozen halfway in the process of lifting the first aid kit from the wall.

"We came to help," I said, pulling away from Evan and collecting myself briskly. "Who's hurt?"

Alban didn't answer right away. He just stared at us.

"Alban!" I said. "Is anyone hurt?"

"Dr Balgobin," Alban replied.

His face was white and terrified; his usual bravado had been stripped away. He stared at the first aid kit in his hand like he'd forgotten why it was there.

I took the kit, his hand yielding slackly, and headed into the classroom. The place was wrecked. Tables and chairs had been strewn everywhere by the fall. Supply cupboards had been torn open and their contents had scattered across every possible surface. Emergency rescue packs of glowsticks and thermal blankets had been opened and dumped on the floor in desperation. The only light came now from the greenish blur of the glowsticks, overlaid by a sweeping, juddery torchlight.

I scanned the silhouettes in the shadows, but I could tell none of them was Mum. I knew she wouldn't be there – she'd gone to the lab with Dr Balgobin, but then Dr Balgobin must have left her there to see to the class.

I took the first aid kit over to where I could see Ysabel and Jacob crouched over a dark shadow.

My stomach lurched when I saw her. A metal chair leg had sheared off and speared her thigh. She lay at an awkward angle, the cruel shard of steel protruding grotesquely. Ysabel stood with her hand at her mouth, her body shaking uncontrollably. Jacob was nearby, saying over and over: "You're OK, Dr Balgobin, you're going to be OK…" Dark blood pooled around the wound and soaked Dr Balgobin's flight suit. She stared at us with wide eyes, her teeth gritted against the pain.

"We need to do something," Ysabel whispered.

"Morphine," I said, stepping forward. "She needs a painkiller. Ysabel, shine the torch on her good leg." I moved on impulse, helped by the natural authority of the first aid kit. Ysabel obeyed and aimed her torch at Dr

Balgobin's good leg. I bent and rifled through the first aid kit. They'd given us first aid sessions at the training centre, but most of it was a blank. The morphine was familiar, though, because it was packaged in a spring-loaded pen, just like Hanna's EpiPen.

The torch beam listed and swung downwards.

"Ysabel, the torch!" I said sharply.

Ysabel flinched like she was coming out of a dream. She adjusted her torch, which had begun to droop in her hand.

I uncapped the morphine pen, took an experimental swing to test my aim, and then pressed it hard against Dr Balgobin's thigh. There was a *click* as the morphine dispensed.

Dr Balgobin's face relaxed. She closed her eyes and let out a shuddering sigh, nodding her gratitude weakly. Her chest heaved as she swallowed a great lungful of air.

"Press this to the wound," I said, passing Jacob a handful of dressings. "You need to stop the bleeding, but don't disturb the…" I trailed off, looking uneasily at Dr Balgobin's leg.

"The chair leg. Gotcha," Jacob said.

He did as he was told, carefully wrapping the dressing pack around the injury. His hands became instantly slick with blood, and when I looked down, I realized that mine were too. Dr Balgobin gasped as Jacob pressed his weight into her wound.

"Dr Balgobin?" I said. "Can you hear me?"

She nodded, her eyes squeezed tight like she was

concentrating on a particularly difficult maths problem. When she opened them again, they were glassy and serene, the morphine doing its work. She offered me a brittle smile. "I appear to have a penetrating thigh injury. I believe the object has ruptured my *vastus lateralis* and most likely fractured my femur, but on the bright side it appears to have missed the femoral artery."

"How can you tell?" I breathed.

She smiled more warmly. "I'm not dead yet." She moved her head slightly so she could call out, her teacher instincts kicking in despite everything. "Class, you should take a look. It's really very fascinating."

"She's high," Jacob remarked.

"Yes," Dr Balgobin agreed, suppressing a knowing smile. "I am so high."

Ysabel and I glanced at each other, and Ysabel let out an anxious snort of laughter.

"What about everybody else?" I asked. "Anyone else hurt?"

"We're fine. Bumps and bruises," Jacob said.

We gathered together, our faces ghostly in the light of the glowsticks and torches.

"Does anyone know what happened?" asked Jacob.

"It was an explosion," Ysabel said. "I saw a battery unit go up through the porthole before we fell."

"The reactor scram must have damaged something," Alban said, his eyes fixed on me.

I felt the tension rise. A circle of accusing looks. *Why did I come here?*

"Lily had nothing to do with it," Evan responded. "It wasn't the reactor scram."

"How do you know?" Alban shot back.

"I was there."

"What?"

"We were both in the ops room when it happened. Lily didn't do anything."

Nobody said anything for a long moment. They stood, watching me distrustfully.

"What happened, then?" Alban said at last.

"The plasma containment ruptured," Evan said. "I don't know why. The eddy fields moved the hab units and they broke some of the polytunnels. I guess the battery units shorted out."

I thought about the CRABs shutting down, the wave of blackness rushing towards us. Hadn't there been a moment when Evan had thought it *was* me? He'd clearly decided it wasn't worth mentioning to the others.

"We need to let them know we're still alive," Ysabel said. "They can come and get us."

"There's an emergency UAC in Dr Balgobin's office," Jacob said. "We can try and contact them."

He darted off, and I watched through the open door as he took the UAC from Dr Balgobin's desk and pulled on the headset.

"Deephaven, this is the edu unit. Do you copy?" he said, sounding serious and far too grown-up. "Deephaven, we have survivors and injured. We need urgent evac. Do you copy?"

Silence.

Evan moved over to the porthole and peered out at the blackness. "The whole rig's down. They've got no power."

"They won't hear us," Jian agreed.

Jacob fell silent and turned to watch us, like he was waiting for permission to go on.

"We're taking on water," Alban said. "We don't have much time."

"They'll come for us, won't they?" Ysabel said.

Nobody responded. We were all doing the maths in our heads. How many polytunnels had ruptured; how many sections had flooded? The ops room was gone. Even if Ari had made it back to the main rig before the second explosion had taken out our polytunnel, he would have had no control of the rig until he got down to the command centre. And then what? He'd have to get the reactor under control, restore emergency power and make sure the rig was safe before he could even *think* about mounting a rescue mission.

"We should rest as much as we can," I said. "Conserve oxygen."

The others agreed, grateful to have a plan, even a meagre one. We found the thermal blankets and discovered some energy bars amongst the emergency packs. We distributed them and used the cushions from the breakout area to make ourselves as comfortable as possible. My body ached and my head buzzed. I thought about Mum. Where was she? Was she OK? The science lab was at the very far end of the site, furthest from the rig. She might be trapped, like us. She might have slid off into the trench entirely.

A deep, black feeling welled up inside me. Panic and constriction. A scream that wouldn't come. And something vast and cold and lonely.

The damp air felt cruel against my skin. I'd removed my wet flight suit and wrapped myself in a thermal blanket, but I still couldn't stop shivering. The only sound was the malicious gurgling in the walls to remind us that we were steadily losing air as the pressurized water forced its way in.

Suddenly, Dr Balgobin sat up and let out a rasping gasp. Her eyes sprang open, and she sang in a scratched, reedy voice: *"There's a hole in my femur, dear Liza, dear Liza! There's a hole in my femur, dear Liza, a hole!"*

Then she slumped back down, her face white, her mouth working silently.

"Dr Balgobin?" Ysabel asked anxiously.

I moved over and sat next to her. Her forehead was clammy, beaded with sweat. We'd wrapped thermal blankets around her, but her hands were still icy.

"Can she have more morphine?" Ysabel asked.

She held the torch for me so I could check the label. "I think it's OK, yes."

We gave Dr Balgobin another dose of morphine, and she heaved a sigh. I sat back and pulled my thermal blanket closer to me, my teeth chattering.

"You're cold," Ysabel said. "Here..."

I allowed her to slide under the thermal blanket next to me and swaddled us both, the warmth of her body soaking into me.

"You were really good earlier," she said, "with Dr Balgobin."

I shrugged. "I just did what anyone would have done."

"Not me. I froze. I was so scared. There was so much blood." Ysabel thought for a moment. "Have you done anything like this before?"

"Like this? I accidentally locked myself in a Portaloo once, does that count?"

Ysabel laughed. "I didn't mean that. I mean a proper emergency."

"Sorry... No. I watch a lot of movies. Maybe that's it."

Ysabel's lips trembled slightly. "I'm sorry we were so mean to you."

I shrugged.

"Alban shouldn't have blackmailed you."

"Did you know?" I asked.

She looked shocked. "No! We squeezed it out of him after the things you said right before you ... well, after what you said." Her face tensed indignantly. "He's just a little brat anyway. You should ignore him."

"I know that now."

Ysabel turned slightly so she could look at me more directly. She looked much younger in this light; I imagined that I did as well. "Why do you do it?" she asked.

"Do what?"

"Break things."

I tensed. Why did that matter now? Surely we had more important things to worry about. But there was no hint of accusation in her voice. It was like our shared fear had stripped away the nonsense, and all that was left was a simple, honest question. It was ironic, I thought, that it took certain death at the bottom of the ocean for me to be able to have a straightforward conversation with someone.

"I didn't push the ERS, you know," I said.

"I wouldn't blame you if you had. We were being horrible."

I drew a breath. "It's not like I think it through or anything. It's just like all the feelings fill me up, like I'm a bag of water, and the feelings are bursting out the seams. They have to come out somewhere, or they'll tear me apart."

Ysabel thought, then she nodded. "I know how that feels." She surveyed the smashed-up edu unit for a few moments, littered with our sleeping classmates, wrapped up in their thermal blankets like tin-foil tacos. "If we get out of this, would you like to hang out sometime?"

I laughed. "What?"

"There's not much to do on Deephaven, but we could watch a movie or something ... or gossip. I miss having a girl to hang out with."

She seemed awkward. Shy. The fact that we most likely weren't getting out of this, and if we did, I was certainly getting sent home anyway, didn't seem to matter so much.

"Yes," I said. "I'd like that."

She grinned and looped her arm through mine. "Evan likes you, you know. I can tell."

CHAPTER 32

I was having the loveliest dream.

Dad was showing me around his latest project. I knew it was a dream because the project was unlike anything he'd ever worked on in real life. It was a brain, and we were *inside* it, and it was *beautiful*. It wasn't how a real brain would look: grey and lumpy like day-old porridge. This one was perfectly black, except every now and then there was a spark and a shower of light that rattled through the space all around us. Brilliant showers of purple and blue thought, branching off in every direction, like being inside a perfectly silent lightning storm. Dad was pointing things out as we walked. *That's the Frontal Lobe, where we plan and think. And here, the Amygdala, where we feel.*

Do you see the memories in the Hippocampus next to it — like after-images?

I woke slowly, not quite remembering where I was. The sound of gurgling water reminded me, and with it came the realization that the water level had risen and the lowest half of the edu unit was completely flooded. Ysabel was breathing heavily in her sleep next to me, just as the others were doing in their chosen spots. The air felt damp and stale, and condensation ran in rivers down the domed portholes.

I shivered. All I wanted to do was drift back to sleep so I wouldn't have to think any more.

But something had woken me. The light was different. Not just green from the glowsticks, but blue and turquoise as well, like my dream.

I sat up suddenly. My sodden flight suit was still hanging nearby. The oversized pocket on the left thigh glowed purple. I reached inside, expecting to see the pulsing dots of the euglenoid. My thoughts were muddled, still half-asleep. How excited I'd been with my discovery, my ability to coax the euglenoid into life! How long ago and irrelevant it all seemed now. I looked at the pressure jar.

And recoiled in terror—

A face!

The pressure jar skittered away from me, across the floor. I stared at it, my chest heaving. A face? No. It must have been my own reflection. I looked around to see if I'd disturbed anybody. It was quiet. Six sleeping bodies. Low oxygen, I thought. It makes it easy to sleep.

Perhaps ... it makes it easy to hallucinate as well?

Nervously, I crept forward. My hands shook. My brain felt like it was trying to claw its way out the back of my skull. There was no denying it. The face hung in the jar like a pickled exhibit in formaldehyde. Or like a reflection in a porthole? I clenched my teeth and reached forward. Every muscle in my body screamed at me to leave the jar where it was, but I needed a closer look. The air shuddered from my lungs. It wasn't just *a* face.

It was *my* face.

Almost my face.

I forced myself not to hurl it away. The eyes were open, they were alive, but it wasn't like looking in a mirror. The image watched me just as I watched it. The eyes were a little larger than I remembered my own to be. The nose looked wrong, like a child's drawing of a nose. At least, I *hoped* that wasn't how my nose looked. It shimmered ever so slightly as the spots of euglenoid jostled for position.

I forced the rigid muscles of my face into a smile.

A moment later, the face in the jar smiled back.

Tentatively, I stuck out a quivering tongue.

The face stuck out its tongue too.

I blinked.

The image blinked.

I winked.

The image tried to wink, but somehow blinked instead. It tried again. A tight, hysterical peal of laughter escaped me.

"What *are* you?" I murmured.

The face watched me, inscrutable. Thoughts raced inside my head: a thousand people talking at once. No, a thousand memories coming all at once. Then, a realization so sharp it made me gasp in pain—

"It was you," I said with sudden conviction. "*You* activated the ERS?"

A wave of horror swept over me. The euglenoid had done it all. Not just the ERS. It had torn the rig apart. *Something big and scared and blind.* It had killed— Who knew how many it had killed? Maybe all of us. *But why?* My head throbbed. If the euglenoid had attacked the rig, then it really was my fault. I'd brought it on board, I'd figured out how to activate it. *My fault.*

The euglenoid watched me.

"Why?" I hissed. "Why did you...?"

I had to think. I couldn't think. The thing that had destroyed the rig was inside my head. But it was inside the rig as well. Thoughts surged through my brain, a deluge of images that didn't belong to me. Black. Ancient. Vast. No, no, *no... I miss him... I love him...* A sound was coming out of me, a dull moan. A coldness. White-hot lithium tears burned in my throat, but they wouldn't come.

"You OK?"

Evan. I jumped, startled, and hastily shoved the jar back into my flight suit pocket. Then I realized that I was wearing nothing but my neoprene underwear and scrambled to pull the thermal blanket over me.

"Um … yes… I'm fine. I'm…"

I pulled the thermal blanket more tightly up to my neck and offered Evan an anxious smile.

"I've been thinking about what happened to the rig," Evan said.

"What do you mean?" I couldn't keep the nervous catch from my voice.

"You told us to shut down the reactor."

"So?" I watched his face for signs of suspicion.

"How did you know?"

"I… Nothing." I was trembling, I hoped he couldn't tell. "I was just scared."

Evan nodded slowly.

He knows, I thought. Or at least he suspected. He'd stuck up for me in front of the others, but what if that changed? If he found out what had happened, that it was the euglenoid that I'd somehow activated, would he hate me for it?

Suddenly, a shaft of bright light from outside lit up the classroom. I flinched, turning and shielding my eyes. It was coming from below us: the floodlights that marked the edge of the telemetry grid. They'd managed to get the power back on.

Evan rushed over and pressed his face to the domed porthole. The others were stirring now, and there was a murmur of excitement as they crowded around him.

"What's happening?" Ysabel asked.

"I think they've got the power back," I said.

Her eyes widened. "That's good, right? We should try to contact them again."

Jacob hurried over to the UAC. "Deephaven, this is the edu unit. We need help. Over. Deephaven, do you copy?"

"They'll come now, won't they?" Ysabel asked. She looked outside, and then her expression dropped. She raised her hand to her mouth. "Oh, no," she breathed.

We stared out of the porthole. The shadow of Deephaven loomed over the ridge above us, but it was hardly recognizable. The main supports had been ripped from their fixings by the coils of electromagnetic flux, and the whole rig had dropped, crashing forward so that the domed windows of the command centre had been rammed into the silty ocean floor. Twisted steel pylons curled around the broken hull like the fingers of a vast hand reaching up, caught in the moment of crushing it.

"Is it still watertight?" I asked.

"Some of it will be," Evan answered.

"But the sub bay is gone," Jian said.

"What does that mean?" Ysabel asked.

"It means there's not going to be a rescue," Evan replied quietly. "Not without the submersibles."

There was a long silence as we tried to make sense of this. Deephaven had multiple redundancies. Every valve, component, door and seal had at least three backups. But all the waterlocks were on the sub bay level. Nobody had anticipated that the rig might be pulled off its mounts entirely.

"Ari will find a way to save us," Ysabel said. "They can send ROVS to us."

"And do what? Wave?" Alban snapped sarcastically. "Remote Operated Vehicles aren't going to be able to get us *off*."

Ysabel stared hatefully at Alban.

"Calm down, guys," said Jacob, coming over. I felt a pang of sorrow for ever being spiteful towards him. We needed a hero now; we needed his sun-bronzed, Captain-America certainty to win us all over and give us faith that rescue would come. "What about topside?" he said. "They'll have sent someone by now, won't they?"

Evan shook his head. "I don't think there was time for Deephaven to send an SOS. Topside will assume a comms failure and wait forty-eight hours before raising the alarm. We're lucky there was already a sub scheduled, but even that won't be here until tomorrow…"

"We'll never last that long," Alban said. He sounded beyond panic now.

"That's just to get to Deephaven," Jian added calmly, precisely. "They won't send someone to look for us right away. They're going to assume we're dead – they have to – and they're going to have other things to worry about."

"Jian's right," Evan agreed. "We're on our own."

I felt numb. I looked at the others and saw that they had the same defeated look about them. We were going to die there, that was a fact. We'd wait, getting colder and colder and the air getting more and more stale until we drifted off to sleep and didn't wake up. It was too big to contemplate, too big to feel real.

At least it would be painless. The water was rising very slowly, so at least we wouldn't drown. That was good.

I shook my head. *Good?* I was sixteen and I was going to suffocate at the bottom of the ocean. That was *not* good. That was *not* OK. But it was happening. There was no getting away from it.

I thought of Mum.

Then I stopped myself. Thinking of Mum was too painful. I could never apologize to her now. I could never make things right.

We stared up at the rig, as if by staring hard enough we could bring about the means of our salvation. But we knew it was impossible.

Something pressed at the inside of my mind, a weight. A memory that was not quite my own. *Go back…* I moved closer to the domed porthole and looked down.

Down? What made me look down?

Down into the red, underworld glow of the telemetry

grid and the sharp white lines of the floodlights that bordered it. A wasteland, dredged and blasted flat and laced with locator beacons so the CRABs could work their way across and gather their chunks of precious metal.

There ... nestled on another furrow in the uneven slope below us, only visible now that the floodlights were back on, precariously close to dropping off into the telemetry grid: the amphipods. Why wasn't I surprised?

"Look!" I said.

The others turned to me.

Evan squinted into the darkness. "The amphipods?"

"They won't be flooded, will they?" I asked. "They launched automatically during the overload, remote piloted themselves..."

Evan nodded. "It's possible."

The others looked one to the other, desperate to understand.

"You can't get to them," Alban said. "The ocean will crush you."

"We can use the survival suits," Evan said.

I nodded. They were still attached to the dock points on the roof.

"Wait—" Jacob said, interrupting. "So, the two of you get down to the amphipods. Then what?"

"We pilot them back to Deephaven," Evan said. "The sub bay is wrecked, but there are emergency dock points on the roof of the main rig just like we have on the edu unit."

Ysabel drew a deep, shivery breath and let it out.

"And then what?" Alban said.

Evan looked stumped. "We'll tell them you're down here. They'll send someone as soon as they can."

There was silence. This wasn't a rescue plan, it was an escape plan, and it could only save two of us. With the sub bay wrecked, there wasn't much Deephaven could do, even if they knew there were survivors down here.

"How come it's you two?" Alban asked gruffly. "We should all decide who gets to go."

"It has to be me and Lily," Evan replied. "The survival suits have moulded to our bodies, and we're the only ones who know how to fly the amphipods."

Alban shook his head vigorously. "That's bullcrap. We'll draw lots. You two fetch the amphipods, and we'll draw lots to see who gets to take them back to the rig."

I felt the atmosphere in the room tighten. A moment ago, we were all expecting to die down here together. Now, we were competing for survival.

"You won't be able to pilot the amphipod," Evan said firmly.

"*Screw* you!" Alban spat.

"You'll crash, and you'll die."

Alban glared at me. "If *she* can fly it, I don't see why *I* can't."

"Lily's exceptional," Evan said flatly.

In spite of everything, I felt a small glow of pride.

"I'll take my chances," Alban answered.

"You'll die for sure," Jian interjected. Alban stared furiously at him but quailed in the face of his unemotional certainty. "You're a rubbish pilot, and you won't be familiar with the controls," Jian continued. "In a pressured situation like this, Lily and Evan are the only ones who stand a chance."

There was silence as the rest of us processed this.

Jian turned to me. "Would you mind taking a note back with you, Lily?" he asked. "There's a good chance you'll die too, of course, but if I have two copies my parents will likely find it sooner."

I swallowed, the words sticking in my throat. "I… Of course."

Alban flung his arms out in frustration and stormed off to the far corner of the room. "It's not *fair*!" he snapped. He sounded young, and petulant, and scared, and not at all the malevolent force I'd once imagined him to be.

Ysabel was staring at me now. I couldn't tell what she was thinking. Was she angry? Did she hate me? Had she realized somehow that all of this was my fault?

"Can I give you a note too?" she said.

I bit back a bitter sob. "Y-yes. Of course."

She left me, quickly finding a pad of paper and a pen amongst the wreckage and crouching down to write.

This isn't happening, I thought. *This* can't *be happening.*

Evan handed me my flight suit, still damp, but wearable. "Here," he said grimly. "There's no point us waiting around now. The sooner we get back the more chance there is for them to find a way to help."

I nodded. I could feel the weight of the pressure jar in my thigh pocket.

"I'm glad it's you," Jacob said.

I turned, surprised. "What?"

"I'm glad it's you who gets to live."

I frowned, shaking my head in confusion. "Why?"

Jacob shrugged, struggling with his words. "I think … I think maybe you'll do something amazing one day. I get that sense about you." He grinned, the same confounded grin he always grinned when he didn't really know what he was trying to say. "You seem the type," he added.

I turned to stare out of the porthole to avoid looking at him. Alban was right, it wasn't fair. Jacob might do amazing things one day as well, and even if he didn't, it didn't mean he deserved to die down here. I stared resentfully at the amphipods. *How did they get down there? Is it really just luck?*

I thought of the others watching as Evan and I headed back to the rig. I'd felt alone all my life, but in a stupid way being stuck here was the closest I'd come to feeling like I was part of something. As irrational as it was, a bit of me wished I'd never seen the amphipods, even if that would have meant not getting out of here—

I stopped.

A thought had occurred to me. It was a stupid thought.

"We'll tow you," I said suddenly.

Evan and the others stared at me.

I started talking quickly. "We'll use the amphipods to tow the edu unit back. Then we'll dock the whole thing directly on to the emergency dock points on the roof of the main rig."

"That's ridiculous," Alban snarled. "Are you trying to finish us off sooner? We'll smash right into the cliff!"

"They told us at the training centre that all the hab units have integrated towlines, right?" I pressed on, scared that if I stopped, the idea would die before I even had time to finish the thought. "They used them when the units were first installed, so we can hook an amphipod to each side and—"

"Are the amphipod thrusters powerful enough to lift us?" Jian asked.

"Maybe," Evan replied carefully. "So long as the unit doesn't take on too much more water."

"So, it might work?" I asked.

"Let me get this straight," said Jacob slowly. "You want to tow the entire edu unit back up the side of the cliff and drop it on the roof of the main rig?"

"Not drop it," I corrected him. "*Lower* it."

Alban let out a bitter *ha!* "You'll kill everyone on board along with us. Just go, please."

I swallowed. Maybe he was right. The others were silent. I could see Jian and Evan thinking it through. Calculating.

"It's not a bad plan," Evan said quietly.

"This is ridiculous!" Alban huffed. He turned to Ysabel. "You're not going to let them do this, are you?"

"Our parents are on that rig," Ysabel said. "You could kill them."

I nodded. "I won't let that happen. I promise. I'll ditch us into the rocks first."

"No way," Alban said. "You'll mess it up."

There was a long, nervous silence. Dragging ten tonnes of edu unit fifty metres up the side of the rockface and dropping it — *lowering* it, sorry — on to the main rig? It was idiotic. But I could see them wavering, desperately wanting to believe that it could work.

The problem was, it was *my* plan. Of all people, their lives and the lives of their families would be in *my* hands. It wasn't just the plan they had to believe in. It was me.

"I trust her," Ysabel said suddenly, turning to the others. "I think we should do it." She flashed me a weak smile. "She must be a good pilot, since she got herself back to the rig last time. And ... if she thinks it might work, then…"

Alban looked outraged.

I looked at the others. Jian. Jacob.

Jian opened his mouth, hesitated, then shook his head

in slow resignation. "I think … I think Lily is smarter than she acts. It's worth a try."

I almost laughed with relief. "Thanks, Jian. Kind of."

"I'm in," Jacob said. "I think they can do it."

That seemed to settle it. The mood shifted. Even Alban gave a short nod of agreement. There was a shifting, scraping sound behind us as Dr Balgobin struggled to sit more upright. "I think it's a *marvellous* idea!" she exclaimed.

Then she slumped back, becoming instantly unconscious again.

"There's a problem," Evan said. "The rectal connectors on the survival suits aren't compatible with the amphipods. We can't dock them. We'll have to hitch on to the outside and use the external control panels."

There were a few moments of silence.

"You want us to fly the amphipods with the survival suit arm-stumps?" I said, scarcely able to imagine how that might be possible.

"We only have to go up," Evan said.

"But also drop us on top of the rig?" Alban said dubiously.

"*Lower you,*" Evan and I said in unison.

"My dad would freak," Jacob muttered.

Nobody said anything for a long moment.

Then Ysabel shook her head. "Wait. Even if you can pilot the amphipods, we're pressed right up against the rockface. There's no access to the emergency towlines on the downward side?"

Evan nodded. "I've thought about that."

"And?"

"I have an idea … but it's a little riskier than Lily's part of the plan."

"Riskier?" Alban exclaimed.

I glanced at Evan. His face was full of determination. He looked like somebody who was in his element, an *experimental-deep-sea-rig* kind of person. I felt like I was seeing, for the first time, the Evan that had existed before his father died.

"We need to move the edu unit to free up the towline," Evan said.

"How are we supposed to do that?"

Jian's face changed to one of delight as he figured it out, one step ahead of the rest of us. "Of course! You're going to release the compressed oxygen in the emergency tanks and use it to push us over the ridge!" His face dropped suddenly. "You're going to *what?!*"

Evan allowed himself the briefest smile. A little bit of him was enjoying himself, I suspected. "If we're lucky, it'll be enough to dislodge us, and we'll slide the rest of the way to the amphipods and stop when we hit the same furrow they're in. The terrain is less steep there; we should still have access to the towline. And being closer to the amphipods will mean we're less likely to run out of power in our suits before we can get to them."

We stood in pale silence, our appetite for the plan dwindling by the second.

Dimly, I wondered how this would have played out at my old school. Whether our willingness to entertain this plan was a good thing, or the result of extreme panic and oxygen deprivation, or just a sign of how stupid you had to be to live down here in the first place.

"What if we ride right over it and plummet into the valley?" Alban asked.

"We'll implode," Jian said matter-of-factly.

"What if we land *on top of* the amphipods?" Jacob asked.

Evan shrugged. "We'll not be any worse off than we are now."

"What if the survival suits run out of power before we get back?" I asked.

"We'll asphyxiate and die," Evan replied, locking eyes with me.

"What if we damage the rig when we drop the edu unit on top of it?" Alban said.

"*Lower* it," I corrected him one final time.

"Whatever."

I sighed. "Like I said, we won't let that happen."

We listened to the quiet gurgling of water leaking somewhere inside the hab unit's internal machinery.

"Let's do it," Evan said.

"Roger that, Captain!" Dr Balgobin responded.

CHAPTER 33

We busied ourselves preparing. The slide down the valley wall was going to be bumpy. Not as far as last time, but steeper, and there was a chance the unit would roll again.

The furniture was designed to be stowable so the edu unit could be moved into place when the rig was first constructed. Dr Balgobin called out half-delirious instructions that hardly made sense, and we re-packed meticulously, dismantling each table and chair and securing it in recesses in the floor like a giant IKEA project. Books, tablets and other school supplies were locked in supply cupboards so they couldn't bounce around and cause injury. Then we pulled out the insulating foam from the far side of the unit and used it to double pad and pack out the side that would hit the ridge. We built padded cocoons for each of us.

We used extra foam padding for Dr Balgobin, carefully packing it around her and the chair leg so there could be no movement.

"I'm going to give you another shot of morphine," I said.

"Righto!" Dr Balgobin said.

When we were ready, I huddled in my foam cocoon and held my breath. Jacob, Alban and Ysabel had volunteered for the dangerous job of activating the emergency air release valves and then doing their best to get back to the safety of their foam cocoons before the edu unit picked up too much speed.

"Is everyone ready?" Jacob asked.

Ysabel and Alban stood poised at their own emergency release valves. Myself, Evan and Jian wriggled ourselves more tightly into our cocoons.

Jacob shot me a look, a smile hovering over his lips. "Three ... two ... one..."

There was a hollow *thump!* as the air canisters vented, and a jolt.

Unpleasant, but not too bad. At first I thought it hadn't worked.

Then, the floor began to tip, and there was a low, grinding sound beneath us.

"Quickly! Quickly!"

Jacob, Alban and Ysabel half ran, half fell the length of the edu unit and plunged towards their cocoons. Ysabel fell wrong, landing half in and half out of her cocoon, angled in such a way that the moment we hit the far edge of the furrow she would get badly hurt.

"Ysabel!" I yelled, scrambling out of my cocoon and throwing myself at her, colliding with her and shoving her into her own cocoon.

The hab unit was sliding end first now, rattling and squeaking, jolting against the ragged slope of the valley. The water and the angle of the slope controlled our speed, but each lump and furrow in the uneven rockface still sent vicious jolts through the floor. There was a sound like a gasp, and a jet of high-pressure water fountained in from somewhere overhead.

"Lily! Get down!" Evan called.

I turned, teetered on the edge of my cocoon, and in that moment, the hab unit hit the bottom. The foam wall rushed towards me at terrific speed, and the world went black—

"Lily… Lily…"

I groaned.

"Lily! *Please!*"

I just wanted the voice to go away.

"*Lily!*"

A sharp pain in my side caused me to yelp, and I opened

my eyes to see Jacob standing over me, his face tense with worry, and Evan next to him, catching his balance after the kick in the ribs he'd just given me.

"Did we make it?" I asked.

"Not yet," Evan said grimly.

The world swam back in an ocean of light and pain. My head rang like a diving bell. There was a firework in the far corner of the unit. No, not a firework. Water, forcing its way in from a cracked porthole, sizzling and spitting with the pressure.

"We're taking on more water," I said.

"Yes, there's that," Evan said dismissively. "Come on, we need to move. We ran closer to the edge than I'd have liked; I don't know how stable we are."

"What about the amphipods?"

"Right next to us. I can see them."

I staggered to my feet and allowed myself to be dragged dazedly over to the ceiling dock points in Dr Balgobin's office. Evan went first, struggling up into his survival suit which was still outside and connected to the edu unit by its rectal connector. Jacob had to place both hands on Evan's behind to help him haul himself back up into the hole.

Alban stepped forward as I started to climb into my own survival suit, and I flashed him an evil look. "Don't even think about it," I growled.

He stepped back, his arms raised defensively. I felt Ysabel's hand on my shoulder.

"Thank you for saving us," she whispered.

"I haven't saved anyone yet," I said.

"Thank you for trying."

I smiled tightly. Then Ysabel leaned forward and gave me a peck on the cheek. I blushed.

"Look on the bright side," Alban said, coming closer.

"Which is?"

"If you screw up, we'll all be dead, so there won't be anybody to yell at you this time."

A smile curled my lips. "That helps actually. Thanks, Alban."

Jacob lingered. He seemed to be trying to say something, but his rugged awkwardness was getting in the way. "Lily... I, um..." He gave up and clapped me chummily on the shoulder instead. "Try not to die out there, OK? Or kill us."

CHAPTER 34

It had only been a few hours, but I'd forgotten how awful the survival suits were. I could see almost nothing beyond the battery warning light blinking furiously in my heads-up display.

I bounced, spaceman-like, across the roof of the edu unit. As I tensed my legs for a final bounce, I realized – almost too late – that I'd reached the edge and was staring precariously at the drop. My muscles stiffened, desperately trying to prevent the further bounce that would take me over. The unit had risen up over the lip further than we'd expected it to, and it was now balanced, just barely, like a poorly built see-saw.

I dabbed the thumbstick, and the ciliate drives fought

to hold my balance, pushing me backwards to safety. My battery indicator dropped in response. *Twenty per cent*. Surely that wasn't enough: we still had to hitch up to the amphipods and make our way back to the rig... A movement caught my eye, and I saw Evan waving frantically for me to join him.

I bounced over to him and flipped open the emergency remote panel on the nearest amphipod.

Evan had walked me through the start-up sequence. It was the same as in the main cockpit, but with less feedback to tell you whether you were doing it correctly or not. I tapped each command in turn, my movements painfully awkward with the survival suit's clumsy arm-stumps and claws.

I glanced over to Evan, and he nodded.

The amphipods burst into life. They hovered in front of us, their ciliate drives stirring up small clouds of sediment. Deephaven bristled with anchor-points and emergency lines. But not even Maximus had anticipated mounting a survival suit on to an amphipod. I wasn't even sure where to begin.

Evan was hovering level with the back of his amphipod. I watched as he clipped himself to the back of it, first to one side, and then to the other, creating a kind of sling for himself. I did the same, a single anchor-point attached to my stomach and two connected from my sides to two anchor-points either side of the main body of the amphipod. If I hooked one of the survival suit's claws into one of the amphipod's panels, I could handle the controls with the other. It wasn't exactly stable, but it was OK.

We piloted the amphipods over to the edu unit, taking our time to get used to the feel of them. The amphipods were easier to control than the survival suits. The survival suits had a tendency to dart forward, further than you'd intended, whereas the amphipods were steadier and seemed almost to know where you wanted them to go. Set against that, I was trying to manipulate the small thumbstick on the amphipod through the thick pressure-foam of the survival suit.

The first time I tried to activate the towline on the edu unit, I missed and clunked heavily against its side instead. I looked up and saw Ysabel and the others watching anxiously through the porthole. It took a few moments of clumsily mashing the amphipod into the hydraulic lever, but finally I had it, and a surge of bubbles signalled the release of the clamps as the towline spooled out.

I clicked it on to my amphipod on each side and looked across to the opposite side of the edu unit. Evan raised his arm to tell me he was ready. This way we would share the load between the two amphipods like we were carrying a heavy trunk.

I gazed back up the jagged slope towards the rig.

Battery: *thirteen per cent*.

There's no way, I thought darkly.

The ciliate drives on Evan's amphipod whirred.

I powered on my own.

Ysabel pressed her face against the porthole. A thin smile. A shaky thumbs up.

I gave Evan a nod, and we pushed the power up to maximum. Our amphipods lifted, carrying us and our survival suits with them until the towlines pulled taut. We hovered there for a moment, straining against the weight of the edu unit.

Then, slowly, we began to rise.

A hysterical giggle escaped my lips. Small, beige and round. We looked like sheep riding mopeds and towing a caravan.

We were rising faster now. *It's working!* Up and forward, tracing the angle of the rockface, which slid past beneath us. The edu unit trailed behind, its drag and weight pulling against the amphipod engines, making them whine bitterly.

Suddenly, there was a *clang!* and a shockwave rippled through the towline, yanking the amphipod back and almost dislodging me. I looked down and saw that the edu unit had clipped a protruding spike of the rock, sending the unit swinging away like a giant pendulum.

I wrenched the thumbstick backwards and pulled away from the rockface before it could swing back down. Evan did the same, but I was a little faster, and now the edu unit was twisting, pulled at an awkward angle by our differing heights. I levelled off, caught sight of the unit as it began to swing back. It hit the rockface again, sending another shockwave through the towlines. Suddenly, I was grateful that we had no comms, so I couldn't hear what the others were saying inside.

I wrestled clumsily with the controls through the survival suit. One more twisting oscillation… I dropped and raised the amphipod to absorb the momentum, and finally we were steady again.

I was trembling all over, my muscles locked rigid in fear.

Nine per cent.

A moment later we crested the ridge, and I saw for the first time the full extent of the damage to Deephaven. Pretty much every hab unit had been shifted or dislodged in some way. Several had been pulled completely from their mountings, their polytunnels shattered, leaving fragments of polycarbonate littering the ocean floor. Three of the battery units had exploded and burnt out completely, leaving nothing but black scars amongst the shadows. At least one of the hab units was similarly burnt out. Another battery unit was still burning, a white-hot lithium fire casting trembling shadows on the rocks around it. The main rig itself was sitting crookedly in its mountings, the domed windows of the command centre half submerged by the silt.

I realized with a jolt that we were moving too fast.

At this speed we were never going to be able to slow the edu unit down before it rose too high and drifted too far away to correct. I looked over to Evan and saw that he'd realized our mistake as well. He was slowing down, and his towline had fallen slack beneath him. I pulled out to the side as far as I could, using the force of the towline to swing me around until I was beneath the edu unit. The edu unit passed between us, rising with its own momentum, and a second later a painful wrench as the towline pulled taut knocked me from my position on the back of the amphipod.

I hit the ciliate drive on my survival suit and pushed myself back into position.

Five per cent.

I slammed the amphipod's thumbstick forward and powered downwards, back towards the rig. Now I was pulling the edu unit *downwards*, using the amphipod thrusters to slow its rate of ascent. Evan was doing the same.

But I'd misjudged; we were closer than I'd thought, and suddenly I was travelling too fast and directly towards the top of the rig. I reached blindly for the amphipod controls, the bare metal of the rig closing on me like a clenched fist.

I hit it hard. The world whirled, and I gasped for breath. The survival suit absorbed most of the impact, which would have killed me otherwise, but I still felt the wind forced out of me. I blinked, trying to make sense of the world. The amphipod lay on its side next to me, its ciliate drives idling.

A shadow was closing over me. The edu unit was falling now.

Falling towards me.

The next moments played out in my mind in slow motion. The edu unit would land on top of me, pinning me to the roof of the rig.

Desperately, I pushed the ciliate drives on my survival suit, and it lurched forward.

Zero per cent.

I mashed its claw into the amphipod controls. Full throttle. No control. Anywhere, anywhere but here. The amphipod twisted, lifted itself, then took off – dragging me, bouncing and twisting, along the roof of the rig. I stared at the row of spotlights that marked the edge of the rig, the slit of open ocean narrowing in front of me. The thrusters whined. The shadow of the falling edu unit grew darker. I watched as its flat bottom scoured the top of my amphipod and sent out a flare of sparks that glowed and died in the water around me—

Then I was clear! I hauled myself on to the amphipod and pulled back, into another arc that led me around the side of the edu unit. I felt the towline pull taut, and I pulled for a few moments more, slowing the edu unit just enough, before I killed the power.

Everything went very still. Below me, the edu unit fell

the last few centimetres. Metal ground against metal as the unit and the rig knocked together with the lightest possible touch. My breath shuddered in my throat. I let myself drift back down towards the roof of the edu unit.

Zero per cent. Zero per cent.

The heads-up display flashed urgently at me.

My mouth opened and closed, but there was no air. No power, no pump, no air. I watched, my vision fading, as Evan unhooked himself from his amphipod and used his own ciliate drives to power over to me. He hooked the claw of his suit on to mine. *No. Air.* My lungs strained. The world had become blurry, insubstantial. Evan's face, and a dreadful sense of hollowness in my lungs, that was all I knew.

Then darkness closed around me.

CHAPTER 35

Dumped unceremoniously back into the edu unit by my survival suit, gasping and dizzy. The sound of water. A headache, and a throbbing grey film across my vision.

The next few hours were a half-conscious, oxygen-deprived blur. Evan had saved my life, again, manoeuvring me on to the rectal connector even as his own battery flashed zero. The others told me he was unconscious too when he finally dropped through the airlock into the edu unit.

We watched in wonder as the water drained through the dripping dock point to the Services level of the main rig below. Ugly as ever: conduits, pipes, rust, metal floors ... but beautiful, oh so beautiful.

The people on the rig arrived at about the same time, drawn by the noise of our landing. They looked like what they were: survivors – dirty, tired and injured. But overcome with relief: they'd expected a structural failure or some other catastrophe, but they'd found a miracle instead.

A confusion of gasps and questions and hugs. But mostly hugs: celebratory and loving and terrified and sorry and glad all at once.

Jacob was swamped by his parents from both sides.

Alban sobbed into his mother's shoulder, his eyes all the time fixed on mine, silently thanking me.

I searched desperately for Mum, a cold feeling pitting my stomach. Had she made it? Had she been caught in one of the hab units that had caught fire?

But then there she was, elbowing her way through the crowd, her eyes streaming, her face swollen.

"I'm sorry," she whispered over and over, rocking me gently. "I'm so, so sorry…"

"No," I murmured back. "No, *I'm* sorry. I didn't mean—"

"I'm sorry I was angry… I'm sorry I wasn't there when… I'm sorry I wasn't there."

My voice cracked with emotion. "Please don't give up on me, Mum."

"*Never…*" Mum breathed. "*Never, never, never…*"

"I want to go with you," I said. "Please. Whatever we do next, I want to go with you."

306

"*Always.* For as long as you want it."

Only Evan stood alone. But not for long; Ari engulfed him in a bear hug that was so intense I wondered if Evan wished he were still wearing his survival suit.

"Evan, my boy," Ari crooned. "I thought I'd lost you! My clever, clever, *clever* boy."

"It … it was Lily really," Evan said haltingly.

Ari looked at me, tears running down his face. "Well, then. The new girl has done us proud, hasn't she? I always knew she would."

We gathered in the canteen. Mum couldn't stop hugging me. Emergency power was back, but two levels were flooded, and the sub bay was still unusable. The mood was sombre. Ari's team hurried here and there, gathering equipment and shoring up damaged conduits. The rest of us sat in a stunned daze. Small groups were scattered along the velour benches. Sleeping, or reading, or just staring. Parents hugged children. Grown-ups hugged each other. They were professionals – brave, sturdy types who'd chosen to work at the bottom of the ocean and understood the risks involved. But they were still people.

The injured nursed their bandaged arms or splinted legs. Quite a few had been hurt. One man in particular, an engineer with a bushy moustache, had burn dressings down one side of his face. They laid Dr Balgobin next to him and she lay clutching her leg and humming quietly to herself. The chair leg still protruded grotesquely – too dangerous to remove before we got topside, we were told.

"What are we going to do?" I asked Mum.

"There's a rescue sub on its way," Mum said.

"But the sub bay is destroyed? It won't be able to dock."

"Ari's team is working on it. It'll be ready for when the sub comes tomorrow."

I nodded and closed my eyes, content to lie in the warm bubble of Mum's arms. It felt like every fibre of my body had been stretched to breaking point, and only now could I relax, returning slowly, slowly, to my regular shape.

"Thank you," said a hoarse voice nearby.

I opened my eyes to see Mike, Jacob's dad, standing over me. He looked haggard. As Safety Officer, he was taking the whole rig exploding thing harder than anyone, I guessed.

"Hello, Mike," Mum said gently.

"Thank you," Mike said again. He swallowed. "Jacob told me what you did, Lily. I was wrong about you," he continued. "You saved my son. You brought him back."

"Um… Well, it wasn't just me," I said, squirming under his intense gaze. "It was a team effort."

Mike continued like he hadn't heard me. "You *saved* them all."

He wasn't the only one who thought so. Everywhere I looked I was catching curious glances. Sure, I was used to people looking at me strangely, but usually they were giving me evil stares, or worrying about what I was going to do next. This was different. These were looks that made me feel wobbly inside.

"What's going on? Why's everyone so weird all of a sudden?" I asked.

"You're a hero," Mum whispered, smiling wryly.

A hero? I liked the sound of that.

I didn't need it, though. I just needed Mum, and that hug that made me feel like I was little again, when life was understandable, and I was utterly safe and cared for.

CHAPTER 36

In the dream, Mum and Dad were fighting again. They were in the kitchen, leaning over the dining table and shouting so furiously it was hard to imagine they'd ever not hated each other.

I stood, rooted to the spot, my body tense. But I knew it was a dream, or a memory, or both muddled together, because they were using the wrong words.

"The human brain is the size of two clenched fists!" Dad shouted angrily. "It weighs about 1.5 kilograms, and from the outside it looks like a walnut, with folds and crevices!"

Mum banged the table in frustration. "There are eighty-six billion neurons inside the brain, and each neuron is connected to one thousand other neurons!"

Dad threw up his arms. "A neuron is a specialized nerve cell that receives information from other neurons through its dendrites."

"But it *sends* information through the synapses at the end of its axon!"

"Stop!" I pleaded. "Stop it, you don't even know what you're arguing about."

I remembered this fight. I remembered being there in the kitchen, Dad standing where he was standing now. The fight hadn't actually been about neurons (that made no sense at all), but it had been about something equally stupid. Mum was angry because Dad had forgotten to cook dinner, and Dad was angry because Mum had started to cook dinner herself instead of reminding him that it was his turn. I didn't know why we couldn't just order takeout.

"Dad—" I tried.

"Wait, Lily." Dad held up his finger. He turned back to Mum. "Four billion years of evolution could have selected networks with topologies and dynamics suitable for intelligence, even though they are *outside the intercellular networks* of a brain we are currently familiar with."

"Dad, please—"

"Intelligence is an emergent property of a complex system!" Mum snapped in response. "It's not *reducible* to the parts of the system in isolation."

"He didn't say it was," I shouted.

"Microbial intelligence is *just as feasible* as human

intelligence," Mum went on, ignoring me. "Mycorrhizal fungi interconnect the root system of a forest and allow trees to coordinate their defence against external threats in far more complex ways than we understand."

"And a complex system of electronics is *just as likely a host* as a human brain!"

I blinked. Now, suddenly, I was outside. I could see Mum and Dad through the window, still arguing across the dining table. It looked warm inside, almost inviting, but I was out here. Alone. Frightened. Confused. Mum was slamming her hand against the wall, punctuating her words. *And they weren't even using the right words!*

Fine, I thought, *if they aren't going to listen to me…*

Bang!

A plant pot. The explosion of mud and pottery and plants looked like a firework and a car crash mixed together. It was pretty cool.

Smaash!

Dad's herb garden had about twenty of these little pots.

Craack!

Mum and Dad were still shouting at each other inside.

Srraash!

If I kept throwing the pots at the wall then sooner or later one of them would notice.

Vraak!

Then they would stop fighting.

Ztting!

And I wouldn't be out here on my own any more.

Fsskk!

And then we could get takeout.

Crra – SMAASH – ang!

OK. So, look – I really didn't mean for that one to go through the window.

"Lily! Lily!"

The world was black and red and full of noise.

"Lily!"

The world was also wet.

I groaned. Why was I wet again? I was so tired of being wet.

"Lily, please!"

When I got topside, I was never going to take a shower ever again.

"Lily! Wake up!"

"OK, OK, I'm awake."

I sat up groggily. Evan was leaning over me, his face stark. Mum was only a second behind him, bundling through the crowd of scared-looking people. Two of Ari's ops team were nearby, desperately sealing off the burst seam that had been showering me.

"What's happening?" I mumbled.

"It started again," Mum said. "Nobody knows why."

"You were dreaming," Evan said. "I think you upset it."

"Upset it?" I asked.

My breath caught in my throat. I stared at him. He watched me in return, unflinching. Was it possible? Had I triggered this somehow? I remembered my dream. The way it had felt to stand outside and look in, hardly understanding. Throwing pot plants at the wall to get their attention so I would feel less alone.

"The fusion reactor is overloading again," Mum said. "They're trying to shut it off."

I closed my eyes, the dream of the window shattering inward was still vivid in my mind. I could hear the noise now, a great echoing, booming sound like something was shaking the rig from the outside. Mum wrapped her arms around me, whispering barely coherent, reassuring things.

She didn't know the truth. She didn't know I'd done this.

"We need to get you down to the command centre," Evan said.

"*What?*"

I shook my head. I wanted to stay here. I wanted things to get back to how they were just a little while ago, when Mum was holding me, and for just a moment everything had felt *normal* between us again.

"I don't know how to stop it," I whispered.

Evan held my gaze. "You'll figure it out."

I drew a shivering breath.

Mum's eyes flicked between us, terrified. "What's going on?"

"We need to get Lily down to the command centre," Evan explained. "She's the only one who can help."

"She needs to stay here. Where it's *safe*," Mum replied.

"Nowhere's safe unless we get Lily to the command centre," Evan said.

A hollow sound reverberated around the walls, like somebody knocking to come in. I stood slowly, feeling the floor rock under my feet.

"He's right," I said. "You need to trust me. I'm sorry, I can't explain it."

"I don't understand," Mum said pleadingly.

"Neither do I."

Mum bit her lip. "You always were a little … special."

"I know, I'm sorry." I hazarded a weak smile. "Mum, I need to go."

"OK, fine." Mum puffed air out of her mouth, defeated. "But I'm coming with you."

We headed down, our feet clanging on the metal grille and the lights flickering and fizzing around us. The pressure doors were sealed shut at the flooded the Recreation level, and a murky blueness glowed from the viewing portals. I pressed my face to the glass.

"Lily, don't—" Mum warned.

The emergency lights were still on. I could see the shattered portholes on the far wall. A football floated past in slow motion. That could have been us. On a different day, if luck had landed differently.

"Lily, *come on!*" Evan hissed.

We hurried down the stairwell towards the bottom level while the rig rocked and shuddered around us. I could almost feel the violent arcs of magnetic field sweeping through the ocean, tearing at the rig with angry fingers. We passed the sub bay. It was still half flooded. The external pressure doors had been repaired, and they were using ROVs to dig out enough of a path for a sub to dock. Ari's team waded urgently through the water, clearing the last of the debris from the waterlock.

The stairs ended as we reached the very bottom of the rig. The command centre looked different to the last time I'd seen it. With the ops room flooded, Ari had moved in several bulky monitors and old-school keyboards from storage and constructed a makeshift operations desk over one half of Carter's slick line of touchscreens. Coffee cups littered the floor, as did several untidy piles of ring binders with the words *EMERGENCY OPERATING PROCEDURES* printed in loud capitals on the covers. Three of Ari's team were yanking unceremoniously at electrical conduits behind the giant screen.

"Kids? Ruth?" Ari looked strained. "It's not safe down here; you're supposed to stay in the canteen."

"We need to see the rig schematic," Evan said before Mum could say anything.

"The what now?" Ari said.

A vibration rumbled beneath our feet like an earthquake.

316

Everyone looked anxiously at the domed windows. They were half covered, pressed into the silt when the sub bay supports had collapsed. There was a crack along one of them, and a knotted line where the aluminosilicate had automatically repaired itself. They weren't designed for this. If the rig moved another centimetre they would fail.

"I can help," I said. "You know I can."

Ari thought for a moment, then gestured towards a nearby workstation. "Take that one. God knows, we need all the help we can get."

I sat down and looked at the schematic. Everything was blinking red. It looked like a traffic jam. The fail-safes had locked again; the fusion reactor couldn't dissipate its energy. The magnetic fields of the containment grid had swollen with the excess power, a feedback loop that was getting worse. They arched through the surrounding ocean, pulling at the steel rig like they were trying to shake us loose.

I could feel the euglenoid clearly now. Inside the rig and inside my head. It was black and cold. It was fury and frustration.

Why are you doing this?

"Keep an eye on the coolant levels," Ari said. "If Battery Room Three goes, we're all done for."

I reached forward and adjusted valve 532F. It rerouted coolant and took the pressure off a bank of heating circuits.

I felt the euglenoid shift. Uncertain. Watchful. *So dark... So alone...*

I traced the energy surge to a series of fail-safes and tripped each one in turn, breaking the circuits in those parts of the rig to force the current elsewhere.

"Lily, what are you—?" Mum started.

"Shh... Let her do this," Evan said, cutting her off gently.

"She's doing OK," Ari confirmed. "The Control Network's gone wild again, but we can get it stable by hand if we need to."

I worked quickly at the controls, chasing the power fluctuations as they coursed around the system, watching the euglenoid blunder through the Control Network. I could see it in the shifting patterns of the user interface, but I could feel it inside my head at the same time. If I anticipated its movements, I could get ahead of it, figure out which part of the rig was going to malfunction next and stop the problems from cascading.

A noise and the sound of a scuffle broke out behind me.

"What in the name of insanity is *she* doing here?" Carter yelled.

"Let her be!" Ari said. "She has a knack for this stuff."

I flushed a conduit that was getting too hot and dumped the superheated water into the Recreation level. I shut down a stuttering bank of CO_2 scrubbers and set them to reboot. But I was just buying time. The failures were getting faster.

Thoughts... *Vast. Black. Lonely.* They scratched at the inside of my head. *Alone. Frightened.*

Stop … please stop, I whispered.

Alerts pinged and I silenced them. Lines of magnetism thrummed through the rig and caused the walls to shudder like vast sails in a gale.

"Why has it started again?" Mum murmured, almost to herself.

"Lily was having a dream," Evan replied softly.

A heavy, twisting metal sound echoed around the walls. Surges of current curled through the rig, squeezing and pulling us like we were a weed being uprooted.

I closed my eyes. Imagine if the rig was alive. Imagine if all those kilometres of conduits were its nervous system, all those thousands of sensors its nerve endings. Taken together, all those interconnections might rival the complexity of a living thing.

That's what Dad had been trying to tell me in my dream. *A complex system of electronics is just as likely a host as a human brain.* Just as the complex system of roots and interconnecting mycorrhizal fungi can enable a forest to exhibit a kind of intelligence. *That's* why Maximus had requested Mum's expertize.

"Get her off that console *immediately*," Carter hissed.

"I can't do that, sir." Ari grunted with the strain of holding Carter back. "I didn't listen to her the last time; I'll be damned if I don't listen to her again."

"When this is over, Ari," Carter spat, "I'll see that you never work a rig again."

"Fine with me," Ari answered sincerely.

"Lily, listen to me," Evan whispered. "Stop thinking about the schematic. That's not what's really going on here. It's in your head. It's in the rig. You need to find some other way to communicate with it. Do you understand?"

I nodded. He was right.

I could feel the euglenoid inside my head. Not words. Not even images. It was moving around inside my thoughts just as it was moving around inside the rig's systems. I could hear Maximus in my mind. *It's learning so fast...* But it was still a child.

Imagine a baby stirring in its cot. Imagine something is disturbing it, making it unhappy. You don't know what the source of the disturbance is, but you know that any minute now it's going to start screaming, and when it does, its scream is going to rip the world apart.

Look, I don't understand any of this, I whispered. *But you've got to trust me. Stop hurting the rig and I can help you.*

Words were useless, of course. It heard only feelings.

I thought of Dad. I formed the memory of him in my head. His big, soft hands. The look he had on his face when he was in his element, figuring out some complex question of maths or computers. What would he say right now?

Chill out, Lilypad.

Chill out? Are you serious? It's trying to kill us!

A bank of fail-safes locked and flashed red, covering the schematic.

It's not the thing, it's the feeling behind the thing, Dad's voice said.

A warning blinked on the screen:

PLASMA CONTAINMENT UNSTABLE.

I opened an alternative path and allowed the current to dissipate.

I had to get its attention. I squeezed my eyes tight shut. With Dad, you always had to make an effort to get his attention – you had to play the user interface game or ask him about work. Only after that could you have a proper conversation.

I formed the memory of school in my head. The assembly where they told us about Hanna's "nearly fatal" accident and the dangers of vandalism, the other children watching me, their bewilderment, their gradual moving away.

How utterly alone I had felt, how utterly alien.

There!

The euglenoid turned sharply towards me. I felt its thoughts sting as they touched my own. So vast, so different.

A tremor caught in my throat. If it could rip apart the rig, what might it do inside my head?

The answer came almost instantly: memories leapt into my mind from nowhere. Bright, technicolour memories that I recognized but had never seen so clearly before.

The time I put the remote control in the blender.

The time I poked a hole in the pipe under the bath with a biro and flooded the living room for the second time in a month.

I drew a sharp, gasping breath. *I'm falling!* No, worse than falling. *I'm sinking!*

"Lily? Are you OK?"

I shook my head, but I couldn't answer. The memories were coming more quickly, the euglenoid rifling through my mind, looking for something, hammering at the walls of the rig.

The police standing at our door, the fear on Mum's face.

Emptying a bottle of milk on to Mum and Dad's mattress.

The day Dad left—

I shrank from the memory. Each memory was like opening a vein. The euglenoid rushed to it, devoured it.

It's trying to kill me.

No, Dad's voice said. *You're thinking about it all wrong.*

Driving the pressure jar into the porthole, wishing one or the other would smash. When something breaks like that … it's like you exhale the shards of glass and the feelings go with them.

You're the interface, Lily. Help it.

I closed my eyes. The shuddering of the rig was constant now. Panicked shouts. Mum was tugging at my shoulder. Ari and Carter were arguing.

Evan's voice was calm and steady near my ear: "It's working, Lily."

I forced another memory into my mind.

Lying in bed with Mum and Dad after the mattress incident. They'd had to buy a new mattress, of course, because the old one stank. We were testing it for the first time. It was Sunday, and it was raining outside, and nobody wanted to get up. So, we lay like that, with me warm and sandwiched between them while Dad read a book to us.

Safe. Calm. Not alone.

I felt the euglenoid shift inside my head. Questioning. Curious.

Another memory: *me and Dad geeking out over his new phone, Dad not mentioning the fact that he only had to buy a new one because I had destroyed his old one.*

Forgiven.

I have a lot of things in my head that I'm not keen to think about. Things that sit like great, ugly spiders inside my brain. I push them down and down and I used to think that was enough to be rid of them ... but it doesn't work. They dwell inside you; they leak out.

I don't want to remember, I thought.

You have to.

Now another memory. *The day Dad moved out. His rucksack sitting by the door. He looked so lonely. Lost, like a little boy.*

The euglenoid moved in, scrambling nimbly over the memory, tasting it, forcing it more vividly into my mind.

I'd prised every key from his laptop. I felt guilty about it. But I could see his face more clearly now. A flicker of a smile behind his eyes, like maybe he already knew. "Chill out, Lilypad," *he'd said.* "It's OK."

Then something else. Something I'd forgotten. *Mum reaching forward and putting her arms around him, hugging him. She had tears in her eyes.* "Look after yourself," *she'd whispered.* "Drive safely."

Loved.

I stopped. The euglenoid stopped.

I felt its immense thoughts halt as if in contemplation. It seemed to understand something ... something more, possibly, than I understood myself.

Then – *clunk!* Like a heavy tool being set down.

CHAPTER 37

The atmosphere in the command centre was ... *tense*. The silence was somehow worse than the sounds of grinding steel.

The others watched me warily: Mum, Evan, Ari, Carter ... the assorted members of Ari's team as well as Holden and the rest of Carter's. They looked dazed, relieved and terrified all at once.

I looked at the schematic. The fail-safes were operational again, routing power around the rig exactly as they were designed to do. The containment field had settled back into alignment and was no longer tearing at the rig's infrastructure.

"Well, I'll be..." Ari sighed. "She did it. Lily did it."

There was a ripple of relieved laughter, but Carter cut through it, shoving his way to the console where I was sitting.

"Does somebody want to tell me what in the blue blazes is going on here?" he bellowed.

"Nothing," said Ari innocently. "Lily's got a talent for this stuff. I've seen her do it before."

"She gets it from her dad," Evan added.

Mum nodded her agreement.

Carter's eyes narrowed. All of the false niceness was gone now. He looked shrewd and dangerous, like a snake sliding through the grass. "Nobody's *that* good."

I felt my heart begin to thud. What had he seen? A teenage girl sitting down at a computer terminal and bringing the rig under control? He was right. That didn't seem very likely.

But what *had* really happened? The euglenoid had understood me. The memories, the feelings they evoked, they'd meant something to it.

Thought and feeling, that's what the euglenoid was. Pure emotion, brooding at the bottom of the ocean for billions of years. *Kāne, sensing that he was separate from the Po, pulled himself free of Po.* And now it was inside my head, I was the interface. I shivered.

I looked around and saw anxious faces. Suspicious faces.

Carter spoke without taking his eyes off me: "You want me to believe that a sixteen-year-old child just realigned a fluctuating fusion reactor when my best man" – he slapped Holden's startled shoulder – "was completely and utterly useless?"

Ari scratched his beard nervously.

"She figured out how to fly the amphipod pretty quickly," Evan said. "Some people just have the knack."

"What other explanation do you have?" Mum asked.

"Sabotage," Carter answered without a moment's hesitation. "She knew what to do all along. She vandalized my rig so she could pretend to be a hero."

"Oh, come *on*…" Ari protested.

"No," Mum said firmly. "Lily wouldn't do that."

"Really?" Carter replied. "She nearly killed her best friend. Who knows what she's capable of?"

Mum's face was set and cold, her work face.

Carter took another step closer to her. "Are you really telling me you believe she had nothing to do with this? Does that sound plausible to you?"

Mum wavered, then shook her head slightly. At last, she said, "I don't expect you to understand, Carter, but I trust my daughter. I don't need any other explanations. If she tells me she figured out how to realign your – frankly, criminally unsafe – fusion reactor, then I believe her." She stood up. "We're done here."

A warm glow of gratitude spread inside me. Mum held out her hand, and I almost reached for it. *Is this it? Will the euglenoid stay quiet now?* I could keep awake until the sub came, would that be enough? But even if it was, I couldn't let Mum leave like this, I realized. If I let her leave now, and then she found out the truth later, she'd never trust me again.

I could still feel the euglenoid inside my head. Somehow my memories had quietened it down, but it was still there. A monster. A cold drop of ocean lodged in the grey soup of my brain. It hadn't gone anywhere. It was waiting. Thinking. I didn't know what it wanted. I didn't know what it would do next.

"There is something I need to tell you," I said.

Evan shook his head, but I ignored him. Slowly, hardly believing I was doing it, I reached into my flight suit pocket and took out the pressure jar. "Mum, you need to promise not to freak out too much."

I placed the pressure jar on the table.

There was a collective intake of breath; a strangled half-scream–half-gasp from Holden or one of the other technicians behind me. Mum's eyes grew wide.

It would have been better if it were just the glowing spots of light we'd started with. But the euglenoid had moved beyond that. *It's learning so fast.*

It had a face now. It still looked a little like me, but in certain lights it looked a little like Maximus, and a little like Mum and Carter and Evan as well … the same way a child looks a little bit like its parent but is different at the same time.

It blinked.

"What in the *abomination*...?" Carter ran out of words and stared instead.

Mum sat heavily, her hand clutched to her mouth.

Ari pressed both hands to his beard and squeezed like he was wringing out a sponge.

"That's ... new," Evan remarked dryly.

"It's the sample we brought back from the Rift," I said. "I think it's the euglenoid Maximus was studying."

"It has a *face*," Ari breathed.

"It has a face now," I said. "It didn't at first, then it figured it out, I think by looking through my memories."

Carter regained his composure. "Explain."

I shook my head. "I... I can't."

"I think I know what's happening," Evan said.

Carter made a sweeping gesture, an ironic yielding of the floor.

"The euglenoid's intelligent," Evan said. "Not individually – they're basically just eukaryotes. But all together, they're like neurons in a brain. We don't know how intelligent they are, but Lily played tag with them at least."

Evan waited while this thought sank in.

"Second, the euglenoid seems to be able to interfere with the rig's systems. Maybe it gives out some kind of electromagnetic field? I don't know. It killed the power on our amphipods when we first encountered it. I think it's causing the reactor to become unstable."

"*The euglenoid* is what's trying to destroy my rig?" Carter said incredulously.

"I don't like the sound of this," Ari murmured.

"Third," Evan continued, seemingly unfazed by whatever Carter thought. "The euglenoid appears to have bonded with Lily somehow."

I opened my mouth. Closed it again. Being the centre of attention for being psychically linked to a previously undiscovered intelligent entity that was trying to kill everyone was definitely *not* a good feeling.

"Bonded?" Mum sounded terrified.

"It's imprinted on her... It reacts to her. I don't know why. But that's how she saved the rig."

"When did you figure it out?" I asked quietly.

"I felt something in the Rift as well," Evan said, facing me. "Just not as strongly as you. Then ... I knew *something* had to have triggered the ERS; I knew it wasn't you." Evan shrugged. "Then the rig blew up, and I was busy with other things. But I saw you in the edu unit with the pressure jar, and I could tell you were hiding something... You were scared, but not just because we were trapped."

"Smart cookie, this one," Ari said proudly.

Carter interrupted. "Hold it. You're telling me that she let an alien intelligence on board my rig without telling anybody? And now it's trying to kill us all?"

"We both brought it on board," Evan said. "And it's not alien."

"And it's not just on the rig or in the pressure jar, it's kind of everywhere," I added unhelpfully.

"But it *is* trying to kill us?" Carter clarified.

Trying to? I wasn't sure. *Going to?* That seemed possible. But it didn't seem like a distinction worth pointing out.

"I don't know," I replied weakly. "I think it's … confused."

Mum heaved a shaky sigh and massaged her temples. "Oh, Lily…"

"I think it might be trying to communicate," I said.

"By ripping us apart?" Carter replied. He snorted. "It couldn't have dropped us an email instead?"

"It's not *human*," I protested. My voice felt very small. "It doesn't think like us…"

Carter threw up his hands in frustration. "I actually don't care," he said. "You scientists can ponder this all you like, but that's not my thing. I'm just a lowly installation manager, aren't I? The fact remains: *that thing* is in my rig, and it's messing with my fusion reactor. I don't care if it's trying to give us pipe organ lessons, I want it *gone*."

"What are you going to do?" I said, fear rising in my voice.

"I'm going to do what I should have done a long time ago."

My eyes flashed to Mum. "Mum, you can't let him—"

She was already on her feet, her expression wild.

"We need to think this through... This is an important discovery. Maybe the *most* important. We need to study it—"

"As of this moment," Carter interrupted, each word quick and sharp and clipped, "we are at war with a hostile intelligence" – he pointed accusingly at me – "which *she* brought on to my rig and remains in secret communication with." His words rang out, stunning even Mum into silence. He turned to the three technicians standing behind him. "Holden, MacMillan – prep the AUVs and go see if the ANFO explosives are still good. As soon as that sub bay is operational, we're going to blast the east ridge to high heaven. That's where it came from; we're going to take the fight to it." He turned to Ari. "When the rescue sub arrives, I want you to start clearing everyone off the rig." He glared at me. "Starting with *her.*"

Ari frowned but nodded tightly.

Mum's sternest work voice rang out in response: "The rig is obliged to allow the science team due access and sufficient time to investigate all potential—"

Carter rounded on her. "There is no *science team.* Or didn't you get the memo?"

"You have no authority to disband the team—"

"I *already* disbanded it!" Carter raged, his face turning red.

"In the light of the circumstances—" Mum pressed on bravely, talking over him.

"In the light of my *arse!*" Carter blared. "This is my rig, and I call the shots, and you can send as many emails as you like, it won't change a pretty thing."

Ari coughed nervously. "Maybe we should wait until we can make contact—"

"*You,*" Carter snapped, "are basically fired and don't get an opinion."

Mum glared coldly at him. "You've been waiting for an opportunity like this all along, haven't you?"

"Yes." Carter smiled, nodding. "Yes, I have."

Mum said something in response, and Carter snarled his answer back, but I'd stopped listening. I felt exhausted, the euglenoid pressed steadily against my thoughts.

"Stop it, please," I said, my voice weak.

I'd had enough. I put my hands over my ears. Something was happening to me; a feeling was building up inside. I hated the sound of arguing. Arguing became a habit for Mum and Dad, years of accumulated argument made their muscles strong in that direction and weak in every other direction, that was all.

"*Please,* stop," I whispered.

The euglenoid didn't like them arguing either. Or at least, it didn't like the way their arguing made me feel.

My heart hammered in my chest. I couldn't stop it.

Sitting in my room, listening to Mum and Dad fighting downstairs.

"*Please!*" I yelled.

CRRHRUNK!

A twisting, tearing metal kind of sound. The crack in the domed window reopened and a jet of water briefly spurted in before the aluminosilicate fizzed and sealed the fissure. My breath shuddered in my throat. The euglenoid twisted inside me, I could hardly tell which feelings were mine and which belonged to it.

"Did she just do what I think she did?" Holden said quietly.

The other technicians nodded, staring at me.

Lily the outsider. Lily the atrocity.

"Mum…?" I said, feeling sick.

Mum threw her arms around me, and I gripped her tightly. I could feel the euglenoid inside my head. Watching. It didn't understand.

"Lock her up," Carter said firmly.

"Lock her— What?" Ari sounded outraged. "She's a kid."

"That's not going to happen," Mum said darkly.

"I'm doing her a favour, Dr Fawcett," Carter growled. "If the rest of the crew get their hands on her it'll be much worse."

Mum gripped me tighter. He was right. I was used to the scared, suspicious looks that came when people didn't understand you. But this was different. Too many people were too scared. I wasn't safe any more.

"It's OK," I whispered. "He's right. It's for the best."

Mum's face strained. She nodded through her tears. "Just for a little while, Lilypad. Until the sub arrives, OK?"

I nodded bravely. I could feel their eyes on me. I felt small, terrified, and alone.

Nobody said anything for a few moments. Then Holden shuffled timidly. "Sir?"

"Yes, what is it?" Carter said.

"Sir, w–where should we put her?"

I watched Carter thinking it over. Lots of areas on the rig were code-locked, but that would stop you getting *in*, not stop you getting *out*. At last, he found his solution. "The stationery cupboard," he said, smiling meanly. "We'll use the stationery cupboard."

CHAPTER 38

LILY FAWCETT: DEEPHAVEN PERSONAL LOG
DAY 18
On the one hand, I patched things up with Mum and saved my classmates from certain watery death. On the other hand, I appear to have psychically bonded with an alien entity intent on killing us all… Oh, and now I'm locked in a stationery cupboard.

Not alien, I thought, correcting myself. *It's been here longer than we have.* Billions of years longer. I could still feel it, a soft presence in my mind. It had followed us back from the Rift and found its way into my head and the rig's systems. It was a mind made from the interaction of billions of tiny eukaryotes, but it couldn't tell the electrolytic solution of the sea from the network of wires and circuits of the rig or the electromagnetic pulses of my brain.

But why had it chosen me? Why not Evan? Maximus had brought back samples to the rig and nothing like this had happened before. I knew the answer. There was something in all those things I didn't like to think about, some sense of them that had leaked out of me, which the euglenoid had recognized and reached for. And then I'd reached out to it in turn. I'd formed memories in my mind like laying breadcrumbs for a squirrel.

But what did it want? My mind felt thick and stupid. I couldn't figure it out. Maybe it was just stuck? Or maybe there was something else.

I gazed hopelessly around me. I was sitting on a cardboard box labelled *Biros*. Two tall racks of shelves loomed either side of me, brimming with printer paper, cartridges and various other supplies. *There should be a rule*, I thought bitterly. *When you design an experimental deep-sea mining rig, you should have to make it look cool.* There should be a theme, maybe a colour scheme or something, and a logo. But most of all … the stationery cupboards shouldn't have locks.

I closed my eyes and thought about the euglenoid. Images flickered in my mind, so vast and incomprehensible they nearly took my breath away. I was terrified. It's a strange thing to be terrified of yourself. To no longer *trust* yourself. It wasn't a new feeling for me.

The euglenoid stirred. The rig rumbled distantly with its dreams. Our thoughts were muddled together. I'd let it rifle through my memories, and now I couldn't tell its memories from my own. If I let my mind wander, I could forget that I was Lily (locked in a stationery cupboard) and start to think I was … something else. Something that didn't even have a name for itself yet. Something that was ancient and new at the same time.

Mum and Carter were still arguing outside. Their voices ricocheted between them like angry table-tennis balls. I couldn't make out their words, but I was sure Mum was sticking up for me, arguing against whatever Carter had planned for us when we got topside, trying to protect the euglenoid. She trusted me now. For whatever reason, as badly as things had turned out, she was standing by me, and that filled me with a warm glow.

But their arguing was also making me anxious. I could feel the low shudder building inside me, and with it the same shudder built inside the rig's walls.

The rescue sub was due any minute, and when it came, I'd be first off the rig.

GHHHRR-NNHKK!

But I couldn't leave.

The realization came to me sharply: *the euglenoid didn't want me to leave.* I was thinking of leaving in the ops room when the first of the overloads began. I was dreaming of home when the trouble started again. I'd bonded with it; perhaps Maximus had bonded with it too, and it was terrified of being left on its own again.

"Lily?" A hiss of static. "Lily, can you hear me?"

I jumped and spun around, looking for the source of the noise.

"*Lily…*"

Hearing things now?

"Who's there?" I said to the empty room.

"Lily, it's me."

Evan's voice crackled in the air around me, and I finally saw the black dome of a security camera set into the ceiling. *Evan!* He'd come. He was here … virtually, at least. I was surprised by how good it felt not to be alone any more.

"How are you doing that?" I asked.

"Intra-rig security system," Evan said. "My dad built in a whole bunch of back doors when he designed it."

"You can hack the rig's security system?"

"Yes."

"Do the cabins have them—?" I stopped myself. "Forget it, I don't want to know."

"I wanted to check that you were OK," Evan said.

I nodded slightly, not sure I had a good answer. "It's sleeping."

"Good," Evan said. "Just try and keep it calm until the sub comes."

My chest tightened. The sub was completely the wrong thing to mention.

"What's Carter doing?" I asked. "And what's an AUV?"

"Autonomous Underwater Vehicle," Evan explained. "He's going to programme them to blast the east ridge and seal the passageway."

"It won't stop it," I said. "It'll only scare it, make it more dangerous."

"I know," Evan replied.

"We have to stop him."

Evan didn't respond. I could tell from the faint hiss of the connection that he was still there, thinking. "There's something that's been bothering me," he said. "You said that Dad had modified Cephalopod to make it play tag like the euglenoid?"

"Yes."

"But it wasn't a modification. It was *already* part of the game. I programmed it a week before Dad died."

I could hear the fear in his voice, the sound of somebody who didn't trust himself any more. How could he have written the same game that the euglenoid had played with his father before Maximus had seen the game for himself?

It didn't know it was alive until we played together.

"I think this all started when your dad went into the Rift," I said. "It's in his notes. I think he woke it up somehow, and when he died, he left it all alone. It's been reaching out ever since. You felt it. Joy and Isaac felt it."

"But it's different with you. Nobody else can do what you do."

"I think we bonded in the Rift," I said. "The deeper we are, the stronger the connection, and I reached out to it down there. I didn't mean to, but it recognized something of itself in me."

"*Recognized* something?"

"I don't know… Loneliness, I guess. Being different." I waited, but Evan was silent. "Evan, if Carter makes me leave, I think something terrible is going to happen."

"What?" Evan said.

If I left, the euglenoid would do what I had done when Dad left: it would smash.

"I need you to get me out of here," I said. "I can't be on that submersible when it leaves, and we need to get to the amphipods and stop Carter blasting the ridge."

Evan's laugh sounded like a burst of static. "You're not serious?"

"I am."

"There are a lot of people very keen to get you off this rig."

I imagined Evan in his room, his laptop balanced on his bare knees, the worried, thoughtful frown on his face that I was starting to feel oddly affectionate towards. All I wanted was to be a normal kid, to go visit him in his room and hang out.

"We can't let them," I whispered.

"OK," he said at last. "I'll think of something."

CHAPTER 39

The rig creaked and groaned like it was in a storm.

My mind creaked and groaned with it.

Ari led me into the sub bay, his hand on my shoulder, Holden and two other members of Carter's team hovering close by, watching me like I was a prisoner at risk of escaping.

"I know it's not your fault, Lily," Ari said gently. "There are just a lot of nervous people out there; this is for your own good."

Tired, resentful faces watched me from the shadows. *They know*, I thought. *And they're furious with me and terrified of me. Carter must have told them.*

"Ari, please," I said. "I need to stay on the rig. This is a mistake."

"Don't worry, Lily," Ari said. "Soon as we're topside everything'll feel different."

"No," I insisted. "You don't understand—"

"It's OK, Lily," Ari said more firmly.

The scene in the sub bay was chaotic. Ari's team had opened the forward hatch of the rescue sub and they were busy hurling the last few fittings into the waterlock. They were stripping out everything that wasn't strictly necessary so they could fit as many people on board as possible. The first batch of the crew – the children, the injured, and the ones most freaked out – were gathered nearby, waiting for the OK. Dr Balgobin was laid out on a stretcher alongside three other members of the crew, her eyes glassy.

I looked around anxiously for Evan. I hadn't expected them to be *guarding* me. How could he possibly get me out of this?

Another ominous rumbling outside caused everyone's eyes to flick anxiously towards the ceiling, and then, after a moment, to me.

"Lily! Are you OK?" Mum threw her arms around me, holding tight. Carter's men jostled closer until Mum warned them off with a fierce look. "I'm going to sue him," Mum told me. "He's acting completely outside his authority. I'm drafting some extremely strongly worded emails."

"Mum, we can't let him—"

"*Shhh…*" Mum murmured. "It'll be fine, I promise. I'll

send a full report to the International Seabed Authority. We'll cement a moratorium that'll stop all future excavation in this area."

"It'll be too *late* by then," I insisted. "He'll have already sealed off the Rift."

Mum didn't seem to hear. I felt a sinking feeling inside, a sense of inevitability. Mum was the only one who could possibly challenge Carter now, but she didn't understand that we were past the point where strongly worded emails would do any good. She kissed me on the forehead. "Get on board now. I'm right behind you, OK?"

Ari ushered me to the hatch. "Children first."

I froze, staring into the cramped darkness below. Where was Evan? If he was going to do something, he'd better do it *quickly*. "Ari, *please*—"

"It's OK, Lily," Ari said. "You'll be topside before you know it."

Somewhere overhead, a rusty sound, like somebody scraping a garden rake across a blackboard, echoed in the darkness. Everybody stiffened. It felt as if a bolt might shear or a seam might burst at any moment, and our time and luck would be gone in one freezing gush of seawater.

"Come on, Lily," Ari urged me. "We all want to get out of here."

I clambered down the ladder into the sub and stumbled along the walkway to the main cabin. The euglenoid scratched at the inside of my mind. It knew I was leaving, and it didn't like it. I thought about Dad's laptop, the keys popping off one by one. I could feel it watching me.

Fretful. Alert.

Where is Evan?

Ari's team still bustled around inside, unbolting and cutting and hurling the last pieces of unnecessary equipment through the forward hatch. The seats had been removed and large straps hung from the roof instead.

"That's it, Ari!" one of the engineers called. "We're all done."

"All right!" Ari called back. "Next batch!"

The rest of the crew bustled on behind me. I could sense their fear just as I could sense the euglenoid's.

They had no idea of the mistake we were making.

The walls felt like they were closing in around me. Another tremor resonated through the sub. The euglenoid's question pressed against my mind, and I tried my best not to let it hear my answer.

"It's getting worse," somebody remarked, casting me a murderous glance.

"Let's hurry it up," another person nearby said.

Evan isn't coming, I thought. Something had gone wrong. Maybe Carter had figured out what he was planning and locked him up as well.

I drew a shaky breath and tried to touch the euglenoid in my mind. *It's OK...* I whispered. But I knew it wouldn't be. The memory of Dad forced its way back into my head. The day he left, in vivid colours, his wrecked laptop in his rucksack by the door. The look on his face as he hugged me goodbye.

The euglenoid needed me. It had been alone for ever, and then it had discovered people. It wouldn't let me leave now. I remembered the two amphipods resting on the rocks beneath the edu unit; it had been trying to tell me what it wanted all along.

"Were you serious?" a voice asked.

Evan.

He stood so close I could feel the warmth of his body. His hand brushed the back of mine, and a shiver of relief ran through me. His face was drawn, his eyes darting around the cabin.

"Tell me you have a plan," I said urgently.

He gave me a sideways look, a whisper of a smile. "Sure I do. But you're not going to like it."

He ushered me towards the front of the sub. Ysabel and Jacob were busy wrapping their wrists into the hanging straps nearby. Jacob winked clumsily.

"Jacob and Ysabel are helping?" I said, feeling suddenly sceptical.

"We need them," Evan replied.

"Is this plan better than your last plan?" I asked.

"Marginally. Come on."

We slipped past the bulkhead at the front to where an

engineer was unbolting a large sonar array on the other side of the small hatchway.

"We'll be launching any moment," I whispered. "If you're going to do something—"

Evan pulled me against the wall, and we waited there a moment. We were so close I could feel his heart pounding against my own.

"Wait for my signal," he whispered, his breath on my ear.

Suddenly, a cry came from the far end of the sub.

"Get us out of here!" Ysabel's voice rang out shrilly. "We have to go *now*!" She rushed to the front of the sub, clawing her way past the others to get to the pilot's console.

"Quickly!" Evan said to the engineer. "She's freaking out; she'll damage something!"

The engineer at the front hatch bustled past us and caught Ysabel by the arm.

Jacob followed. "The rig's flooding! Um … again!" he yelled, rather less convincingly than Ysabel.

Panic swept through the sub. Instant. Visceral. The nervous crew shoved backwards and forwards like a tide. Some were crowding around Ysabel, trying to calm her down; others had concluded that there was a problem with the sub and were attempting to get off; yet another group had heard the commotion and decided that the sub was the safest place to be and were forcing their way further inside.

"Get on, get on!" somebody shouted. "We need to *leave*."

"Lily!" Mum's voice screamed through the furore, on board with the others now.

"I'm here! I'm fine," I called back.

"Stay where you are!" Mum shouted.

"*Now!*" Evan whispered close by.

We turned, two steps, and slipped out through the hatch and on to the deck of the sub. We stood precariously, the water of the waterlock slopping wetly against the side of the sub below us. We could see Ari across the deck at the rear. His back was to us as he ushered the last of the nervous crew on board.

"Let's go! Let's go!" a voice yelled from below.

I heard Ysabel scream from inside again, making doubly sure that the sub would launch and nobody would do a final roll call: "The hull's cracking like an egg!"

And Jacob: "We're ... going to get really wet!"

Ari hit the emergency launch lever and stepped back. In the same moment, the forward hatch snapped shut, and the water around the sub began to boil as the thrusters kicked in. My feet trembled near the edge of the sub, barely managing to avoid slipping into the water beneath me.

"Now what?" I asked.

"We have to jump or the sub will pull us down with it," Evan replied.

I stared at the black, icy water below us. "Jump? You didn't tell me that was part of the plan!"

"*You* wanted to stow away on a half-flooded rig," Evan

said, his voice rising. "I don't think *you're* in a position to complain about *my* plans."

"Have you any idea how cold the water in a waterlock is?"

"It's heated," Evan said defensively.

"To, like, one degree?"

"Slightly less," Evan admitted.

"I really wish you'd think through your plans more carefully!" I yelled.

But then there was no time for anything else. The water rose up around our feet, and the bitter cold bit into me as the sub dropped from beneath us.

I took a breath. And jumped.

CHAPTER 40

It was like jumping into stone. The icy water slammed the air out of me. I tried to scream. Sank. Saltwater rushed into my mouth and burned my lungs. I kicked and my head burst above the water; I thrashed with my arms and legs to stay afloat.

The decking of the sub bay was only a few metres away, but it might as well have been a kilometre for all the chances I had of reaching it. If it wasn't for the churn of the departing sub beneath us, Ari and the others would have seen me in an instant.

I felt the currents of the waterlock and the disappearing sub dragging me down. I felt the walls shuddering, the euglenoid taking my fear and turning it back on to the rig.

"Float!" Evan gasped. "You have to float until the shock reflex passes."

I opened my mouth to reply, but the water choked me again and my head went under. The current clawed at me like fingers reaching up from below. I fought my way back to the surface and emerged to the sound of grinding steel. I gulped air like a beached fish.

"You're in shock," Evan said. "Lie back and float."

Absurdly, Evan was floating on his back nearby, looking for all the world like he was playing Starfish in the local swimming pool. His hair formed a loose halo around his head.

I drew a long, shuddering breath and forced myself to hold it. He was right. They'd taught us this. Cold water shock. The natural tendency to panic, to thrash around until you ran out of energy. I leaned back, copying, letting my legs rise to the surface.

"The first ninety seconds after you fall into freezing water, your body will want to fight, but you have to float," Evan recited breathlessly. "Lie on your back until you can control your breathing."

I felt calmer. I was beyond cold now. My arms and legs felt like clay.

"Didn't you listen ... to anything ... in your safety briefing?" Evan gasped.

"Not particularly," I replied.

"OK, now paddle slowly," Evan said. "This way ... not where they're working."

Above our heads, we could hear Ari and his team prepping the sub bay for the rescue sub's return. I took a moment to appreciate the elegance of Evan's plan. If we'd tried to slip away before we were on the sub, they'd have just held it until they found us. They had to *think* we were on the sub when it left. That was the only way.

I clenched my teeth and paddled. Below me, I knew, the sub had most likely just exited the waterlock and entered open water, Deephaven's outer doors sliding shut just as they had after I launched myself out in the amphipod.

My arms moved beneath me like planks of wood. The water welled around my head and threatened to swamp me. One of Ari's team only had to glance in our direction, and we'd be seen. But we were hidden in the dimness of the emergency lights, and they were too busy making last minute repairs to pay attention to anything else.

I felt the reassuring bump of the metal grating, and I turned and hauled myself on to the walkway, dripping and heavy. I collapsed and lay helplessly on my back.

Evan whispered, "In here…"

I dragged myself on my hands and knees towards the noise. A storeroom of some kind, more of a cubbyhole. Then a pleasant warmth spread down my side, and I noticed an emergency space heater.

"You got us a space heater?" I said, through chattering teeth.

"Yeah. We should be OK in here for a little while," Evan breathed.

I listened to him shifting about. My body felt dead. I stared at the emergency lights glowing dimly in the ceiling, too tired to think.

"You need to get out of those clothes," Evan said, tugging his flight suit off his shoulders.

"Can't," I muttered. "Sleepy."

"*No,*" Evan said. "Don't sleep. You need to warm up."

I turned and coughed, fighting back a wave of nausea. I tugged weakly at my flight suit, but my hands felt like boulders. Evan helped me undo it, then he took my hands and rubbed them vigorously, breathing warmth into them.

"Velcro, see?" he said softly. "For safety."

The warmth of the heater against my shoulders slowly gave me more energy. I sat up, and Evan passed me a space blanket that I hastily wrapped around myself. Once fastened, it made a kind of makeshift, silvery – very unflattering – flight suit. Hanna would have been horrified. Or maybe she'd have found a way to make it work.

I shook my head and tried to concentrate. Evan sat heavily next to me, fastening his own space blanket.

"That was a really stupid plan," I said.

He laughed through chattering teeth. He reached across and put his arm around my shoulder. I leaned into him, feeling the warmth of his body.

The thought of Mum came to me with a sharp stab of regret. She'd have realized by now that I wasn't on the sub. She'd try and make them turn back. My god, she'd be formidable.

But it wouldn't work. There was no way the pilot would turn back.

That gave us two hours while the sub was out of contact before they returned for the next load and told Carter that we were missing. Maybe three hours, tops. I hoped it would be enough.

"What now?" Evan said.

"Get to the amphipods and stop the AUVs before they blast the east ridge."

Evan nodded shortly. "Fine. This way. Try not to be seen."

I glanced at my shining flight suit. "In this?"

Evan smiled as he turned away. I rubbed my fingers, squeezing the last of the bitter coldness out of them. We crept around the outer gantry of the sub bay. Ari's team still milled around, shoring up burst seams and doing their best to make the sub bay secure for the sub's return.

Nobody looked in our direction.

We darted into the main corridor and headed towards Maximus's lab and the amphipods. It was eerily quiet. Normally, the rig hummed with the distant rumble of the fusion reactor, the electrics, the life support systems. After a while you stopped noticing it. But Ari had cycled down even the emergency power in the hope of keeping the reactor more stable, and the silence of it felt shocking.

"It wasn't easy getting a new access card," Evan remarked.

"I'm sorry."

"I stole it from Dr Balgobin while they were loading her on to the sub."

"I'm sure she'll understand," I said.

Onwards, into the chevroned no-access area, the sound of our footsteps impossibly loud.

A noise made us freeze: the heavy shivering of the grated floor, two people striding this way. We hunted desperately for somewhere to hide, but it was too late.

Carter's voice: "Head back to the command centre to monitor the AUVs on sonar."

"Yes, sir," Holden replied.

"How long until we're ready to blast?"

"About half an hour."

They appeared around the corner and stopped dead. Carter blinked in surprise. "Are you *kidding* me?"

I hazarded a winning smile. "I guess I missed the bus."

Evan's eyes were wide, his body tense like he was planning to run or fight. Carter looked bigger and more immovable than ever, his body made of steel and gristle and malintent. I turned, thinking we might make a run for it, but MacMillan had appeared behind us and blocked the way.

"Do you know how long I've worked on this rig?" Carter said grimly. "Ten years. Ten long years." He drew a breath. "Do you think the suits back at head office know what it's like? Do you think they come down here to see how I'm doing? No. They just set the quotas. 'Fifty tonnes of this, Carter. Seventy tonnes of that, Carter.'"

I felt Evan's hand close around my own and then draw away. I didn't dare look, but I could feel that he'd left something in my palm. Sharp edges dug into my skin – a key card.

"All I'm trying to do is make this place a *success*," Carter said imploringly. "I'm just trying to make this place *commercially viable* so we can build *more*. Because we *need* the copper, the nickel, the manganese and the cobalt. And do you know what makes my life *harder*?" Carter licked his lips. "*You!* All the families, and research, and *kids* roaming around this place. '*Not like that, Carter, you'll hurt the rocks*,'" he sang in a mocking voice. "I will get rid of you, and that … *thing*. I will get rid of *all* the distractions. Do you understand? I'm not *losing* to you."

"It's intelligent," I said. "The euglenoid. You have no idea how intelligent it is."

I could feel the pressure building inside me. The rig groaned under my feet and a small, rapid vibration began deep within the rig's walls.

Carter glared at me, fear flashing in his eyes. He raised his voice defiantly. "Don't make me out to be the bad guy!

I dig this stuff up because people like you *want* it. You want me to dig up less down here? You want me to be more *careful*? Then you've got to use less up *there*!"

SHUCKTHUNK!

The rig lurched to one side, and I felt the wall slam against my shoulder. In the same moment, Evan threw himself forward. He caught Carter off balance and rugby-tackled him to the ground. His long arms and legs pinwheeled through the air. Carter let out a bellow of rage as he hit the ground.

"*Go!*" Evan shouted. "*Go!*"

Holden stood in my way. I kicked wildly and felt my foot connect with soft tissue. He coughed, crumpled. I turned in time to see Carter elbow Evan viciously in the face, Evan's head snapping backwards.

I ran. I cannoned into the pressure doors that led to the amphipod bay and slapped the card against the reader. The hydraulics hissed as the door ground to the side. Carter's feet hammered on the metal floor as he came after me. I slipped inside.

Carter appeared at the end of the corridor, his face red. "*LILY!*" he screamed.

A moment of hesitation. And then resolve.

"You lose!" I shouted. And hit: *Close.*

CHAPTER 41

There was a power switch to disable the pressure doors. I flipped it. I could hear Carter banging on the other side, his furious voice muffled.

"Lily! Open up! Lily, you need to *stop*!"

I hurried over to the control console. I drew a shaky breath and tried to calm myself. A bewildering array of digital readouts and systems diagrams confronted me, all manner of diagnostic displays clamouring for attention. How was I supposed to do this? The last time I'd been here it was Evan who had activated the amphipods. I'd only launched one.

I tapped a few keys. Hopeless.

But Evan must have thought I could figure it out, or he

wouldn't have given me the card. I stared at the blinking displays.

Then I saw it: one of Deephaven's standard prep sequences, just like they'd shown us at the training centre.

I hit the keys. The rack with the remaining two amphipods ground into action, sliding into view.

The amphipods lowered and the cockpits sprang open.

I smiled, feeling pleased with myself. *I am pretty good at this stuff*, I thought. *Exceptional*, some would say.

I clambered into the nearest amphipod and strapped myself in. I pulled on the shoulder straps. Servos whined as the controls adjusted themselves. My hands were already moving over them, running the diagnostic checks, warming up the ciliate drives. The gangplank withdrew. The cockpit hissed shut.

What am I doing?

I took a breath. I hit the blinking red light.

My thrusters strained as I tore through the ocean. I was numb with fear, my thoughts narrowed to a single point. I dropped fast. My ciliate drive pushed me over the uneven seabed towards the telemetry grid.

"Lily!" The sudden squawking of Carter's voice made me jump. "Lily, you've got to stop." He actually sounded worried.

I checked the console. It was OK, the UAC signal was coming from the rig.

"Those AUVs contain high explosives. You *can't* be in the water near them, do you understand me?"

"Shut them down, then," I said.

There was a pause in which I imagined Carter thinking this through. He came back levelly, almost regretfully. "I can't do that, Lily."

"Can't, or won't?"

"Come back, Lily. This is your last—"

A blast of static cut across him.

Then silence.

Out of range.

The telemetry grid blinked red beneath me. Carter wouldn't shut down the AUVs – I knew that much. Even if his conscience got the better of him, the limited range of the communications meant that they were probably too far away by now anyway.

I pushed my throttle up to maximum, watching the polymetallic nodules that littered the ocean floor rush past beneath me. They made a strange, unearthly sight. How peculiar, I thought, that the world should leave us everything we need to live and thrive harmlessly, if only we had the ingenuity to see it.

The east ridge loomed up ahead. I stared through the murk, desperate to see some sign of the AUVs. What if I couldn't find them? What if I was on the wrong part of the ridge?

Then I saw it. A trail of silt and bubbles blurring the line of rock ahead. The faint, jerky movements of the AUVs, their safety lights blinking.

My heart thrummed in my chest. My thoughts narrowed to a point. They were just ahead of me now. Three stubby, red lozenges, the whine of their thrusters loud even through the aluminosilicate cockpit. I could see the explosives crudely lashed on to their undersides. Carter wanted the passageway buried and the euglenoid sealed away for ever. He thought that would give him the freedom to blast the east ridge and extend the telemetry grid as much as he wanted. But he was wrong. He didn't know how disastrous it would be to try and force the euglenoid back into isolation now, after it had learned what it felt like to be near other minds.

I moved in on the nearest AUV. The turbulence of its thrusters shook my amphipod, pushing me backwards. I moved out to the side and came around its wake. The ridge was getting close, fast. I tapped the control and the amphipod gripper knocked heavily against the AUV's side.

Water is incompressible; they'd taught us that at the training centre. That meant that an explosion would not be absorbed, and the blast radius down here would be many times more deadly than the same size explosion topside. If they detonated now, I thought, there would be nothing left of me.

I adjusted my position and tried again. This time I got

a decent grip on the place where the thrusters connected to the main body.

I hit my reverse thrusters. The AUV tugged and bucked against the amphipod, forcing me forwards and then backwards in my harness. Its thrusters were no match for the amphipod, but the angles were all wrong. I leaned the amphipod back to get more leverage, and the AUV reared upwards, its thrusters straining. It was no good. I couldn't stop it this way. And all the time, the other two AUVs were speeding ahead.

Change of plan. I accelerated, pushing the AUV forward, catching up with the other two. What would happen if I made them collide? I wasn't sure. Would the explosives detonate on impact? Hopefully not. Down here, proximity detonators would be a safety hazard. They would be on timers.

I forced the AUV's stubby nose into the tail of the AUV in front of it—

CCRASHH—

A jolt ran through the amphipod, so hard my head connected with the cockpit and bright blue stars filled my vision. I blinked away the pain. I could feel blood streaming from my nose.

Again, I accelerated. Another jolt. One of the AUV thrusters howled as something caught in its rotor. Then it broke away, fragments of plating shearing off and disappearing behind us.

I gasped, sobbing in frustration. It wasn't working. The ridge was looming large in front of me now. Thirty seconds away, maybe less. When they reached the ridge, they would detonate.

I had to stop them.

I tried again, one last time.

SLAM!

This time the torn plating caught more fully in the thrusters of the second AUV. The plating ripped away and the rotor pulled the first AUV tight against its body. The pair of them swung upwards, connected now, dragging the amphipod with them. There was a terrible sound of straining metal and another sharp jolt as I pulled away, biting my tongue in the process.

The two AUVs spun around in the water, tangled up in each other, twisting around and around. They were sinking! They hit the seabed, their thrusters still at full power, writhing and churning up a silt cloud. I tasted salty blood in my mouth.

I grinned, satisfied. A detonation here would be OK. The crust was thick enough, and they were a good distance from the rig.

I looked up in time to see the last AUV disappear into the line of the ridge.

No, no, no, no... I hit the thrusters and accelerated towards it.

The ridge towered over me. I couldn't see the AUV any

more, but I didn't slow down. I knew where it was going. The location was already showing on my amphipod's navigational computer. I let the autopilot take over.

Darkness swallowed me as I plunged into the passageway. Stalactites and jagged spears of rock rushed past. I caught a glimpse of the AUV's safety lights as they disappeared around a bend ahead of me. I pushed the thrusters to maximum, ignoring the warning lights on the autopilot as it struggled to navigate the twisting passageway at speed. *This is stupid*, my mind screamed at me. *Turn around.*

The passage gave way and opened out into the staggering blackness of the Rift. My breath caught in my throat. The AUV loomed in my spotlights, appearing to grow larger as I approached. I slammed on my retro-thrusters and slewed to a halt.

Perfect stillness. And black. I missed this place. It felt like home, although I knew that feeling was probably not mine.

But what now?

It must be timed to detonate just inside the passageway, I thought, to ensure that it was closed from both sides. It would go off at any—

The sound of an explosion shook me, and a rush of bubbles and rocks forced its way through the passageway. A piece of something clonked heavily on the amphipod, and the pressure wave knocked me sideways. The amphipod's thrusters buzzed to regain control. Console lights flashed warnings. The other two AUVs had detonated.

My breath caught in my throat.

This one would go next.

My mind seemed to accelerate. A thousand thoughts falling over each other. There was nothing I could do. It was too late.

Would I feel it? Even for a second? Would I feel myself torn apart?

A scream filled my head.

A deluge of memories. Thoughts. Feelings.

A question. *What? What? What? What?*

The euglenoid felt my fear. But it didn't understand.

What? What? What? What? I felt it sifting through my mind, searching, trying to extract meaning. Memories cracked open inside my head; shattered fragments tore through my brain. *Pouring a pint of milk on to the mattress. Poking a hole in the pipe under the bath with a biro. Cutting the last twenty pages out of the novel Mum was reading.* All the little things I'd done to make the universe stop and look at me for just one second.

People thought I broke things because I was angry and vengeful. But they didn't understand. I wasn't breaking laptops and mobile phones. I was calling out, trying to make the universe listen to me in the only way I knew how.

I needed to warn the euglenoid about what was about

to happen. I needed to explain to it so it might forgive us, at least. I drew the memories together, forced them into something the euglenoid would understand: *our house after everything had been packed up. How small our boxes of things had looked. How large and cold our unfurnished living room had been. My insides – as empty as the house.*

Hearing the door click shut and then posting the keys back through the letter box for the estate agent to collect later—

The last AUV detonated.

CHAPTER 42

I should be dead. I certainly shouldn't be seeing the explosion.

I watched the water swell, a ball of hot gas erupting outwards, glowing white-hot from its centre. Its lazy, impossible expansion, like watching a balloon inflate. At the same time, the glowing euglenoid rushed towards the fireball, swarming it, consuming it.

Slowing it.

Is it hurting the euglenoid to do this?

I hoped not.

It was working.

It would stop the explosion from smashing the passageway and sealing off the Rift. It would save the euglenoid. But it was not enough to stop the ever-growing ball of fire from reaching and engulfing me. I felt myself thrown backwards, the world becoming pure white. Then the rocky underside of the seabed rushed to meet me, and everything was blackness once again—

I woke, shivering, a half-choke, half-sob caught in my throat. Red lights blinked urgently. An alert buzzer keened. OXYGEN LEAK. OXYGEN LEAK. There was a hairline crack in my capsule, the aluminosilicate still fizzing as it sealed the fissure.

The euglenoid had done it. It had stopped the destruction of the east ridge. By the time Carter was able to send a submersible down to find out that he'd failed, Mum's emails would have done their work, and it would be too late for him to try again.

I'd won. We'd won.

I checked the console. My oxygen level was dropping, but not that quickly. The ciliate drives appeared to be functioning. At full throttle, I could make it back to the rig before my oxygen leaked away.

But I wasn't going back.

I silenced the oxygen alarm.

I'd always known this would be a one-way trip, I just couldn't tell Evan. The euglenoid would never let me go; we were connected now, and it had been alone for so long. It didn't understand, and the rig wouldn't be safe until it did. I hoped that I could explain to it, but I had to be closer, deeper, so that it could see me more clearly, and so that I could see *it* more clearly.

I hit the buoyancy control and started to drop.

Blackness swallowed me. Above, the underside of the ocean floor vanished from view. It was my last connection with home, the last tangible thing I'd ever see. Without it, there was nothing.

I shivered. I was a penny dropped into a well, so deep the universe might forget me.

I was vanishing.

I listened to my heart beating in my ears.

My mind felt as black and empty as the Rift. I used to feel so angry with myself. Angry for the things I did, for not fitting in, for not being like other people. But if this really was the end of me, then I was OK with that. I was sad for Mum; I knew she wouldn't understand. I was sad for Evan, for what might have been. But for the first time in my life, I knew I was doing the right thing. I was doing the *only* thing that could be done. Dark shadows. Disjointed lines.

I fell deeper. Beyond the reach of any submersible.

At the training centre, they'd told us that squid were notoriously social animals; if there are no other squid, they will swim with a shoal of fish rather than swim alone.

That was the euglenoid, brooding at the bottom of the

ocean, the loneliest creature on the planet. I could feel its loneliness inside me, my own loneliness reflected back. All my life I'd been having a one-way conversation with Dad. I'd struggled to connect, to feel that I wasn't alone when I was around him. That's what the euglenoid felt in me; that's why we'd bonded. It had lost Maximus, and then it had found me.

Still deeper I fell. I must have passed out.

When I woke, the world was still black, but the euglenoid was growing larger in my mind.

It moved through my memories. Eager. Curious. It wasn't human, but it had human traits. It could want, and need, and suffer. What did it understand of me? Probably no more than I understood of it. But it *wanted* to understand! That was the most human thing of all.

I slept. I dreamed.

Something must have woken me – a light? I strained forward and peered down past the amphipod's ciliate drives. *Purple!*

A band of colour beneath me, impossibly vast. I was falling through it; it was growing denser. The noise of the euglenoid filled my thoughts now. A kind of low chatter, like voices, but too many to understand. It was like standing in a storm, a relentless wind pressing against my mind. I blinked and shook my head. *I must be hallucinating.* I fell further, drifting, squinting into the growing bands of colour.

I pressed my forehead against the cold aluminosilicate

of the amphipod. I could see the bottom now. A ridge of rock. Then, beyond the rock...

An ocean of colour!

I let out an involuntary gasp of wonder. It was so beautiful. It rolled and swelled with invisible currents. It grew brighter, became so bright it hurt my eyes.

Billions of euglenoid.

I hit the ledge with a jolt. The euglenoid's thoughts were more intense than ever, straining against the boundary of my mind. Its colours had multiplied; no longer just turquoise or purple, but every colour I knew and more besides. So much colour. So much thought. A human brain is about the size of two clenched fists. But this ... it was hard to imagine what thoughts it was capable of.

A shape nearby caught my eye. For a long moment I couldn't understand what I was seeing. Then I realized—

Maximus. His survival suit was slumped against the rockface just as I was, his face waxy in my spotlights, long dead. I bit back a cry.

When his submersible had failed, his survival suit must have saved him. But not for long. He would have known he had no way back, so he did what any scientist would have done: he'd gone down.

I'd been feeling his last memories muddled up with my own since I'd arrived. I could feel them more clearly now than ever. Like dwindling echoes. *Oh, my boy ... my boy... Sinking... I'm falling... I'm alone... I'm darkness...*

That would be me, an hour from now – no, forty minutes. That would be me.

But I had work to do first.

The sound of the euglenoid's thoughts grew louder in my head: a flurry of noise – surprise – disappointment. *Why is he silent? Will I be silent too?*

A question: *what?*

Alone in my capsule at the bottom of the ocean, I smiled ruefully: how strange that I should be the one to try to explain what *human* was, when I had never really understood human all that well myself.

But where do you start with a distributed consciousness that might be as big as a continent for all I knew? What do you tell a microbial intelligence that evolved in isolation at the bottom of the ocean for billions of years?

I thought of Dad. I remembered movie night together, the excited way he could tell me all about the hidden meanings of certain movies (mostly sci-fi movies) and yet be utterly bemused by others. You had to make allowances for Dad, even though it was painful sometimes. How could I help the euglenoid understand that?

They should have sent a poet.

That was from an old book Dad had made me read: *Contact*, one of his favourites. I remembered reading the book and then watching the movie together: Dad pointing at the screen as he told me about Carl Sagan.

I felt the euglenoid rush to the memory. I felt it

pull the thought of Dad closer to it. *Loved in spite of his otherness.*

Then I thought of Hanna. She'd texted me! I wondered what she'd wanted to tell me. I remembered a moment at school, not so long ago, when we were still friends: her head thrown back in laughter, the sun bright against her skin.

Loved, even though we were different.

The sea of euglenoid was stirring now, twisting and curling back on itself. I could feel its excitement. *Yes... Yes...*

I thought about being trapped in the edu unit, how awful it was, but how that awfulness was lessened by being with other people.

I thought about Mum. There were times when Mum was a kitchen full of work, a glass of wine, and a feeling that I was distracting her. But there were other times when I came home from school and she snapped shut her laptop and asked me about my day. When she did, she liked me to tell her *everything*: what I'd had for lunch; what topic we were covering in biology. The more mundane the better. She'd sit at the kitchen counter, smiling, watching me chatter away with that sense of quiet wonder that parents sometimes have.

Cared for.

A rush of colour – a deluge, an outpouring.

What vast and lonely creatures we were! Specks of dust

lost in monumental darkness, visible in glimpses through twisting passageways. The euglenoid saw it all, and the thought plunged into my own mind. Those flashes, those times when someone else's torchlight falls across us and we see and are seen … those are the moments we call love.

I exhaled. I felt the euglenoid become calmer, closer. The memory rose in my mind of being held by Mum after I'd dragged the edu unit back to the rig. *Yes! Yes!* It understood. It knew what we were: we were *each other*, the sum of the people we loved and who loved us.

I formed one final thought in my mind: the thought of not seeing them again; the thought of never speaking to Mum or Hanna again; the memory of Dad's big, soft hands. Gone.

The euglenoid convulsed inside my head.

Grief.

It already understood grief. It had lost Maximus, but it hadn't understood why. Now, it understood the winking out of thought and the hole it leaves behind. It understood how fragile we were. It would protect us now…

And the rig would be safe.

It was over.

I stared at the rolling waves of colour. I was far too deep to get back before my oxygen ran out. But it was OK; I'd done what I came here to do. I'd wait here, I thought, and then I'd sleep. I was fine with that. I felt happy. I was in the loneliest place on Earth, but I'd never felt less alone.

"—ily... L–ll–ily."

My UAC crackled.

"Evan?" I said.

I twisted in my seat, not sure if I was really hearing him.

"I'm here." Evan's voice came through more crisply. "I can see you."

And then, there he was, his amphipod drifting slowly down next to mine.

"*Evan!*"

I shook my head, unable to find the words. He was here. I was so relieved to see him, I felt like I might choke. But it was awful as well: awful, awful, because I knew, of course, that he couldn't get back any more than I could.

"You shouldn't *be* here!" I exclaimed.

"I followed you."

"But you'll *die*—"

"Shh." He couldn't touch me, but he leaned forward in his amphipod and pressed his hand against his capsule so that it was only a few centimetres from my own.

"It's OK," he said.

"*No!*" I sobbed. "Go back. Please ... go back."

"It's too late," he said. "I'd never make it."

"Then why did you come?"

Evan looked troubled for a moment, as if he hadn't thought to ask himself this question until now. "I couldn't leave you out here on your own, could I?" A sad, regretful expression settled on him. "I thought... I thought maybe

I could save you again. But we're too deep, I know that now. I'm sorry."

I shook my head. I could feel the euglenoid's restive movement stirring inside my thoughts again. It was worried about us. It knew grief now; it knew why this was so much worse for me than when I thought I was down here on my own. The sea of colour grew more intense, sharpened. Evan watched, the colours reflecting against his capsule and flickering in his eyes.

"I see why you wanted to keep this to yourself," he remarked.

A small laugh escaped me.

Tears streamed down my cheeks.

I hadn't cried since Dad left. I'd wanted to, so many times, but I'd never known how. Now that I'd started, I didn't know how to stop.

I couldn't speak. It was meant to be just me down here. I was OK with that. But no one else was supposed to die because of me. My throat strained; I cried some more. Evan waited, his own face wet. He turned and stared into the rolling colours of light.

"You were always planning to do this, weren't you?" he said after a moment. "How were you going to get rid of me?"

"I was going to launch the other amphipod before you had a chance to get in. I forgot because you weren't there."

Evan nodded. "That probably would have worked."

"How did you get past Carter? And the doors?"

"He was too busy freaking out about you to pay any attention to me," Evan replied. "And Dad had an override code for the doors."

I'd stopped crying at last. My throat was dry, and I desperately wanted a drink of water. My brain was so full of the euglenoid I could hardly separate it from my own thoughts.

"Do you think it worked?" Evan asked. "Whatever you came here to do?"

I nodded. "Yes, I think so."

The sound of the euglenoid's thoughts were getting louder. It knew there was something Evan needed to see.

Evan must have felt it too because he looked across and saw his dad.

"Don't look," I breathed.

He let out a rough, shivery sigh. "I knew he was dead... I did. I knew it." After a long moment, he turned back and stared out at the shining sea before us. "I'm glad he saw this before he died. He'd have liked seeing this."

We fell silent, watching the swirling colour. Pink. Blue. Orange. Purple. Red. Orange. Grey. Yellow. Beige. Marine. Silver. Black. Other colours too...

"What colour do you suppose that is?" Evan asked, pointing to a ridge ahead of us.

"I'm not sure... I don't think it has a name. Black-gold maybe."

"Or silver-black?"

"Yes."

"This one?"

"Indigo–scarlet."

"You're right."

"I think he was OK," I said. "I know it sounds weird, but I can feel him... The euglenoid was inside his head when he died. He wished he could show it to you, and he was sad, but he was OK." I searched Evan's face. "I'm sorry, I didn't mean to—"

"It's OK," Evan said. "I feel it too."

An oxygen warning light had turned red on my console. "Evan—" My voice was suddenly a long way away. "I think I might need to sleep now."

His mouth twisted. "Wait! No. Not yet."

"I'm sorry—"

Something was happening to the euglenoid. I felt its panic, its realization that I was fading just as Maximus had faded. Great clouds of colour pulled together and formed new shapes. Something was coming towards us from the colour. I blinked and shook my head, sure that I was hallucinating.

"Do you see that?" I whispered.

Evan turned and gasped. "Dad?"

I recognized Maximus now. A ghostly turquoise shadow taking form as it approached. The figure smiled, the same self-confident, action-hero smile I'd seen in the videos. Warm and playful, a joke designed to set you at ease.

"We found your code!" Evan said through his tears. "Decrypted your notes."

The euglenoid buzzed inside my head.

Clever lad, Maximus replied.

"I know you're not really here," Evan went on. "I know it's not really you... But I'm glad I got to see you again."

I watched, feeling myself grow more distant as the figure gestured towards the cables at the top of Evan's amphipod.

Evan's eyes widened. "You want us to share oxygen?"

Maximus nodded.

I shook my head. "No, you can't."

"It wants me to."

Evan nudged his thrusters and positioned his amphipod alongside my own, our aluminosilicate capsules knocking gently together. He tapped a control and an oxygen line snaked out from his amphipod and connected to mine.

"No, please..." I protested.

A rush of cool, fresh air filled the cockpit. It was a relief, but I was crying at the same time. I took a deep, grateful breath. My vision came back to normal. Evan's dad was smiling, the same smile I'd seen in the pressure jar.

The euglenoid seemed pleased with itself.

"You don't understand," I told it. "We can't survive this."

The image of Maximus gave Evan one last, gentle look, and placed its hand against the capsule of his amphipod. Then it seemed to step back or fade. It disappeared into the swirling lines of colour. I could feel its grief keenly. How it had loved Maximus. How much it loved us. And how much Maximus had loved his son.

"It's OK," Evan said to me. "It's better. Neither of us will be left on our own now."

I opened my mouth, but I didn't have any words.

"I wish we had a picnic," he said thoughtfully. "Whenever we went topside, Dad used to take us for picnics in the sand dunes. It looked a bit like this." He thought for a moment, then corrected himself. "Except it wasn't purple." He gazed at the rolling waves of colour. Then he said, "Hey, we should go sometime. We could get a train up from Tokyo, take a picnic or something... What do you think?"

"What? Like a date?" I smiled.

Evan flinched. "Kind of."

I turned back to the colours, my face burning. We were dying at the bottom of the ocean, and somehow I'd made it awkward. Evan was right: we could pretend, for a moment, that we were just two kids who were maybe going on a date one day.

"Yes," I said. "I'd like that. It's a date."

Evan's face lit up, delighted even though it was a date we couldn't possibly keep. I pressed my hand against the capsule at the point where the two domes of aluminosilicate touched, and Evan did the same. I knew it wasn't possible, but I felt like I could feel the warmth of his skin.

The flow of oxygen was beginning to fade already; there wasn't much when it was shared between two. I felt the euglenoid's thoughts growing louder again. A buzzing urgency. *Wait. Wait. Wait.*

Wait. Wait. Wait. Wait. Wait.

"Are you feeling that?" I asked.

"What does it want us to wait for?" Evan said.

I shook my head. "I don't know."

"The euglenoid freak me out a little bit," Evan remarked.

"Different is always scary," I said.

"Yeah."

I looked over to Evan and his eyes were closed.

"It's inside my head," he said.

"I know."

The thoughts of the euglenoid rose higher and higher. I was breaking apart. Fading.

It was possible, I thought, that the euglenoid wasn't just inside our thoughts, but that our thoughts were inside it. That dying here didn't have to mean the end of thought.

Then something happened.

There was a burst of light from above, so bright it carved through the coloured waves like a laser. My eyes flicked open. I'd been dreaming. Our amphipods cast long, black shadows that moved across the rock in front of us. I gasped in surprise, struggling to crane my head upwards and see what was happening.

"What is it?" I asked.

"I don't know," Evan murmured, pulling himself back into consciousness.

"Lily? Evan? That you?" A voice crackled over the UAC.

"*Ari?!*" we exclaimed together.

A submersible swung around as it descended, hovering directly in front of us, its thrusters whipping up clouds of glowing euglenoid. Ari stared at us from inside his capsule. He looked exhausted, worry etched into the dark lines of his face. But his eyes shone with relief.

A rush of exhilaration boiled up inside me. Not just me – the euglenoid.

Saved?

Saved.

"You gave us quite a scare, kids," Ari said. "You're lucky I managed to find a sub that was still watertight."

"How did you find us?" I gasped. "Why haven't you imploded?"

Ari flicked a switch, and the lights of his submersible dimmed, and as he did so the many coloured lights of the euglenoid blossomed around him.

And Kāne created the light to push back the darkness...

Ari grinned, his bronze beard shining in his cockpit lights.

"You've made some pretty interesting friends down here, Lily Fawcett."

A sob burst out of me, and I gazed at the trembling ocean of light that surrounded us. "I did," I breathed. "I really did."

CHAPTER 43

LILY FAWCETT: PERSONAL LOG
DAY 107
The good thing about a rig that looks like a caravan park is that it's pretty easy to repair.

The rig needed new electrics and quite a lot of redecorating. They sank replacement hab units and tethered them into place. They had to sink a specially designed crane to lift the main rig back on to its supports so they could fully restore the sub bay.

It took three months, and they relocated us all to Tokyo while the work was done.

Tokyo was pretty cool. I mostly explored the city

with Mum and Evan. Dr Balgobin put us all to shame by somehow managing to become fluent in Japanese while she sat by the pool with her leg in a cast. As soon as she was able to hobble around, she set up a morning school for us, and we resumed our wild, meandering lessons about anything and everything, sitting under the furnace-like colours of an autumnal cherry tree.

In the afternoons, we explored the city, or sat by the pool, as the mood took us. Ysabel confessed to me that she had a crush on Jacob, and I laughed, and told her that everyone else had figured that out weeks ago. I told her that the feeling was most likely mutual, but she'd have to make the first move, because growing up on a solar pontoon makes you good at almost everything, it turns out, except girls. Now that I knew them all better, I found that I fitted in with my classmates more easily than I'd thought was possible. I still wasn't sure if I'd completely forgiven Alban, and Jacob could still be hard work at times, but we got along well enough.

I spoke to Hanna. I got a new phone, and texted her, and she texted back right away. I told her that I was sorry, that nothing I could say would change what had happened. She told me that she forgave me because she missed me too much not to. She asked me what had happened. The news had reported an accident and a narrowly averted catastrophe but nothing more. I wanted to tell her the truth, but I didn't know where to start.

It was weird talking to her. I felt like she was friends with a different version of me, an older version 1.0, filled with glitches that only she had figured out. She kept saying that I sounded different. Version 2.0 of me is better, I told her. She had loved version 1.0, she told me, but she'd learn to love version 2.0 as well.

About a month after we arrived, Dad came to visit! He'd finished his contract, and he was as relaxed as I've ever known him. We explored the Akakusa, bought ridiculous gadgets in the Ginza district, and geeked out for hours at the Akihabara. It was pretty great.

Then, one crisp morning in October, not long after Dad left, Evan and I packed a bag and caught the Inokashira line to Shōnan. We filled a rucksack with snacks bought from a stall near the station – this was his dad's version of a picnic apparently. He was smiling a lot, and he leaned forward and kissed me for the first time as we stood outside the street stall sorting through our carrier bags. He took me by surprise, and it was kind of awkward, but I didn't mind. We laughed. Then we kissed again, properly this time.

When we got to the beach, the sun reflected off the sea like a million tiny shards of glass, as if somebody had exhaled every useless, mixed-up feeling inside them in a single breath. We swam and sunbathed and chatted about our dreams like we were normal kids.

In spite of everything, the decision to come back to Deephaven was an easy one. Mum's unique ability to activate the euglenoid samples (yeah, right!) won her instant admiration and she was offered Maximus's old job on the spot. What the universities know about the euglenoid, what Mum knows even, is hardly a scratch compared to what Evan and I saw. But it's enough to keep them happy, for a while at least.

Mum has never been more in her element. But that's not why we came back. I don't know when it happened, but somewhere along the way, Deephaven started to feel like home, and neither me nor Mum can imagine being in any other place.

"Welcome to Deephaven!" Ari exclaimed as we stepped back into the rig's canteen for the first time in months. It hadn't changed much: it had new seating and a fresh coat of paint, but the ceiling was still yellow, and they'd kept the same food counters.

"What do you think?" Ari asked, grinning hopefully.

"She's beautiful," I said.

Ari seemed delighted. "And what about me? Will I do?"

He raised his arms and gave a small twirl, his chest thrust out proudly. He was wearing a suit that looked a size too small for him and a purple tie that even my dad would have been embarrassed to wear. I burst out laughing before I could stop myself.

Ari looked crushed. "It's not me, is it?"

"You'll make a fine Installation Manager whatever you wear," Mum said kindly.

"Just … not that tie," I added.

"Or that jacket," Mum agreed.

Ari pulled off the tie and slipped the jacket from his shoulders. "There's hardly any pockets in these things anyway," he grumbled.

He disappeared off in search of a flight suit. The rig would run differently now that he was in command. It would meet its quotas, more or less, but it would do so with a larger science team than ever, finding new ways to extract the minerals the world needed in ways that wouldn't harm the euglenoid or anything else down here.

Carter had been allocated an administrative role topside. A reprimand for overstepping his authority, and for being in charge of the rig when it had inexplicably nearly exploded. And Mum had plenty of plans of her own beyond the euglenoid. If the world understood more of what it was like down here, she reasoned, they'd use less up there.

"Football match on the Recreation level!" Jian called as he darted past.

"We got new balls!" Jacob yelled delightedly.

I looked at Mum. "The world's first experimental deep-sea mining rig and they're excited about new footballs? This place should have, like, a *holodeck* or something."

"Go," Mum said. "Meet you back here for dinner."

I headed off to join the others, and when I got there

Ysabel bounded over and threw her arms around me in delight. "Hey, I got a new phone! I need your number again."

"You live, like, one cabin over from me!" I exclaimed. But I gave her my number anyway, smiling and shaking my head.

"You obviously haven't heard about the new broadband situation," Ysabel enthused. "*Four* new lines. We can send each other cat videos and ... whatever else people do with their phones topside."

Jacob joined us. "I've decided. I'm going to teach you how to play football."

I shook my head. "No... I'm serious, I can't play—"

"I'm going to insist," Jacob said profoundly. "It's an important life skill."

I gave him a pained look. "Nobody our age uses words like '*life skill*'; you know that, don't you?"

Jacob looked bemused. He disappeared on to the pitch and a moment later I heard a shout in my direction.

"Game's starting!" Jian called.

He kicked the ball, and I saw it arc towards me. Time seemed to freeze. I watched as the ball hung in the air. Then it reached me, and my leg responded automatically, flashing out and walloping it away.

"*Ayaui!*" Dr Balgobin shouted. "Watch out!"

It was too late. The ball spun off the edge of my foot and veered sharply towards the ERS. I felt a cold, sinking feeling as I saw what was going to happen. Then Alban reached up, almost lazily, and caught it.

"Idiot." He smirked. "We are totally putting a protective cover on top of that thing."

I headed over to my usual spot at the edge of the pitch. Evan was there already. He was hunched over his tablet, his tangled hair hanging loosely over his face, his eyes tense with concentration. He was dressed for football. His long, bare arms and legs were like a puzzle I wanted to solve.

He didn't see me right away. He rubbed his forehead with the back of his wrist and flicked to another page of whatever he was studying. When I sat down, he looked up and smiled, his dark eyes catching mine and sparkling with excitement. He shuffled a little closer so that our legs touched and slipped his arm casually across my knee.

"Not playing?" I asked.

"In a minute," he said. "I wanted to show you this first."

I looked at the tablet in his hand, a schematic of a modified amphipod, a ream of technical information. "We need more range, more ... air." He pulled up another layer of detail. "This is what the team topside came up with."

I nodded. "It looks good. When will they come?"

"Prototypes next month."

He grinned and leaned forward and kissed me: so soft and natural and easy that it felt as if this was just the way things had always been between us, and the way things always would be.

"OK, wish me luck," he said, standing, and heading over to the pitch.

I watched the game start: Jian jumping lightly on the spot to warm up; Ysabel re-tying her ponytail; Evan stretching out his sinewy legs and rolling his shoulders. I felt content, as if I was a vast and peaceful stillness in a world of swirling chaos. I was still me... Still different... Still rubbish at football... But I wasn't alone any more.

Somewhere deep inside my brain the euglenoid turned and shifted in its sleep. I took a breath and held it. We'd learned so much, but we still had much to learn.

There's plenty of time, I thought. *We're safe. We're with our loved ones.*

We are home.

DEEPHAVEN CREW ROSTER

Meg Riddington. . . . . Drilling Supervisor

Gilbert Connors. . . . . Drilling Foreman

Evan Connors . . . . .Drilling Roughneck

Kathy Allen . . . . Drilling Operations

David Allen . . . . Directional Drilling

Amy Allen. . . . . Fluid Supervisor

Jon Curl . . . . .Plume Consultant

Isaac Curl . . . . Well Head

Peter Allen . . . . .Tong Operator

Carma Alicaya . . . . Medical Officer

David Riddington . . . . Proofreader!

Janet Riddington . . . . Rig Mechanic

Tom Riddington. . . . . .Motorman

Lisa Riddington . . . . Rig's Librarian

Madoc Threipland . . . . .Shale Shaker

Nick Drew. . . . . .Spline Reticulator

Angela Tam. . . . . .Shark Midwife

Eva Drew-Tam. . . . . The Random Person

Piers Hudson. . . . . Roustabout

Kate Hudson . . . . .Driller

Richard McBarnet . . . . Directional Survey

Helen McBarnet. . . . . .Drilling Analyst

Natalie Bear . . . . Casing Operator

Nellie Preston-Bear . . . . Toolpusher

Betsy Preston-Bear . . . . Drill Safety

Tom Coward . . . . Rig Architect

Jo Wratten . . . . Education Team

Imogen Coward . . . . Drilling Hand

Samuel Coward . . . . Casing Floorhand

Jim Martin . . . . Rig Performance

Pippa Martin . . . . Completion Consultant

Daisy Martin . . . . Rig Technician

Eliza Martin . . . . Drilling Analyst

Rob Hueting . . . . Tool Assembly

Nic Hueting . . . . Rig Supervisor

Skye Hueting . . . . Rig Floorhand

Ryan Hueting . . . . BOP Inspection

Josh Hueting . . . . Casing Hand

Linas Alsenas . . . . Derrickman

Kate Shaw . . . . Platform Operator

Imogen Cooper . . . . Rig Manager

Kiran Khanom . . . . Crane Operator

Jamie Gregory . . . . Ballast Controller

Emma Greenwood . . . . Drilling Workover

Gary Willington . . . . Roughneck

Robin Wyatt . . . . Artist in Residence

Patrik Sundberg . . . . Hill Consultant

Alex Benton . . . . Rig Welder

Limor Elhayani . . . . Barge Engineer

Daniel Jones . . . . Chief Scientist

Anna Brooke . . . . Bogey Operations

Annaliese Avery . . . . Celestial Mechanisms

Helen MacKenzie . . . . Fracturing Supervisor
Urara Hiroeh . . . . Hydraulic Pumps
Yvonne Banham . . . . Dangerous Gifts
Sharon Boyle . . . . Tool Hand
Angela Murray . . . . Well Service Supervisor
Michael Mann . . . . Cloud Technician
Harriet Worrell . . . . Mud Pumps
Sarah Dutton . . . . Rig Superintendent
Jenny Glencross . . . . Torque Consultant
Genevieve Herr . . . . Well View Manager
Chrissie Sains . . . . Rig Operations
George Poles . . . . Flexible Pipe
Georgia Benjamin . . . . Drilling Safety
John Malone . . . . Morale Officer
Sarah Mackie . . . . Dynamic Pressure
Amy Cooper . . . . Fluids Consultant
Jenny Tong . . . . Drilling Team Manager
Alex Edden . . . . Well Control
Kate Perry . . . . Spooling
Kerry Mintern . . . . Crew Chief
Cheryl Lambert . . . . Electrical Rig
Elizabeth Shapiro . . . . Cheese Supervisor
Cathie Kelly . . . . Drilling Coach
Rosie . . . . Rig Dog

With many thanks to my long-suffering friends,
family and colleagues who helped to build this rig.